A NEST OF

VOODOO DOLLS

A NEST OF
VOODOO DOLLS

B. K. KNIGHT

authorHOUSE®

AuthorHouse™
1663 Liberty Drive
Bloomington, IN 47403
www.authorhouse.com
Phone: 1-800-839-8640

Published by AuthorHouse   02/15/2013

ISBN: 978-1-4817-8216-6 (sc)
ISBN: 978-1-4817-8217-3 (e)

Prologue

Sergeant Duski Lôcha stared at the ceiling. She was oblivious to the stale, stagnant, hot air circulating inside her tiny bedroom. Despite the heat, all the windows were still shut—they'd been shut for the past couple of days. It was midday, and as usual, it was sweltering. Sweat was pouring out of every pore in her exhausted and traumatised body, but the soaring temperatures were the least of her concerns. Likewise, her splitting headache barely registered.

Missing private parts, clean-swept crime scenes, and poisoned arrows all point to the same killer. She tossed the thought round and round her head a gazillion times. She knew the investigating team was also aware of the similarities among the three murders. Fear had prompted an early closure of the other two cases, and they were now filed under "unsolved murders." It was common knowledge that most police officers weren't too keen on investigating alleged ritual murder cases.

Who can blame them, considering the risks involved? she thought gloomily.

This case, however, was different. One of their own, a police officer, was murdered in the same ritualistic manner as the others. And this time, they had a suspect—or so they thought. His private parts, like the others, had been sheared off and gone on a walkabout too. Duski knew she had to find them as a matter of urgency.

Chapter One

The call came two hours before the end of her shift. The charge office was unusually quiet for a Saturday night. The section leader, a rather overweight police sub-inspector, was dozing off in the inspector's office. The duty driver, a hippo-sized constable, was sleeping with his head resting on the windowsill. The rest of the section was out on beat patrol duties.

Sergeant Duski Lôcha sat alone in the charge office's main desk, desperate for something to do—anything to take her mind off the impending ritual. She'd been trying all day to put it out of her mind.

During a moment of spiritual weakness, she'd let a friend talk her into a visit to a witch doctor—a wizened old man, apparently experienced in helping women find true love. She'd chuckled a little when she met the toothless but friendly witch doctor.

At thirty years of age, Duski was now officially a *lefetwa* (a spinster). Most of her peers were married or had live-in boyfriends. It wasn't like she hadn't tried hard enough to find a marriage-worthy man. It turned out to be an impossible mission from which she'd learnt a very important lesson: not every frog can be turned into a prince, especially African frogs. In her case, not a single one of the many frogs she'd kissed over the years had panned out. Southern Africa is blessed with a wealth of frogs, and she had kissed quite a number of them: the shovel-footed squeakers, the snoring puddle frogs, the olive and red toads.

She knew she was pretty though, so that wasn't the reason she was the oldest spinster in Gaborone city. She had the curvy hips, the smooth espresso skin tone, and the oval baby face—a package that had attracted all the frogs she'd kissed. It was their fault that she now bore the label *lefetwa*. All they'd wanted was for her to be their *bit on the side*, a mate.

For some bizarre reason, she started thinking about the story of the beautiful long-haired Rapunzel, freed by a handsome prince from her tall-towered prison after hearing her haunting song. Her thoughts, once again, went back to the witch doctor. *Will he help me bag my own African prince charming? Will he turn one of those frogs into something I can marry?*

Duski's problem was that she'd never consulted a witch doctor before in her life. She was dreading the appointment, but she was determined to start the New Year with someone special. She tried to get her mind off the impending ritual, but the eerie silence all around her was making it quite difficult to focus on less daunting thoughts.

The streets had all gone strangely quiet, save for an occasional roar of a vehicle driving by. Even the street kids (who lived in the skip outside the station) had retired unusually early for the night.

She looked all around the rather dull interior, scanning the office like a vulture searching for fallen prey. She was desperate to find something to occupy her mind. Framed pictures of all Botswana's presidents and police commissioners stared back with nothing to offer, with nothing to stimulate the mind. The big concrete counter that separated the charge office from the reception area stood solid in front of her.

Too late, it seemed to say. The whitewashed walls failed to cheer her up either.

You have signed a pact with the devil—their whiteness seemed to utter—*the devil*.

The thought made her heart skip a few beats. *What will my father say? The daughter of the village Zionist Christian Church priest consulting a witch doctor?*

Father will . . . She didn't even want to think about it.

Duski was beginning to doubt whether it was wise—let alone safe—to take the prescribed ritual bath, to get *muti* all over her Christian body. Suddenly, the shrill of the charge office phone made her jump.

"Gaborone central police station, Sergeant Duski Lôcha speaking, how can I help you, sir?" She recited the words with relief as soon as the constable on duty at the reception had put the caller through.

"*Dumela mma,* I'm um . . . the lion keeper at St. Claire's Lion Park," an elderly male voice stammered in greeting.

3

"*Ee Rra,* what can I do for you?" Duski asked, wondering why he was hesitant.

"This might . . . um . . . be a completely false alarm, but I . . . um . . . I think that there might be a dead body inside one of the lion enclosures," he faltered.

"A dead body?" Duski shuddered as she asked the question, recalling an incident at the park about a year ago when a young man was mauled to death by lions during a music festival a few years ago. She hoped the caller was wrong. Still, something in the man's voice sent a cold shiver down her spine.

"Just checked the main enclosure where the three adult lions are kept," the caller said. "The male is roaring and fighting with the two females over something on the ground. I couldn't see much with a paraffin lantern—got a really bad feeling bout this," he concluded apologetically. "There's a festival in the park," he reminded her.

"*Tankie rra,* we'll be there as soon as we can." She replaced the receiver and hurried off towards the inspector's office.

"Sir, looks like the park lions have done it again," she said and stamped her right foot to attention, immediately jolting the section leader out of his nap. "Shall I attend to the report, sir?" she asked breathlessly.

This meant that she didn't have to sit and watch the clock slowly ticking away for the remaining two hours.

By the time I get back from the park, Duski thought, *it will be time to go home, and then I can get that* muti *business out of the way.*

Sub-Inspector Bale blinked, rubbed his eyes, and wiped a trickle of spit from one corner of his mouth with the back of his fat hand. He regarded the sergeant standing in front of him with narrowed, sleepy eyes.

"Sergeant, how many times have I told you not to stamp your foot like that? It's completely unnecessary."

"*Sori*, sir," Duski replied, an amused smile hovering around her lips as Sub-Inspector Bale scowled and sucked his teeth at her.

"What is it sergeant?" he asked and shifted his protruding stomach to an upright position. He looked her up and down as if conducting a parade inspection. He sucked his teeth again.

"I've just had a 999 call from the lion park keeper, sir. He suspects that there might be someone inside one of the enclosures, probably someone trying to get into the music festival without paying," she added. "I'll attend to the report right away, sir."

"Okay, Sergeant. Take Constable Moji with you."

"Thank you, sir," she responded and stamped her right foot—lightly this time—to stand to attention. The sub-inspector yawned and dismissed her.

5

Duski immediately headed back into the charge office, straight to the corner where the duty driver was sleeping. She shook him roughly by the shoulder before throwing a bunch of car keys in front of him. The constable yawned and stretched. "Where are we going, Sarge?" he asked unenthusiastically.

"The lion park," she said, pulling out her white shirt only to tuck it back into her greyish blue skirt neatly. After throwing her police hat on, she marched towards a white police bakkie parked in front of the station. The constable stood up, stretched again, and farted before picking up his police hat and keys and following her.

"I'll drive," Duski suddenly announced, immediately walking over to the driver's side. She hopped into the driver's seat, started up the bakkie, backed into the main road, and sped off with screeching tyres and flashing lights towards the Gaborone Lobatse single carriage way.

The lion park was about fourteen kilometres from Gaborone. A couple of kilometres into the journey, live music blaring out from the direction of the park drifted their way. Franco, a local musician, was performing there that evening. Though St Claire's was a lion reserve, it was used occasionally as a venue for live music festivals.

The road to the park was a narrow dirt track that suddenly appeared on the right side of the main road. Duski hit the brakes hard, immediately swerving the bakkie into the track. The two were

6

immediately thrown up into the air before landing back on the hard, springy seats. And then they were thrown up again, tossed around as the wheels juddered and bounced about.

"Slow down, Sarge!" Constable Moji, who'd never had faith in women drivers, shouted, worried that Duski was losing control of the bakkie.

"I'm trying!" she yelled as the rutted track sent violent tremors throughout her body.

"Look out, Sarge," Constable Moji shouted out again, grabbing the dashboard. A man in a green boiler suit and a paraffin lantern suddenly appeared in the middle of the road. Duski slammed on the brakes just in time, nearly sending them both flying through the windscreen.

"Over here," the man gesticulated frantically.

"It must be the keeper," she said, selecting the first gear and driving slowly through clouds of settling dust towards the man.

He looked quite old, gaunt, and slightly hunched. She observed him as he led them to a poorly lit metal-framed entrance with an adjoining little office on the side. A younger man came out of the office to let them through, and the old man they'd been following immediately signalled them to a stop. Cloaked in a mist of dust, he hurried back towards the bakkie.

A few metres away from where they were parked stood a netted wire enclosure, which served as one of the park's many lion enclosures. All the enclosures were lit by a couple of paraffin lanterns hanging from nearby trees.

Duski rolled down her window. The air was rank with lion urine and faeces. She shivered slightly as another faint, yet distinctive, smell caught her sharp nose. Fresh human blood—she recognised the smell from countless fatal road accidents she'd attended since joining the force.

"*Dumela rra*, the keeper, I presume?" She composed herself and offered the man her hand.

"*Ee mma*," he replied, shaking her hand rather firmly. "Body is over there," he announced as soon as the greetings were over, his voice barely audible over the music still blaring from the arena. The man pointed towards the nearest enclosure with the smoky paraffin lantern he was still holding.

Duski and the constable followed the direction the flickering lantern was pointing towards. Once their eyes were accustomed to the poor lighting, three dark lion shapes began to emerge. One had a mane running from the back of the head to the shoulders. The predators were busy pulling and tearing aggressively at something on the ground.

She turned the ignition off, took out a torch from the glove box, and jumped out of the bakkie. One of the female lions sensed her approach and went into a stalking posture. Head and body held low, it watched her intently.

"I wouldn't do that if I were you, Sarge," the constable warned, his piggy eyes widening with fear. He immediately shuffled over to the driver's seat. *Just in case*, he thought, closely watching the shadowy figure on the other side of the enclosure behind the safety of locked doors.

"The fence isn't that secure, it'll be safer to drive closer to the fence instead," the keeper advised. "These lions have clearly developed a taste for human flesh," he added, running over to the bakkie's passenger door.

The constable reluctantly unlocked it to let him in. Once he got his breath back, the keeper pressed the lantern's glass shade lever down and blew out the flame. Paraffin fumes immediately filled the cab as he placed the lantern by his feet.

Ignoring the keeper's advice, Duski slowly walked towards the enclosure. The smell of blood became stronger as she got closer to the fence, almost overpowering that of the predators' faeces and urine. Just a few metres away, she could clearly see the three lions. The beam, however, was not bright enough to reveal the prey. The male lion had also sensed her approach, and it immediately adopted a killing pose. It roared in warning above the music, sending a cold sweat down her spine.

Duski switched off the torch and slowly retraced her steps back to the vehicle. She quickly jumped into the driver's seat, forcing Constable Moji's bulky body into the small middle seat behind the gear lever. She immediately started up the bakkie and drove slowly back towards the fence.

Turning off the ignition but leaving the headlights on, they all sat quietly as the beams revealed a sight that sent cold chills down their spines. The horrified trio sat silently, staring at the scene before them.

"Oh no! No, it can't be!" the keeper suddenly cried out, breaking the silence and making Duski and the constable jump. He was shaking his head vigorously as if to rid it of the horrific scene before him. A pair of stringy and deeply veined hands flew up to cover his face. He hunched over and trembled violently.

"Recognise the victim?" Duski and Constable Moji asked, almost simultaneously. They both stared at the half-eaten corpse, which was now visible from the car. The victim's shaven head immediately identified him as male.

The female lions, bored of watching the car, resumed tearing away the flesh from the victim's lower body while the male stayed crouched by the fence, his reflective eyes fixed hungrily on the vehicle.

"His name was Boiki—he worked here," the keeper whispered, "He was from Lesetlhaneng ward in Ramotswa," he mumbled to himself.

"Trying to get into the festival without paying, I reckon," Duski said, putting a sympathetic hand on the keeper's shoulder. She knew the enclosure presented direct access into the park. But Duski realised that her own conclusion was wrong before the keeper highlighted it.

Boiki must have known about the lions, why risk his life?

"We were paid this afternoon—Boiki has never been tight with money, wasn't his style. Would've bought a ticket, I know that," the keeper said, still shaking his head. "After last year's incident, we'd started moving the lions to the enclosure at the end of the park with the cubs whenever there was a festival here," he explained. "The lions haven't been fed for days—they've been very aggressive recently." He paused as if to let his system digest the horrific scene. "The boss is away, you see, we couldn't move them without him."

Duski too shook her head, perplexed. "Then Boiki must have thought the lions had been moved. What a waste," she sighed and turned off the headlights.

"He knew," the keeper muttered, as if to no one in particular.

"He knew?" she looked at the man's withered face, wondering whether she'd heard him correctly. "Are you sure?"

"We're the only ones trained to handle the lions," he muttered, "When the boss phoned this afternoon to tell us to leave the lions in the big enclosure, Boiki was the one who took the call."

"But why this? How come he's in there?" Puzzled, she searched the man's face as if it held hidden clues to his colleague's mysterious death. The keeper shook his head uncertainly. "Was Boiki depressed?" she fired questions at the keeper, her

11

mind racing through a list of rational explanations. "Troubled relationship?" The old keeper shrugged.

Could it be suicide, she wondered.

Duski knew that was how a lot of young men ended their lives, especially when love affairs had turned sour.

What a cruel way to end one's life though, she thought. Shootings and hangings she'd seen, but suicide by lions was something new—bizarre to say the least.

"Any close friends here at work, someone who might know if he was depressed or troubled?" Constable Moji, who'd been speechless thus far, fired his first question.

"He was friendly with everyone, always happy. He'd a son with some woman from Molepolole village—only found out bout it last week when the woman came here looking for him. Apparently Boiki spent money on other women—not on the child."

"The woman's name? Do you think she might have anything to do with this?" Constable Moji asked, ready to scribble down some notes.

"She didn't give the poor chap a chance for introductions—she'd basically come down to scream and hurl abuse at him."

"What did she look like?" Duski interjected.

"A typical *Mokwena* woman—light skinned and short with a huge bottom," the keeper declared in a sorrowful tone.

As Constable Moji jotted down the details, Sergeant Duski Lôcha was deep in thought and scratching her head.

Ninety five percent of Molepolole women had sandy-coloured skin and short statures. And almost all are fat with big bottoms, she thought despairingly.

If the woman had anything to do with Boiki's death, she knew that tracking her down would be an impossible mission—unless someone who knew her came forward with contact details.

"I'm going to drive closer to the enclosure to take another look at the body," she announced, turning the engine and lights back on in order to drive up to the other side of the enclosure. Suddenly, she brought the bakkie to an abrupt halt. "I knew there was something not quite right about all this." Craning her neck forward, she continued, "Look carefully at his legs."

"They're cuffed! Sarge, we better call CID," the constable said, immediately reaching for the bakkie's radio.

"Think we've a homicide on our hands," she said looking at the old keeper with narrowed eyes, as if he had all the answers to her questions. "Was he forced in there?"

"Or thrown in already dead for the lions to eat away the evidence," Moji added after radioing CID.

"That's a possibility—but why?" she said staring into the distance.

*The only people with access to handcuffs are security
guards and police officers. If Boiki was deliberately cuffed,
murdered, and thrown in there, fingerprints left on the
handcuffs will lead us directly to the killer or killers,* she
thought, wondering who could have committed
such a heinous crime.

"Can't really do much now except wait for
CID," she explained to the keeper.

*   *   *

Crime scene officers arrived twenty minutes
later and immediately cordoned off the area before
proceeding to take several pictures of the scene.
Soon after, they led the keeper to their vehicle to
take his statement. Half an hour later, the keeper
left the CID vehicle for his little thatched hut
behind the lion enclosure, holding dearly to his
unlit lantern.

It was well after midnight when Duski and
Constable Moji left the crime scene officers to
continue their work and to protect the scene from
contamination.

"What made you think the victim was
already dead when he was thrown into the
enclosure?" Duski suddenly asked as they hit the
Gaborone to Lobatse road to head back to the
station. She almost wished that it were the case,
shuddering at the thought of what it would be like
to be eaten alive by three very hungry lions.

"The keeper said he didn't hear any screaming—except the roaring lions," Constable Moji said, yawning.

"Whoever's done it must be sick in the head—completely crazy. If caught, *they too* should be thrown alive into the enclosure without a trial," she stated after a few minutes of reflective silence, but loud snores coming from the passenger seat soon alerted her that she was talking to herself. Duski sucked her teeth loud and long at the sleeping constable.

Her thoughts soon wandered back to the story of the Molepolole woman.

Was she involved in some way? She mulled over the possibility again, but she found it hard to believe that any woman—no matter how scorned—could be capable of such a cold-blooded act.

One thing was clear; the victim's death wasn't an accident or a suicide.

Duski was the sort of officer who never took work home. But this case was one of those cases she just couldn't leave behind, safely tucked away inside some steel cabinet. As she went home, she found herself wondering about the victim and what had led him to such a nasty end. Determined to track down his killer or killers herself, Duski headed home, exhausted and feeling sick due to a lack of sleep and visions of the half-eaten corpse that kept popping up inside her head.

Chapter Two

Duski reached for the portable stereo on her bedside table and switched it on in an effort to rid her mind of the dead man's face. Eddie Holman's girly voice filled her tiny bedroom. She concentrated on the lyrics, desperate to delete the previous night's events from her head. Her thoughts stubbornly lingered on the horrific incident and found herself pondering Moji's hypothesis.

Could the enclosure be a secondary crime scene?

Someone was trying to make the young man's death look like an accident. And why the cuffed legs?
Finding it difficult to make sense of the case, she forced her mind to think about less gruesome thoughts. The ritual bath she was due to have that morning now seemed a more agreeable subject to dwell on.
Wherever you go, you always leave behind a little bit of yourself at each stop, she found herself thinking about the case again. Her mind was right back at the crime scene. She desperately wanted to believe, that sooner or later, the perpetrators would be caught and brought to justice.

There is bound to be a fingerprint or two on those cuffs . . . and a footprint somewhere, her inner conversation carried on, regardless of her efforts to stop thinking about it.

Duski stared at the ceiling for a while, trying to focus her thoughts on her life instead—even if it meant having to remember all the dishonest, unreliable men she'd been in relationships with.

This ritual better be worth it.

She closed her eyes to say a short prayer:

Jehovah, forgive me for what I'm about to do this morning. You'd send me a sign, wouldn't you? You'd let me know if I was sinning by taking this bath, right? Thank you, Lord. Amen.

Like a silent movie, the dead man's face appeared in front of her—the eyes staring vacantly. Duski opened hers abruptly, propping herself up to take a deep breath in an attempt to clear her head. Though shaking with fear, she was intrigued by the apparition's sudden appearance. The air around her was reverently still—so still she could hear her own heartbeat. She knew then she'd had a visitation—that she wasn't losing it (she hoped).

Was this a sign from above, or was Boiki trying to tell her something about his death?

She closed her eyes again, this time to bring the face back into focus. *Can I read something in those vacant eyes?*

Again, still and expressionless eyes reappeared before drifting out of reach like a ghostly mist.

Puzzled by what the significance of the apparition might be, Duski got up to draw the curtains aside. Blinding rays of the early morning sun immediately flooded her tiny bedroom. Outside, the sky was bright—almost white, a sign of yet another scorching day. Although it was still early in the morning, the sun's rays were intense and burning. She loosened the rusty window screw, lifted the lever, and opened the creaking window. A gust of hot dusty air immediately filled the room.

The house was quiet. Constable Kowa, her housemate, was out. Duski emerged dressed only in her favourite pair of blue cotton granny panties. She dragged her feet on the polished concrete floor towards their shared and unkempt bathroom. As soon as she pushed the bathroom door open, she was greeted by the faint smell of dead cockroaches mingled with the ever-present fragrance of Super Doom insecticide.

Duski scowled at the unpleasant scenery before her. A grubby, dusty, caked windowsill, an old wicker laundry basket covered with her housemate's panties, and a rusty towel rail laden with more of the leathery, dry, greyish-white underwear.

"Great," she muttered under her breath. "Why can't she keep her bloody panties in her room?" She surveyed the bathroom, cursing the day Constable Kowa moved in with her.

Duski scanned the bathroom once more for a space to hang her own panties after her bath.

The rim of the once-white enamel bath seemed the only space not already laden with her roommate's underwear. She looked at the fresh dirt at the bottom of the bath and sucked her teeth in disgust.

Reaching for Jik powder and Handy Andy cream from the windowsill, she emptied half the contents of both bottles into the bath before she started scrubbing and rinsing. She worked until the bath was almost spotless.

Finally, she filled the bath, and stepping out of her big blue panties (which fell on the floor to be hand-washed later), she stepped into the inviting warm water. She immersed her entire body and closed her eyes to shut out her repulsive surroundings and tried to reach a meditative state. Once her mind was clear, she brought the crime scene into focus again.

It was the staring eyes that appeared first, followed by the head—a blurry image of a body devoured to the bone manifested. She could clearly see it. Her eyes suddenly flew open as something cold brushed past her. The renowned ghostly chill—one she'd read about in gothic novels and witnessed in horror films—suddenly enveloped her. She screamed, immediately jumping out of the bath. Her heart was pounding fast behind her ribcage like a boxer's fist.

What the hell is wrong with me? Come on, girl, get a grip!

Her heartbeat steadied a little.

"What do you want from me?" she asked scanning the bathroom for the ghostly intruder before stepping back into the bath. She ran the cold water tap and splashed her face before opening her eyes. Just as she thought she'd imagined everything—another chill presence brushed past before the spectre reappeared. This time, It was just a man's torso in jeans and a beige T-shirt. It lasted a brief second before it turned into a fine mist and drifted out through the keyhole.

Why me? Am I being haunted or simply being irrational? She wasn't a clairvoyant or crackers—of that Duski was certain. But the face was there, all right. Fear might have created the misty torso, but she did feel a cold chill. Was the man trying to tell her something?

Being a born and bred ZCC follower, Duski was closer to the spirit world than she was aware. She was now certain the man had been murdered. What she saw the previous night was enough to suggest it. Still, she wondered what the motive behind such a vicious and brutal murder could have been.

It was a well known fact, that most homicides were committed by people known or close to the victim.

Which means Boiki must have been killed by someone he knew, she thought trying to put her thoughts in order.

Still trying to unravel the lion park murder mystery, Duski got out of the bath, picked up the granny panties she'd thrown on the floor and gave them a good scrub before hanging them on the rim of the bath to dry.

*   *   *

Later that morning, Sergeant Duski Lôcha stepped out with a brightly coloured umbrella held high above her head. Marching along the dusty hot streets of Block Eight, she crossed Dithutwana Road and headed towards the nearest kombi stop. She was already running late for her witch doctor appointment—the incident with the misty spectre had made her lose track of time.

A kombi that had just driven past stopped and reversed, creating a cloud of dust as it reared off the tarmac and onto the dusty edge of the road. She made a futile attempt to protect her face and hair from the fine dust with the umbrella.

The vehicle appeared full, but the conductor opened the door to let her in. "Mogoditshane *mma?*" he asked. She nodded. He moved everyone on the second row of seats along until 'the notorious pit latrine' was revealed. "*Tsena mma,*" he said, pointing to the gap.

She eyed it uncertainly before she perched a bottom cheek on either side as if she were relieving herself. The kombi was legally overloaded, but she knew that if she pointed out the offence, she would have to wait for another kombi in the intensifying heat.

21

After numerous stops, the kombi finally reached her destination. She got off, her rear end feeling a little numb. She stretched and massaged her bum before taking the short walk from the dusty kombi stop to the old man's house. It was a welcome relief, and in no time, her rear end reverted to its normal shape.

*   *   *

Once her turn came, the witch doctor showed her to a building well hidden behind the main house. She pushed the wooden door open, cautiously stepping inside. The floor was damp and smelled of fresh cow dung. It had just been decorated, probably early that morning, she noted. Memories of numerous crack-of-dawn-cow-dung-collection trips with her mother to a neighbour's kraal temporarily took her mind off what she was about do.

She studied the roofless mud hut and its bizarre furniture. An old, cracked mortar and pestle, a rusty tin bath and an old traditional leather armchair were all scattered around the hut. She closed the rickety wooden door and began to disrobe.

This is it, ready or not, she thought, tucking her jeans, T-shirt, and bra neatly under her armpit. She kicked her flip-flops off before looking around for somewhere to put the clothes. The withered armchair seemed the obvious place.

22

"Can I come in *mma?*" the witch doctor called out from outside the ritual hut. She quickly covered her breasts with both hands before allowing him in.

"You'll need to take everything off," the old man commanded, looking disapprovingly at the big brown panties she still had on. She hesitated and watched him while he poured the contents of the aluminium bucket he was carrying into the bath. "I will be right back," he said, shutting the door firmly behind him.

As soon as he was out of sight, she quickly stepped out of the panties and placed them on the armchair with the rest of her clothes. One hand over her breasts, the other on her privates, she stood with her bum to the wall and wished that she had three hands.

The wall will have to do, she thought, grateful that there was one. She recalled the story of a friend's ritual that had to be performed outside.

A couple of minutes later, the witch doctor came back in, armed with his ritual weapons. A black horsetail and an old leather pouch.

"Are you ready *mma?*" he asked. She nodded. "Come closer *mma*," he ordered, looking amused. "*Mma*, there is no need for embarrassment. I'm an old man," he laughed, revealing a big gap between his teeth. "And remember, I am a doctor and a professional," he said reassuringly.

But Duski refused to move. There was no way she was showing him her bottom.

The old man realised she wasn't going to move. "First, we need to throw the bones," he said. He sat crossed-legged on the floor, and emptied the contents of the pouch on it. "We need to make sure that there are no obstacles in your way," he continued, scooping up the bones. He mumbled something she didn't quite catch before he threw the bones on the floor again. His dark brown eyes hovered over them, examining the pattern they'd formed.

Sergeant Duski Lôcha took the opportunity to study the old witch doctor. He looked quite old, somewhere between seventy and eighty. His face was lean and haggard. It didn't strike her as the face of a man who held the key to the elusive concept of *true love*.

"Why are you here?" the old man suddenly asked, as if reading her mind, "Your scepticism is written all over my bones." He accused her before she could think of an answer.

Being naked, the sergeant felt vulnerable, at a disadvantage. She moved closer to the wall for support. The rough mud walls rubbing against her naked bottom reassured her. She shrugged off the accusation.

"This is the bone of the duiker," the old man continued, flashing a toothless grin. He was looking at the floor again. "It's a bone used widely to divine women." He paused to look at her. Duski thought that she saw pity in his eyes. The old man picked up the bones and signalled her to come closer. "*Di khuele mma,*" he instructed, giving her the bones. Duski accepted them hesitantly before blowing hard into them as instructed. "*Di latlhe,*" the old man ordered.

With shaky hands, Duski threw the bones on the floor, wondering whether she'd ever be accepted back into the Church. Her father would disown her if he ever found out—of that she was certain. She'd sinned beyond redemption.

God might forgive me for taking a ritual bath, but definitely not for touching evil bones. These bones are the devil himself, she recalled her father once saying. *Was the old witch doctor sent to test my faith?* She looked suspiciously at the haggard face before her.

"Bad and good news," the witch doctor suddenly announced, making her jump slightly, "You will lose someone very close to you, and you will be implicated in their death."

She looked at the haphazard pattern. It meant nothing to her. For all she knew, the old man could be talking complete nonsense.

He looked at her with an amused smile. "You don't have to believe me you know, I'm just telling you what I see," he said before putting his finger on another bone and stating, "He knows that you're the one."

She looked at him, wondering if he had lost his marbles.

"The man who was murdered yesterday, he knows you're the only one who can bring the murderers to justice."

She nearly laughed out loud.

Of course! The old witch doctor had heard about the lion park murder, she thought dismissively.

But how did he know that I am a police officer? Her heart missed a few beats.

"You'll meet someone soon," he continued to say—changing the subject before she could ask how he knew what she did for a living.

Again, there was a hint of sadness in the old man's voice, pity in his eyes. She shrugged and calmed herself by concluding that the old witch doctor was nuts. His predictions, a pile of elephant shit.

"This *muti* is very powerful," the old man announced, ignoring her unspoken scepticism. He knew she didn't believe anything he'd said. Nevertheless, he led her to the rusty bath he'd filled earlier with the ritual concoction. "It'll get you sorted in no time," he explained with confidence.

Duski examined the murky brown liquid dubiously as the old man stirred it round with the horsetail. She wondered whether she should call it off.

"It's time to get in the bath now *mma*," the old man commanded before she could summon enough courage to change her mind. Once she was in the bath, he dipped the horsetail in, swished it around, lifted it up and flicked the *muti* water at her naked body. He repeated the action until she was soaked from head to toe.

The force of each spray unleashed her father's anti-witch doctor sermons from deep

26

within the crevices of her unconscious mind. She could hear his voice—it hovered ominously inside her head and in the air circulating around the roofless hut. She shut her eyes in an effort to fight an overwhelming urge to run, knock the old man down and end the satanic ceremony. Yet she couldn't. Her legs had grown heavy, turned rebellious. She felt helpless. Still, the witch doctor's demonic chants and swishing horsetail did very little to quieten her father's voice.

The ordeal was over in twenty minutes—save the echo of her father's voice, which stubbornly lingered on. She stepped out of the bath, muddy brown water with tiny pieces of bark and leaf particles still clinging to her. She stood for several minutes to dry before getting dressed.

"As soon as Mr Right has revealed himself," the old man winked mischievously, "I'll prescribe you *moratiso*, a special kind of love potion to sprinkle in his food."

Quite convinced that she wasn't ready to delve deeper into the dark side, she politely laughed off the offer and thanked the old man for his kindness.

*   *   *

It was nearly lunchtime by the time she'd dressed and paid the old man. She called the police station soon after she'd left the witch doctor's yard.

The officer who answered the phone reported that no arrests had been made.

"We seem to have hit a dead end already," he continued, "Nobody seems to have seen the victim at all yesterday, and he doesn't appear to have had enemies."

"What about the mother of his child? Have you tracked her down yet?" she asked the perplexed officer.

"The family doesn't know anything about her."

"The child?" she persisted.

Have they actually bothered to look for this woman? she wondered.

"Nope," he said with a finality that made her heart sink.

"One suspect was mentioned, however. We brought him in for questioning, but we had to release him. Had a water-tight alibi," the officer concluded.

"Could I have a look at the forensics report sometime?" she asked, determined to track down the woman herself.

The keeper did say that she came to see Boiki last week. She's the only person, it appears, with a motive. Surely, someone, somewhere knows who she is.

There was a long pause at the other end.

"Why?" the officer's voice came back on the line, sounding suspicious.

"Just curious to see what you found at the scene," she explained.

"Can't show you the file, not while the case is still under investigation," he said, much to her disappointment.

"I thought you said you'd hit a dead end. Who knows, I might be able to pick up something you've overlooked," she insisted. "Your office is under pressure to identify a suspect ASAP," she reminded him, "the pressure could lead to rushed decisions and conclusions." She added the last part cautiously.

"I can't show you the file, not right now anyway, Sergeant," the officer said after a short and thoughtful pause. "Maybe after the investigation is closed, I might let you have a read then."

"Have you found anything significant at the scene?" she asked, knowing that she was pushing her luck. She wanted to have a look at the file right away, but she knew it would be impossible.

Any information I can get, she thought.

"*Sori mma*, you know I can't give you that information either. Got to go now," the officer said before the phone went dead.

Chapter Three

After that morning's experience on the kombi's pit latrine, Duski decided to take a taxi home. The nearest rank was a few minutes' walk from the witch doctor's yard.

"Taxi?" a short and very dark-skinned man who was leaning against a white VW Golf asked as soon as he spotted her walking towards him.

He was the second victim.

She studied the driver as she walked across the road towards the taxi. The man had a funny face: a sort of pointy beard and a bison's head on his shoulders. He wore a pair of baggy khaki double-pleated trousers and a snakeskin belt which hung loosely beneath an overflowing stomach. Judging by his clothes, Duski could tell he was a northerner. He looked familiar. She was sure she'd seen him before—somewhere.

"Block Eight, please," she said.

"*Forty pula mma,*" the man replied, holding the passenger door open for her. She gave him a couple of twenty pula notes before jumping in. The man slammed the door shut as soon as she'd sat down and had pulled and clipped the belt on. She was just about to wind down the window when the man started the engine.

"No need, this car has air con *mma,*" he announced rather proudly. She obediently rolled up the window again and fanned her face with her handbag instead, waiting for the air con to come on.

It was midday, and it was hotter than hell. As they pulled out of the taxi rank, she could see the driver's bloodshot eyes checking her out through the rear view mirror. Duski pretended not to notice. She looked straight ahead, but she couldn't help noticing that there was a ring indentation on the man's ring finger.

As they joined the dual carriageway to head towards the airport and Block Eight, the internal heat subsided as the car's air conditioning slowly kicked in. A few minutes into the journey, the taxi left the airport road and turned right into Dithutwana Road, towards a row of red-bricked police bungalows.

"Which part?" the driver asked as they entered Block Eight.

"Police quarters please. Just drop me off at Ditjaube Crescent T-Junction, *rra*."

"What number? Can't let a beautiful lady like you walk in this heat, will spoil your complexion," the driver said, smiling at the rear view mirror.

"Plot number 36559," she responded absently.

"Constable Kowa's housemate?" the man asked.

"I knew I'd seen you before," Duski suddenly exclaimed, "I've seen a photo of you in my housemate's room."

"She used to be my girl—once upon a time, that is," he said. "She didn't approve of my marital status—ended the relationship when she found out I was married."

Duski surveyed the indentation on the man's ring finger and wondered what his current marital status was.

"Call me any time you need a taxi," the man said as he brought the taxi to a stop in front of Duski's house. He took out a business card from the glove box and handed it to her.

She studied the card. "How much will it cost to drive me to Ramotswa and back?" she asked.

After the unsatisfactory phone call to the station, Duski had been toying with the idea of visiting Boiki's home village. She knew the villagers would be holding pre-funeral prayer service in the evenings.

Hopefully someone there might know the whereabouts of the victim's mysterious ex. The woman might even be there, she thought wondering why the team had not arrested anybody yet.

The taxi driver regarded her for a while before he responded. "For a pretty woman like you," he began, studying her face with evident lust, "a hundred bucks."

"You wouldn't mind waiting there, would you?" she studied the driver's bison-like face. "Got to see a few people in the village, might take a while to find them."

"*No mathata mma*," the man said. "We going now?"

"This afternoon," she said, shoving his card in her purse. "I'll ring you."

"What time?"

"Bout 4ish," she replied, looking at her wristwatch.

"See you then," the taxi driver said, waiting until Duski had turned to walk into the yard so he could ogle her backside before driving off.

*   *   *

The white VW Golf taxi beeped the horn at the gate of plot number 36559 later that afternoon.

Duski grabbed her purse and hurried out.

"Thanks for coming—could you take me to the bus station instead?" she asked as soon as she'd made herself comfortable in the backseat.

"Why?" the taxi driver asked, clearly disappointed. "I was looking forward to driving you to Ramotswa."

I bet you were, Duski thought. "Sorry, change of plan," she said without bothering to go into details.

She'd been thinking about the best way to carry out the investigation—she'd concluded that taking the bus to Ramotswa would be the most productive way. It would raise less interest from the locals, and it might give her a chance to find out more about the victim on the bus journey. She was also planning to speak to the victim's parents regarding the mysterious woman's whereabouts—she was still convinced the woman was connected to the case in some way.

The drive to the bus station took ten minutes.

"Seabelo's bus is just about to leave *mma*," the taxi driver announced as soon as they arrived. He carefully manoeuvred the taxi through parked buses before bringing it to a halt in front of her bus.

Duski jumped out and fumbled with some notes in her purse.

"Pay me later," the man said waving her off to reverse out of the bus's way.

"*Tankie rra*," Duski said, hopping onto the waiting bus and immediately scanning it to see whether there were any unoccupied seats.

She spotted one towards the rear, between two men in dark looking boiler suits. She made her way towards them and greeted both men before occupying the empty seat. The man sitting by the window was reading a copy of the daily newspaper (which had the story of the case as its headline). She saw an opportunity to start her enquiries.

"It's such a horrendous way to die," she said, craning her neck to scan the contents of the paper. The man took his eyes briefly off the paper and regarded her for a few seconds.

"He used to go out with my cousin—still can't believe he's gone," the man replied, shaking his head. "It's hard to believe we'll never see him again."

"I'm so sorry," she said sympathetically. "Did they have any children?" Duski asked.

The man looked at her suspiciously. She realised that she'd to say something to explain her interest in the deceased man's affairs.

"I've heard a rumour the deceased had a child with some woman from Molepolole—was just curious if your cousin was the woman." *If the man realises I'm a police officer,* Duski thought with a sinking feeling, *he may not be as open as he would be with a civilian.*

"My cousin's a Molete—born and bred in Ramotswa. She does have a little boy, but he's not Boiki's," the man eventually said.

"Will she be at the prayers this evening? Your cousin, I mean."

"Why do you want to know?" The man turned and surveyed her with evident interest and suspicion.

Duski shrugged. "I would like to meet her—to offer my condolences of course. I'm going to the prayers myself." She spoke as casually as she could, hoping the man would not ask her how she knew the deceased.

"CID's been asking a lot of strange questions about this mysterious woman," the man said, not quite buying her explanation. "I'll introduce you as long as you are not from CID," the man suddenly said, putting the newspaper on his lap.

"Oh no, I'm not—but thank you, would really like to meet her" she said, wondering whether to ask the man for directions to the deceased's yard or not.

Better not, it could blow my cover, she thought realising she'd to find her way to Boiki's home without the man's help.

Three quarters of an hour later, after numerous stops, the bus finally rolled into the village. Duski got off at a bus stop not far from the police station. She had been to the village a few times before, but she didn't know the place well enough to find her way round. She'd decided to call by the station for help instead.

"*Ao, dumela* Sarge," a constable behind the reception desk asked.

"Hi, Ali, didn't realise you'd been transferred here," Duski said with apparent relief. Her heart was quickening despite her efforts to stay calm.

She was still in love with him—she'd never stopped loving him, in fact.

Duski had dated Ali for a few months when they were both police recruits. It all ended when she found out he was no different from all the others—he'd cheated on her.

"On attachment for a few days—you—still at CPS?" Duski nodded. "Anyway, what can I do for you?" he asked.

"Heard about the lion park incident?" Duski started, avoiding eye contact.

Is he still in love with me? Will the muti make him fall for me again? She wondered. "I'm here to find out if anybody knows anything about the victim's movements before his death."

"Why? Surely CID would've already done that," Ali said, puzzled.

"I was the first officer on the scene last night. Anyway, that's not the reason I'm here. CID don't seem to be doing their work. I'm sure someone knows what happened to Boiki last night. He couldn't have been on his own," she explained.

"What makes you think locals will wanna talk to you? Could be wasting your time, you know."

"Rumours are probably circulating. Villagers love gossip," she said, confident she was doing the right thing.

Ali smiled, remembering how stubborn she could be. "That might be all you'll ever get—rumours—that's what villagers are good at," he warned.

"The rumours could be just the break we need to solve the case."

"Does CID know you're here?"

"Nope. This is my own investigation," she said stubbornly.

"What can I do to help?"

"A lift to the deceased's home would be much appreciated."

37

"I'm afraid I can't take you—it'll blow your cover." Ali paused thoughtfully before continuing, "But I can ask my girlfriend to take you." He took out his cell phone and added, "If you don't mind, that is."

Her heart sunk. *Why would I*, she wanted to say. She made a face and shrugged as he made the call.

A few minutes later, a white Ford Bantam pulled up at the front of the charge office.

"Your lift has arrived. Good luck," Ali said as he walked her to the door. She didn't say goodbye or thank him for his help—she was pissed off he'd moved on, that he'd found another woman to replace her. As she entered the car, Duski mumbled something resembling a greeting to the woman, slammed the door, and sat quietly. She took an instant dislike to the woman.

*   *   *

The villagers were already congregating at the victim's home when Ali's girlfriend dropped her off. She thanked the woman and joined a crowd of mourners entering a shrub-fenced yard. These were the first evening prayers, and the entire village had turned up. Like Duski, most people were there merely to find out what really happened to the deceased.

Duski mingled easily with the crowd—her eyes focused at bottom level. Any protruding bottom that caught her eye was suspiciously scrutinised in the hope the owner might turn out to be the mysterious woman she believed knew how Boiki died. She was so engrossed that she nearly bumped into the man she'd met earlier on the bus.

"Halo, sista!" the man greeted her. "My cousin," he said, putting a heavy hand on a young woman's shoulder standing by his side. "Hope you are not from CID—my cousin's been interrogated enough this morning," the man warned before he left her with the woman and disappeared to join a crowd being served tea and greasy fat cakes.

"Dumela mma," Duski said, studying the woman's tear-stained face. *Her bottom is too thin; she's too dark to be the woman I'm after*, she thought. "I'm so sorry *mma*," she added.

"My cousin said that you wanted to talk to me," the young woman stared vacantly at Duski. "Who are you?" she asked.

Duski realised she had to tell the woman the truth if she were to get anything out of her. "I lied to your cousin about knowing Boiki. I'm a police officer, not from CID though," she added quickly. "I was the first officer at the scene last night. I know the investigating officers have already talked to you." She showed the woman her ID. "This is going to sound very strange, but the deceased has been . . . what I mean is, his spirit has been in contact with me. Call me superstitious, but I'm convinced he's trying to tell me something. The strange thing is, since making the decision to come here today, he hasn't made contact. Do you see what I mean?" Duski felt embarrassed; she knew how ridiculous her explanation sounded. "I'm sure that you want to know who killed your boyfriend as much as I do," she added.

"What do you want to know?" the woman asked looking at Duski strangely.

"Everything and anything you know about Boiki."

"Like what, exactly?"

"Like how long you have been together, who he was seeing before you met."

The woman stared past her, into the distance. Tears fell freely from her bloodshot eyes.

"Can we go somewhere quiet," she said, leading the way out of the yard.

Duski followed. Once out of the shrub-fenced yard, the woman stopped.

"Boiki and I had been together for nearly two years. He'd been with other women before me, mind."

"Do you know who they are?"

"The bar lady at Salt and Pepper," she said, pausing to sniff back a tear.

"Boiki lied to me when we met, he said they'd split up. He was seen with her last night at Salt and Pepper after he'd told me he was working late," she cried.

"Is she single?"

"Married—I've told CID about her. I am sure her husband killed Boiki."

"What does the husband do for a living?"

"He's a security guard. CID arrested him this morning, but I hear he was released without charge because his wife claims he was with her all night."

Duski looked at the woman thoughtfully, wondering whether the cuffs used to handcuff Boiki could have been the husband's, but for some reason her mind kept going back to the mysterious woman.

"Has Boiki ever mentioned a child or a woman he'd had a child with?" Duski asked.

"He's talked about his little girl, but never about the mother. I had a feeling he didn't like talking about her, so I never asked."

"Have you seen any photos of her—this woman or of the little girl?"

The woman stared into the distance again. "I think we've met, but we were never introduced—suspected it was her, anyway," she said and paused for a while—it was as if she were unsure whether to carry on before she hesitantly carried on. "It was about a month ago—I was at Salt and Pepper when I saw him talking to someone, a woman I've never seen before."

"Did you ask him who the woman was?"

"No, I didn't. But I'd a feeling it was her," she said.

"Has he ever mentioned her name or where she was from? Do you think she's here now?"

"Like I said, we never talked about her."

"Do you remember what she looked like?"

"Short, fat, and very light skinned. She looked like she was a Mokwena or someone from villages around Molepolole," she said. "Do you think she's involved?" the woman asked looking up at Duski, eyes full of hope.

"Don't know yet. Thanks anyway," Duski said, realising it was going to be difficult to track down the mysterious woman. Molepolole was a big village, and most women in the village would fit the description. "Got to head back soon. Is the bar woman here tonight?" Duski suddenly asked.

"She is—the shameless whore," the woman said with a voice full of hate and outrage.

"Do you mind pointing her out?"

The young woman turned to walk back into the shrub yard. Duski followed silently. As they entered the yard, the woman stopped.

"She is over there," she said, pointing to a rounded and short woman serving tea and fat cakes to a group of elderly people sitting inside a low walled enclosure in front of the main hut. "Promise me you'll do whatever it takes to find whoever is responsible for Boiki's death," she grabbed hold of Duski's arm, her big bloodshot eyes fixed on hers pleadingly.

"Will do my best," Duski said, "And thank you for everything—really appreciate you agreeing to talk to me and the information you've given me." With that, Duski headed towards the Salt and Pepper woman.

"*Dumela mma*, I'm Sergeant Duski Lôcha from central police station. Can we find somewhere quiet to talk?" Duski said introducing herself—she'd now completely abandoned the idea of working undercover. She showed the woman her ID.

The bar lady put the tea tray on an empty table by the fireside. "How can I help you? My husband has nothing to do with Boiki's death," she started to say as soon as they'd moved away from the crowded fireplace.

"I was told you were seen with Boiki last night."

"He came to see me, and as usual, he wanted free beers. I gave him the beers and he left. Can I go back in now?" the woman said, folding her arms defiantly.

"Look, I'm not trying to accuse you of anything. I believe you," Duski said in an effort to win the woman's trust. She knew how ruthless CID could be in their interrogations. "All I'm trying to do is talk to anybody who saw Boiki yesterday, and this doesn't imply whoever saw him or was with him is guilty. I'm just hoping someone would give us information to help us piece together what happened," Duski explained in the hope the woman would be more cooperative.

"I know you're all trying to pin the murder on my husband. He didn't even know about this affair until you lot came asking questions. My husband has nothing to do with what happened. It

43

was his night off; he came to see me at the bar, and then we went home together at eleven," the woman said.

"Do you remember seeing Boiki with anybody else, perhaps someone you've never seen before?"

"No, but he did mention he was going to the music festival. That's why he wanted a free case of beers."

"Did he say who he was going with?"

"No."

"Thank you *mma*, and please do ring the station if you remember anything you haven't told us about last night," Duski said, realising the woman was probably telling the truth. "Even if you think it's minor or irrelevant," she added, taking out her cell phone to ring the taxi.

"Any luck?" Constable Ali asked, making her jump.

"You nearly gave me a heart attack," Duski said. "What are you doing here?"

"Thought you might want a lift back to Gabs—anyway, did you find out anything useful?"

"Not really," she said, clearly disappointed.

Told you, Ali was tempted to say, but the look on Duski's face told him it wasn't advisable. He kept quiet and led her back to his car. On the drive back to the city, Duski mulled over what she'd heard so far. Both women seemed genuine and honest; she'd no impression they were lying to her.

The only person who knew what happened to Boiki, she kept thinking, *was the mysterious woman.* Unsure how long the case she'd unofficially assigned to herself would take to solve, Duski stared ahead, determined. *I will find her,* she promised the dead man.

Chapter Four

Duski sat in front of a large fan, her face in the direct path of the cool air that was swirling around like an invisible mini-tornado. Outside, the heat had intensified, and the inside of the house had turned into a large furnace. Everything was quiet except the distant, but constant chirping of crickets and the occasional drone of a lone plane descending towards the world's smallest international airport. A week had passed since the lion park murder, and neither she nor CID had made any progress at all. The case had already gone cold.

Any leads or clues that could have been followed, Duski and the investigating team had exhausted. She'd even gone back to interview the victim's work colleagues, his family, the girlfriend, and the bar lady. Their stories never faltered.

None of them were with the deceased on the night he died.

Duski was desperate to see the forensics report, but getting her hands on it was her biggest challenge yet. She extracted herself from the fan and was about to dial CID when heavy footsteps approaching the front door interrupted her thoughts.

"Koo koo," a man's voice called out.

Duski's heart skipped. For a brief, mad second, she wondered whether it was Ali. She'd been so engrossed in the murder case that she'd almost forgotten his promise to pop in to see her sometime. The appearance of a clean-shaven head and a pair of bulging, bloodshot eyes at the doorway immediately lowered her heart rate.

"*Dumela mma*," the owner of the eyes and shaven head said in greeting. It was the taxi driver, and he was waiting to be invited in.

"Come in *rra*," Duski said, disappointed that the old man's *muti* seemed to have attracted the unwelcome attentions of the taxi driver instead. As the rest of him filled the doorway, she noted that he'd made an effort to dress less formally. The light blue denim shorts he wore exposed a pair of rather unattractive and spindly hairy legs. A brown leather belt held everything in place and stopped the overflowing stomach from wobbling all the way to his sandled feet.

"*Dumela rra*," Duski greeted the man, and she was relieved when Constable Kowa walked into the sitting room at the same time.

"Mudongo, what the hell are you doing here?" Kowa frowned disapprovingly at the awkward figure at the doorway.

"My, you look well fed, babes," Mudongo said, licking his lips while checking out Kowa's well-stuffed thighs and behind.

Kowa sucked her teeth, "You don't look too short of food yourself," she responded sarcastically, surveying Mudongo's protruding belly. "I can see the old cow has been feeding you up."

"Still single?" he asked, moving closer to inspect Kowa's right hand.

Duski watched with amusement.

"Yep, and you—still married?" she asked looking pointedly at his ring finger. "What are you doing here, Mudongo?"

"Came to see you, babes," he said, giving her puppy dog eyes.

Kowa sucked her teeth, "Do I have MUG written here," she said, pointing at her forehead.

Mudongo smiled sheepishly. "I'll make it up to you, babes, I promise," he said, rubbing his shaven head. "Would you ladies like to go to Mokolodi game reserve?" He looked at Duski, pleading. If she agreed to go, he hoped, Kowa would too.

"I'm expecting a visitor later this afternoon, actually," Duski said quickly before excusing herself. She retreated to her bedroom to mull over her non-existent love life and the frustration over the lack of progress in the lion park case.

Chapter Five

Duski was lying in bed, staring vacantly at the ceiling. She'd been back with Ali for a couple of months now—she was mulling over the old man's offer of a stronger love potion. Ali had told her he'd ended the relationship with the woman she'd met in Ramotswa and that he'd be faithful this time. But Duski didn't believe him—it was hard to trust someone who'd cheated on you before. She'd a nagging feeling he was still seeing the woman—that they were probably still together.

The only way to make him completely hers, she'd concluded, was to spike his food—to give him the love potion.

Duski was debating whether to consult the witch doctor again when the sudden shrill of the landline telephone rudely interrupted her thoughts.

Who the hell is ringing at this time, she cursed checking the time on her cell phone.

5:06 a.m., it read.

Duski decided to let the phone ring for a while with the hope the caller would eventually give up and hang up.

But the caller was persistent: five long minutes later, Duski picked up.

"Is this Constable Kowa? This is Babedi," an angry female voice said. She could tell the woman was furious—the clipped tones said it all.

"You might not know me, but I'm calling because I was going through my husband's mobile last night and happened to come across your phone number," the voice at the other end said sharply.

"*Mma* I'm not—"

The caller slammed the phone down before Duski could finish the sentence. *Must be Mudongo's wife*, she thought, shaking her head. *Some men!*

The taxi driver and her housemate were back together—he'd been spending a lot of time in Block Eight—the man practically lived there. Duski was actually surprised it had taken the wife so long to realise that her husband was having an affair.

After the interruption, Duski decided to take a bath. She was on her way to the bathroom when she heard the sound of screeching tyres approaching Ditjaube Junction.

Constable Kowa was on an early shift that morning and usually got a lift from one of the mobile patrol cars. Duski looked through the window to see whether the screeching tyres announced the arrival of Kowa's lift. Instead, a white VW Golf was approaching the house as if the devil himself were behind the wheel.

The car crashed into the metal tube-framed gate.

It was Mudongo's taxi—a rather overweight and heavily made up woman was behind the wheel. Two seconds later, the woman rolled out of the driver's seat and wobbled towards the front door.

Duski suspected she was Mudongo's wife, but she'd no time to warn Kowa. She rushed to the door instead—but it flew open before she could lock it, nearly whacking her in the face. The woman bulldozed her way in. In response to Duski's keen greeting, she grabbed hold of her by her dressing gown collar and pushed her back into the house.

"You've been fucking my husband," the woman screamed, pushing her farther into the centre of the living room.

"*Mma* you've got the wrong person," Duski said as patiently as she could. Gently but firmly, she tried to remove the woman's hand from her collar.

"You lying bitch," the woman screeched. She sucked her teeth and raised her hand to slap her.

Duski grabbed hold of the woman's arm, restraining her with surprising ease. "Take a seat and tell me what your problem is," she said quite firmly.

"You're the fucking problem," the woman screamed again, this time trying to grab Duski's short dreadlocks.

"Leave her alone," Kowa interjected. Her short, stocky figure stood in the middle of the corridor like a baobab stump. "If you have a problem, *mma*, talk to me. I'm the one sleeping with your husband," she blurted out, walking into the room with deliberate slowness. She stopped and faced Duski's attacker.

The woman's jaw dropped—her eyes widened with dismay. She quickly pulled herself together and charged at Kowa like an injured rhino.

Duski threw herself in between the two women.

"*Mma*, if you want to do a shit, go find yourself a toilet," Constable Kowa warned before pushing Duski aside. "Your husband doesn't want you anymore. Move on, find yourself another husband," she said yelling obscenities at the woman before storming back to her bedroom.

The taxi driver's wife stood mortified for a few seconds before she broke into a short, barking laugh and followed Kowa out of the room. "Is that what he's been telling you?"

"Why can't you leave him alone?" Kowa asked, sucking her teeth.

"*In sickness and in health, in poverty or in wealth, till death do us part,*" the woman chanted the wedding vows as she marched behind Kowa into the bedroom. "That's the promise he made, and I expect him to keep it," she said. She pounced at Kowa, screaming and kicking. "Hope he splits your vagina next time he fucks you, you fat little slut!"

Kowa suddenly stopped, turned round to look at the woman. "You calling me fat?" She laughed, shaking her head and wagging her finger at her, she said. "A fat, ugly slug like you is calling me fat?"

Duski, who had also followed the two women into the bedroom, grabbed hold of Mudongo's wife and forced her to sit on the bed.

"Look here, *mma*, if you don't leave now, I'm gonna have to call the . . ." She paused and gently eased her hold.

To her horror and utter disgust, the woman suddenly jumped onto the bed and lifted up her georgette skirt. She exposed massive and dimply brown thighs and a bottom to match.

"Is this where he fucks you? Is it?" she yelled while excavating a pair of large, black thongs from the crevices of her bottom cheeks and urinated all over the bed. When she was finished, she grabbed the pillow to wipe herself before pulling up her panties. She jumped down and stared at Kowa—pursing her mouth in a self-satisfied smirk.

Duski boldly placed herself in between the two women. She forced Kowa to sit down on the dry side of bed.

"Stay there and don't move," she ordered, looking sternly at her housemate. She then turned her attention to Mudongo's wife. "You better go home now if you don't want to be charged for criminal trespass and common assault." She said in a firm and authoritative tone.

The woman cursed and left.

*   *   *

Later that day, Duski was sitting at her desk
in the charge office thinking about that morning's
incident when the second murder was reported.
She was on a nightshift and the office was quiet.
Most of her men had gone out on beat patrol
duties, as usual.

The duty sub-inspector was busy going
through the cell register and cases handed over by
officers from the previous shift. Constable Moji
was, as usual, glued to the latest edition of his
favourite paper, *The Voice*.

"Are you bored, Sarge?" Moji suddenly
asked, putting away the paper. "Why don't we go
and hunt for illegal immigrants?"

Duski's face brightened and Moji added,
"We won't even have to go far to find them—they'll
keep us occupied till morning."

Sub-Inspector Bale looked up from the cell
register he'd been studying since the beginning
of the shift. "I need you both here." Duski didn't
even have a chance to respond to Constable Moji's
suggestion. "There are officers on foot patrol
whose job it is to question or arrest anybody they
find loitering on the streets," he added before going
back to studying the cell register.

Duski looked at him and complained, "But
sir, there is nothing to do here at the moment." She
knew she sounded like a stroppy teenager, but she
added anyway: "I'm bored—it's frustrating sitting
here doing nothing," she muttered. She'd spent the
first hour of the shift on the phone, unsuccessfully

trying to persuade a new detective constable to let her see the lion park forensics report.

The sub-inspector ignored her. Duski sighed and reached for an old copy of the penal code. She was leafing aimlessly through it when two boys in their mid teens suddenly rushed into the charge office, out of breath.

"There is a dead man in our skip," one of the boys announced, his eyes wide with fear. Duski recognised them immediately as street kids who slept in the skip at the taxi rank next to the police station.

"Boys, been sniffing glue?" Sub-Inspector Bale asked, towering above the frightened street boys and added, "Now, how do you know this man is dead?" He continued to look at the two boys in a stern manner.

"He is not breathing or moving—he's got blood all over him," one of the boys said.

"I'll go and check it out sir," Duski offered, relieved that, at last, she had something to do. Without waiting for the sub-inspector to respond, she rummaged through the charge office main table drawer for a torch.

"Come on, you two, show us where this dead body is," Constable Moji said thumping one of the boys on the head before he led them out of the office.

But the urchins were reluctant to go back to the skip. He grabbed them both by their tatty T-shirts and dragged them out of the police station.

Duski followed while Sub-Inspector Bale posted himself at the station's entrance and watched them until they'd disappeared behind the public toilets where the skip was.

"Now where is it?" Constable Moji asked pushing the boys towards the skip. Meanwhile, Duski shone the torch inside.

"Jesus Christ!" she exclaimed as soon as beams revealed a bison-like head, the pointy beard, and the big bloodshot eyes—they were staring at her from the bottom of the skip. She backed away, staggering like a drunk as far away as possible before turning the torch off.

Duski sat down to steady herself.

"What's the matter, Sarge?" Constable Moji asked suddenly letting go off the boys and walking over to where Duski sat. Without awaiting her response, he took the torch from her to investigate the contents of the skip himself.

If her reaction is anything to go by, Moji thought as he slowly approached the skip, *whatever is in there must be pretty unpleasant.* He mentally prepared himself to face whatever nastiness lay at the bottom of the skip.

"Jesus, this is messy!" Moji exclaimed.

On top of some old cardboard boxes lay a naked, mutilated, and bloody corpse. It was already attracting a few blowflies. He shone the torch all over the body and around the skip. The victim's hands and legs were tied up with a thin copper-coloured wire. A bloodied goatee and hairy

chest were the only features that identified the body
as male. The groin area was hollow and covered in
blood—the penis and testicles had been cut off.

"Sarge, I think I know who he is," he
suddenly shouted out as the light revealed the
victim's face.

"Boys, get back to the office," Duski
ordered. She steeled herself before joining
Constable Moji at the mouth of the skip. "I know
him too. He is a taxi driver," she said as soon as
the boys were out of earshot. "He's married, and
he's been cheating on his wife with my housemate."
She rambled on like a mad woman as she recalled
the two women fighting over him that morning.
"Now he's dead—dead," she whispered, wondering
whether his wife had anything to do with his death.

"Constable Kowa? Was she seeing him? Are
you going to tell her?"

Duski shook her head.

"Would you like me to?" he asked before
saying, "Why would anyone want to cut off
someone's privates? What have they done with
them?" He looked at Sergeant Duski Lôcha who
was still shaking her head as if she knew the
whereabouts of the missing body parts. "This is,
without a doubt, the work of witch doctors. This is
a ritual killing," he ranted on before handing back
the torch. "Do you realise that this is the second
gruesome murder we've attended in a short space
of time. Do you think that he was killed here?" he
suddenly asked.

"No, too risky to carry out a ritual murder in the city centre," she replied, looking around the inside of the skip for signs of a struggle . . . and for the missing parts.

She thought, *During a ritual murder, the victim cannot be killed before the important body parts—in this case, the sexual organs—have been removed.*

Duski knew it was vital that those essential body parts were cut off while the victim was alive. Apparently, ritual murder was very much like a hunting expedition (except that the kill would have been identified before the outing). *The killers get a thrill out of chasing the victim prior to mutilation.*

Mudongo's body looked like it had been dumped after being mutilated . . . and after he had been killed. There was no blood anywhere else inside the skip (apart from where the body was lying), and there was no sign of the cut-off organs either.

"Any blood outside the skip?" she asked, shining the torch around it. "If he was brought here like this, I'm sure there will be footprints and blood stains somewhere around here," she added, hopeful.

On the opposite side, Duski's torch immediately revealed a small trail of blood that led to a set of tyre marks not far from the skip. "It looks like the body was driven here," she said, a little bit excited by the discovery. "I'll stay here, you go back in and let the sub-inspector know what we've found. And call CID, will you?"

The constable nodded.

"Oh and take statements from the boys, please. We need to establish when the body was dumped into the skip," she ordered before saying, "Judging from the few blowflies already seeking moist areas of the corpse to lay the eggs, I would guess he hasn't been dead that long."

Duski walked back to the skip just before Constable Moji disappeared behind the toilet block and headed back to the office. She stood and stared at the mutilated body for some time. Mudongo's wife was the only person she could think of with a good enough motive to want him dead.

But why a ritual killing?

She was puzzled. Again, she started thinking about that morning's fight between Mudongo's wife and Kowa.

Was it a revenge killing? Was Mudongo's wife guilty? Did Mudongo try to leave his wife? Is that why she'd paid them that dramatic visit? Is she involved in his murder?

She churned out the questions, but she found no answers.

Why would she have him killed just after fighting over him?

The mutilated corpse lay still and unresponsive. The secret of how it got there—safely buried beneath the rubble inside the skip—eluded her. The body clearly bore characteristics of a ritual killing, which was a business not suitable for the faint of heart. Duski had heard stories of ritual killings and read ritual murder case files, but now she was getting some first-hand experience.

The victims are handpicked by either a witch doctor or someone working in collaboration with one. Usually, the body parts, which are believed to bring business and quick profit to new businesses, are sold to entrepreneurs who are also involved in the killings. The way the victim's body parts are removed, the way the victim is killed, and how long it takes before the victim dies—those factors are all believed to add strength to the muti *made out of that particular victim's body parts.*

Suddenly Duski had a strange feeling that she wasn't alone, that someone or something was watching her. She looked up to be met by the ghostly face of the lion park murder victim.

The face floated into the skip and hovered briefly among the blowflies—over the mutilated body—before it settled on the dead body's groin and stared.

Duski shut her eyes—hoping the face would go away—her heart was galloping as if the devil himself was riding it. Someone or something blew stale warm breath at her closed eyes before brushing swiftly past her. She grabbed the rim of the skip to steady herself.

She began to rapidly recite Psalm 91 before opening her eyes. As if she'd imagined it, the face had gone. It left no trace. Though it was a very warm night, her arms and back suddenly broke out in great rashes of goose bumps.

What's wrong with me? She wondered, frightened and confused.

"What have we got in here," a voice said behind her, making her jump.

"Detective Inspector Marvellous and this is Detective Sergeant Boy," the man said, introducing himself and his partner. "I understand you know the victim," he peered inside the skip.

"Yes, his name is Mudongo. He is a taxi driver licensed to operate from this taxi rank," she said. "This is all very bizarre," she mumbled, as if to herself.

"Why?" the Detective Inspector asked.

"His wife paid us a visit this morning," she blurted out, staring at the skip, "I think she'd just found out he was having an affair with my housemate," she concluded, wondering whether it was a good idea to involve Kowa in what would obviously be a murder investigation.

"We'll need to speak to your housemate," Detective Inspector Marvellous said. "Looks like we might have a ritual killing on our hands," he added.

"Someone needs to speak to the deceased's wife too," Duski reminded. "I'm sure my housemate will have the address," she added, dialling Kowa's number.

Duski had started walking back to the office when she heard a familiar ringtone coming from deep inside the skip.

"That's Mudongo's cell," she said, turning round and hurrying back towards the skip. Her own cell phone was still glued to her ear.

The ringing came from somewhere deep underneath the body. Detective Sergeant Boy—already geared up to start collecting evidence—pulled the body to its side. Detective Inspector Marvellous (who had been taking photos of the body), photographed the phone before Detective Sergeant Boy fished it out with a gloved hand.

"Kowa's cell is busy—must be her ringing Mudongo's cell," Duski announced as Detective Sergeant Boy put the retrieved phone on loud-speak before answering it.

"This is Detective Sergeant Boy, who is this?" he asked.

"Sorry, wrong number," the voice on the other side apologised.

"Constable Kowa?" Duski asked as soon as she recognised her housemate's voice.

"What's going on? Why've you got Mudongo's cell? Is everything all right?" Kowa asked, clearly alarmed.

"Are you at the house?" Duski asked. "Wait there, I'll be over in a few minutes," she said before Detective Sergeant Boy switched the cell phone off.

"I'm coming with you. I don't want you giving her too much information yet. We need to eliminate her from our investigations first," Detective Inspector Marvellous announced as soon as the phone was safely put into a marked exhibit packet, ready for a thorough examination later. "Constable, you need to radio CID South to ask for more officers on the scene. The body needs to be moved, and the area needs to be cordoned off for a thorough examination in the morning," he instructed.

*　　*　　*

"I'm afraid we've got some bad news," Duski started, unsure what to say when they arrived at her house in Block Eight later that night.

Kowa's lower lip quivered; she shook her head. "Has anything happened to him?" she cried.

"I'm afraid Mudongo is dead, Constable," Detective Inspector Marvellous said. "When was the last time you saw or spoke to the deceased?" he carried on, not wanting to waste too much time.

"Sir, she's just lost a partner for goodness sake," Sergeant Duski Lôcha reproached the DI.

"I'm afraid we can't afford to waste time. This is a homicide—she's to come down to the station with us, Sergeant," he said. "I am sure you are aware that, if we are to catch the perpetrator, we need to treat everyone close to the victim as a potential suspect," he added stubbornly.

Duski looked at him indignantly.

Has the man no feelings at all? How could he be so insensitive? She wondered, but she said nothing to stop him from dragging her housemate down to the station that night.

"I'm really sorry *mma,* but I need to know when you last saw the victim, the nature of your relationship, and anything you know that might help us in our investigation," he added quickly when he noticed Duski's disapproving look.

"Where is he? Can I see him first?" Kowa asked, staring past the DI.

"You'll be able to see him once our investigations are over," he explained, leading her out to the waiting police bakkie.

"Do you know Mudongo's home address by any chance?" Duski asked once they were all in the car. "We need to inform his wife," she added cautiously.

Kowa stared blankly into the darkness for a while before she looked at the sergeant as if she weren't sure who she was. "G West, near Satchmo's night club," she whispered as if in auto pilot.

"House number?" the DI asked.

"Don't know," she replied, staring past him—into the darkness.

"I'll drive to Gaborone West police station once I've dropped you two off at the station. Someone is bound to know where he lives," Duski said before all three fell silent to commune with their thoughts.

Chapter Six

The journey to Gaborone West police station proved fruitful. Within half an hour of dropping off Kowa and DI Marvellous back at the station, Duski was parked in front of Mudongo's house. She turned off the ignition and sat in the car for a while contemplating what she was going to say to the woman. Once composed, she opened the car door, took a deep breath, got the torch out of the glove box, and walked determinedly towards the house.

Mudongo's taxi was parked outside the gate, which was locked with some kind of bicycle lock. The house was in darkness. Duski checked the time on her cell. It was nearly two o'clock in the morning. She walked towards the taxi, switched the torch on, and shone the light inside. Nothing seemed out of place, except for the keys which had been left dangling in the ignition.

She walked back to the police car, took out a pair of blue latex gloves from the glove box, and went back to the taxi. She put a gloved hand on the bonnet. It was still warm. Wondering if Mudongo's wife was its recent driver, Duski walked round to the driver's side, opened the door, and pulled a lever just below the steering wheel to unlock the boot. She wasn't sure what she expected to find inside the boot, but something prompted her to.

With caution, she lifted the boot up and was immediately hit by the fresh smell of blood and death. She knew then that the taxi had been used to transport Mudongo's body to the skip. Duski took another long and deep breath before she shone the light inside the boot. The missing body parts were not in there, she noted in relief—that would have been a difficult discovery.

She was about to shut the boot when she noticed an arrow lying not far from the bloodied area where Mudongo's body must have lain. It was a lightly constructed arrow. She picked it up, curious as to why Mudongo had an arrow in the boot of his car. She put it back where she found it and radioed the DI about the discovery. After, she radioed Gaborone West to ask for assistance before confronting Mudongo's wife.

A few minutes later, a police vehicle appeared from around the corner. She immediately recognised the face at the wheel—it was the constable who'd given her directions to the house earlier.

"How can we help you, Sarge?" the constable asked, jumping out of the car as soon as he was parked behind the taxi.

"Great, you brought another officer with you," she said as a second constable jumped out from the passenger side to join them. "I want you to guard the taxi until someone from forensics arrives to collect it," she instructed the second constable. He immediately stood to attention before he took his post in front of the taxi. "And you," she turned to face the first constable. "Come inside with me please. I'm afraid we have to jump over the fence," She began scaling the locked gate, and the constable followed suit.

"Police, *mma!* Open up, we know you are in there," she shouted, pounding on the door several times. "Can we come in for a few minutes Mrs Mbulawa?"

Reluctant footsteps approached and stopped behind the door.

"It's the police *mma*, open the door or we'll be forced to kick it in," she warned. Someone unlocked the door and opened it a crack, just enough to peer through. Duski showed her ID.

"If you are here to ask me to let that cheating bastard in, you are wasting your time," a woman's voice said before slamming the door in their faces.

"*Mma*, we are here about something far more serious than that," Duski said, wondering whether the woman was playing games or whether she was genuinely unaware of her husband's death.

"Shall we come back in the morning? It doesn't look like she's going to let us in," the constable said. He'd been standing patiently behind her. "She's probably gone back to bed now," he added.

"We've got to speak to her tonight—she needs to know that her husband has been murdered. Besides, she might be the murderer,"

Duski said before turning her attention back to the door. "Mrs Mbulawa, you've got to let us in. We need to speak to you. Something has happened to your husband," she said quite authoritatively to the locked door.

Firm and angry footsteps approached the door again. "Come in and make it quick, whatever it is you want to ask me," the woman said. She opened the door and immediately cast a suspicious glance at the taxi. "I know that bastard is in there. What has happened to him this time? Caught with his pants down and got beaten up?" she barked, eyeing Duski from head to toe and sucked her teeth.

"*Mma* I think you'd better sit down," Duski said, leading the woman back into the living room. She looked at her with eyes full of pity, and begged her to sit down.

"*Mma* I'm sure you recognise me," Duski started, embarrassed as she recalled their earlier encounter. Mudongo's wife frowned and sucked her teeth contemptuously. "I understand how you feel," Duski added, desperately searching for the right words to broach the subject of her husband's murder and wishing she hadn't volunteered herself for the task.

The woman looked at her wristwatch impatiently. "Is that what you came here tell me? You think you know how I feel?" she laughed and suddenly stood up, ready to march them out of the house.

"*Mma* when was the last time you saw your husband?" the constable interrupted, coming to Duski's rescue.

The woman looked at them both for a long time and sighed. "Have you come here to laugh at me?" She looked at Duski, eyes full of unshed tears.

"*Mma* your husband is dead. His body is lying, as we speak, in a skip at the main mall taxi rank," Duski said. She walked over to where the woman stood and sat her down again on the nearest sofa. "We came here—" She paused, not sure whether to tell her the truth, and then continued, "simply as bearers of the bad news." She couldn't bring herself to tell the woman that she was a suspect—it would have been too cruel. "I'm so sorry *mma*," she finally said, touching the woman lightly on her shoulder. "I know this is not the right time, but we also need to know when you last saw him." She continued as cautiously and sensitively as possible.

The woman's face hardened. She bit her lower lip to stop it from quivering.

"This afternoon," she started, but then hesitated and looked at Duski for a while. "As you know, he was at your house last night."

Duski nodded sympathetically.

"Well when he came home this morning . . . well, you know the rest," she said, hanging her

69

head in shame. Tears were streaming freely into her folded arms. "I confiscated the taxi keys and his phone. He spent the day in bed. About three in the afternoon, someone rang his cell for a taxi. It was a man, said he wanted to be picked up at five from Gaborone West shopping centre to go to the airport. Told him about the call before I gave him back the phone and keys. He left the house bout five, promising to come straight home after the job. That was the last time I saw him," she said, using the hem of her nightdress to wipe away a stream of incessant tears.

"Do you recall the cell number of the person who rang?" Duski asked.

"Caller ID was withheld. I only answered it because I thought it was that woman he'd been messing around with," she said, eyes glaring with anger and pain.

Duski sighed. She knew that if the last passenger was the killer, it would be difficult to trace the number. Virtually no cell numbers in Botswana were registered.

"When we arrived here earlier, you thought that we were with your husband—I assume you didn't see who drove the taxi back to the house." The woman shook her head. Duski looked at her for some time before asking, "Did you hear it arrive?"

"Yes. It wasn't long before you two showed up. That's why I thought he called you here," she said.

"Did you hear anything else? People talking outside or another car driving away?"

"Yes, a car door being slammed and next, you lot pounding on my door," she said, sniffing away tears. "What am I supposed to do now?" she cried. She was looking at Duski, helpless and desperate. "How am I to live without him? What am I to tell the children?"

"*Mma*, we are doing all we can to find your husband's killers," Duski reassured her. "But we'll need your help to find out if there was anybody who could have wanted him dead, someone's husband or partner for instance." The woman said nothing, but she looked at Duski, eyes full of grief and pain. "I'm sorry *mma*, but we do need answers in order to build a picture of what might have happened to your husband," she added. "You found out he was having an affair with my housemate. Was it the first time he'd ever had an extramarital affair?"

She shook her head—wiping away a lone tear with the hem of her nightdress again—and stared at the ceiling, hands clasped under her chin as if she was praying. "The others were young girls only after his money," she responded after a while.

"Their names or addresses?" Duski asked.

The woman shook her head. "Never stored their names on his cell"

"Thank you very much for your help *mma*. I would like to once more say how truly sorry we are about the death of your husband," Duski said. She

71

put a sympathetic hand on the woman's quivering shoulders.

They were just about to leave when a white government vehicle pulled up at the gate next to the taxi. It was the forensics team coming to collect the vehicle. Duski realised that she still had one more unpleasant request to make. She turned round to face the woman again.

"By the way, we need to take your husband's taxi away for a forensic analysis," she started but immediately paused to look at the woman apologetically. "We also need you to formally identify the body," she added as if it were an afterthought, shuddering as she recalled Mudongo's mutilated body. She wondered whether it was fair to put the woman through any more pain. Duski had deliberately avoided giving her full details of her husband's death, but she knew that soon, the woman would have to be told about the condition of the body.

Chapter Seven

A couple of weeks had passed since the discovery of Mudongo's mutilated body in the taxi rank skip. His wife and constable Kowa were both eliminated as suspects. The taxi's last passenger, like the mysterious woman in the lion park murder, was still at large.

Walking into the charge office that morning, Duski noticed a large brown government envelope on her incoming mail tray. She was excited, wondering whether it was a copy of the forensics report on the skip murder case. After the brief handover, she reached for the envelope with anticipation. She tore it open, wondering whether evidence collected from the skip would give her a better grasp of what had happened to the taxi driver. Yet, to her surprise, the envelope revealed a different forensics report. Her face suddenly brightened, she'd been so preoccupied with Mudongo's death that she'd almost forgotten about the lion park murder case. It had been nearly six months.

She made herself comfortable before spreading out the contents of the envelope on the desk in front of her. The report contained detailed photographs of the crime scene. At the top of the pack were photographs of the victim . . . or whatever remained of him—the head and stomach.

Lions, apparently, never eat the stomach contents of their prey.

The second set of photographs showed a trail of bloodstains leading all the way into the enclosure. A set of barely visible tyre tracks—just a few metres away from the enclosure—indicated where the trail came from.

Moji's theory was correct; the enclosure is a secondary crime scene, Duski thought as she scrutinised the photographs.

Something else caught her eye—in one of the pictures, next to Boiki's cuffed legs, she noticed an arrow exactly the same as the one she found in the boot of Mudongo's taxi.

What is the significance of the arrow? she wondered. She knew Bushmen used poisoned arrows to hunt large prey.

Could the arrows have been used to paralyse the victims before mutilation? She pondered. However, the report mentioned nothing about any poison found in the victim's system. It however mentioned that there were no footprints outside the enclosure—not even the victim's.

"Remember the lion park case?" Duski suddenly asked, looking up at Constable Moji who'd been staring at his cell phone since he walked into the office that morning. "According to this," she paused while he put the cell phone away. "The victim must have flown into the enclosure," she said looking back at the report suspiciously as if it were hiding something from her.

"Someone obviously wanted the victim's death to look like an accident or suicide," Moji said, walking around to the sergeant's desk to examine the photos himself.

"I don't think so. Why the arrow? The murderer must be trying to tell us something. According to the report, the investigating team hasn't got much to work from," she said looking up briefly at the constable before focusing on another set of photographs of the crime scene.

Her attention was immediately drawn to a close-up of the victim's groin. The area was circled with a pencil to draw attention to some distinct marks. Scribbled notes next to the area stated that the marks were inconsistent with those made by the lions' teeth on the rest of the victim's body. The inscription went on to explain that the victim's groin area appeared to have been cut by a sharp instrument, most probably an okapi knife.

She studied the groin closely. It was hardly touched apart from a cut round the area. It was very similar to Mudongo's mutilated groin.

"It looks like Boiki might have been mutilated and murdered in the same way as Mudongo was," she finally said, stuffing the report back into the brown envelope. She was now sure that the two murders were connected. But who was behind them, and what was their motive? She stared into space and reflected on the facts. "I wonder how CID is getting on with their investigations into Mudongo's murder," she suddenly said and sighed.

"I wonder if Mudongo's killers have also been meticulous in covering up their tracks."

Having finished reading the report and studying the photographs, Duski had nothing else to do. She paced around the charge office aimlessly. She wondered who could have killed Boiki and Mudongo. Her gut feeling was that both men were killed by the same person or people. Suddenly, she was overwhelmed by a strange, almost premonition-like feeling that the two men weren't the killer's first or last victims.

Later that morning, she was still preoccupied with the forensics report. She was scanning it and re-examining it when a young man suddenly burst into the charge office.

"I'm handing myself in," he cried, standing pathetically in front of her. Duski, whose mind had been so occupied by Boiki and Mudongo's mysterious deaths, immediately thought the young man was the elusive killer.

"I have stolen and killed one of my master's cows. I have shared the meat out among my family and sold the rest," the man confessed breathlessly, much to her disappointment. "Look at what he's done to me for stealing and killing one of his cows," he said, turning round to show her his invisibly handcuffed wrists.

For the first time, she noticed that the man's wrists were bizarrely locked behind his back by some kind of invisible cuffs. She went round the table to where the man was and ordered him to turn round again before attempting to pull his wrists apart. To her amazement, the invisible force holding the man's wrists together felt strangely like real handcuffs. The man declared that the only way of releasing them was to ring the cattle owner who held the key to the mystery cuffs.

"Please ring him. Ask him to forgive me," the man begged pathetically, "I've got his cell number. Please ring him." He looked at his cell phone which was inside his shirt pocket.

"How do you know this has anything to do with him? Besides, what will he do even if he were to come here?" Duski asked, reluctant to believe the man's locked wrists had anything to do with the cattle owner. She was desperately trying to find a more rational and plausible explanation for the man's locked wrists when Constable Moji rudely interrupted her train of thought.

"Sarge, don't you know most cattle owners still consult traditional doctors to protect their herds against theft? This is clearly one of those cases," Constable Moji said. "Let's call the man, Sarge," he added before reaching for the man's phone. "What is his name, *monna*?" he asked the bewildered man. Moji's thumb hovered over the menu button of the man's cell phone.

"*Rre Mannathoko*," he said, his face brightening up with anticipation.

"Constable Moji, I'm the officer in charge today. Remember, it's my duty to make decisions."

"Sorry Sarge—was only trying to help," he apologised.

Duski sucked her teeth. "What will your master do that we can't do?" she turned round, resuming the questioning of the man who was beginning to look anxious and agitated again.

"Sarge, the man will be able to bring his witch doctor—who's probably responsible for this," Constable Moji explained while the man nodded. Duski eventually let Moji call the cattle owner, though she didn't believe the man's locked wrists had anything to do with witchcraft.

"He took his bloody time," Duski said an hour later as a white, four-wheel drive Toyota pulled up at the front of the station. The driver was a typical, rich Motswana, short in stature with a stomach that looked ready to burst. A little, stringy-looking man with prominent Bushman facial features jumped out from the passenger seat.

His witch doctor I guess, she thought turning to the cuffed man. "Is that your master?"

"Ee mma," the thief replied, shifting uncomfortably on his seat.

Constable Moji popped his head up from *The Voice* newspaper he'd been devouring with gusto while waiting for the cattle owner.

"Do you want me to bring them in, Sarge?" he asked.

"No, thanks," she said, marching out to meet the two men herself. *"Dumelang borra,"* she greeted them as soon as they walked into the station's reception area. "I'm Sergeant Duski Lôcha, and this is constable Moji," she said shaking the men's hands. Moji, who'd followed her to the reception area, also extended his hand in greeting.

"Where is the thief?" the big-bellied man asked.

"Follow me, he is in here," she said, leading them into the charge office.

"*Rra,* you see what happens to people who steal livestock?" the fat man said, addressing his disgraced herd boy.

"*Rra,* I beg you sir, forgive me, *ke kopa maitshwarelo mong'ame*" the cuffed man said, kneeling pathetically at the man's feet.

"Take a seat," Duski instructed the visitors. "I'm a bit confused," she started looking at the two men. "This man here claims you're responsible for his condition. Now how can that be?" she asked, looking at the cattle owner and then the witch doctor sceptically.

"I am. It's true," the cattle owner admitted.

"And what did you do exactly?" she asked, looking at both men.

"To cut a long story short, I consulted my doctor here—he's the one who saw to it that this scoundrel handed himself in to you lot," he explained with an air of pompousness and self-satisfaction.

"Now that the man has confessed to the crime, do you want to free him before we can charge him?" Constable Moji eagerly chipped in.

"Don't want to press charges," the cattle owner replied, "Just wanted to teach him a lesson," he said before instructing his doctor to free the herd boy.

Without a word, the little stringy man took off a leather pouch strapped over one shoulder. He rummaged inside for a few seconds and brought out a small, rusty round tin, which he opened to reveal a foul-smelling greasy concoction. Still without saying a word, the little man put his finger into the tin to bring out a snot-sized portion of the concoction. He rubbed the mixture on his hands before grabbing hold of the herd boy's locked wrists to pull them apart.

"There you go. You are free to go now," the cattle owner said.

"*Tankie rra, tankie mong'ame,*" the herd boy said with relief, bowing his head humbly and repeatedly before the little man and the cattle owner.

"*Rra* we'd appreciate it next time if you didn't take the law into your own hands. Leave the handcuffing to us, it's our job to bring criminals to justice and not that of witch doctors," Duski said looking sternly and reproachfully at both men.

"No disrespect *mma*, but you police officers are useless when it comes to livestock crime. With all the evidence of the crime long devoured by the thief, how'd you have caught this man?" He had cynicism in his voice. "*Monna*, you've still got a job, but if you kill any more of my cattle again without my permission, you might not be so lucky next time." He gave the herd boy a stern look before marching out of the office with the witch doctor and herd boy in tow.

After the departure of the cattle owner and his witch doctor, the office was quiet once again. Constable Moji decided to go into the mall to buy himself a drink, and Duski sat quietly, staring at the holding cell's courtyard. Her mind was occupied by the witch doctor's performance.

Her thoughts eventually strayed to the subject of the love potion—the potion that could make Ali only hers. She couldn't help but dwell on the history and role of traditional doctors in modern day Botswana. She recalled Kgomotso Mogapi's book on the Setswana culture and way of life. In one particular chapter, the author explained how, before colonialism, traditional doctors were regarded as the very backbone of the culture. *Every Motswana's life*, the chapter had stated, *was very much dependent on the services of the traditional doctor. People went to traditional doctors to seek protection for their households, to protect marriages or burials against witchcraft and for all sorts of things.* But why, she wondered, trying to make sense of what she'd witnessed that morning, *do people still seem so embarrassed about this dark side of their culture. Is it because the forces of the dark side are still as much a part of their lives as they were before colonialism?*

We accepted the white man's god and lied to him that we would banish the dark arts from our lives, and

81

now we are forced to practice our culture in secret, she thought. Yet she knew the answer. *For the white man who colonised our ancestors, anything that couldn't be tested, measured, or probed couldn't be real—didn't exist.*

However, the incident hadn't convinced her she needed the old man's love *muti* to make Ali completely hers. As she sat staring at the courtyard, she decided that it was unnecessary to go back to the old man for the love potion. Duski trusted Ali loved her enough not to mess around with other women behind her back. Eventually she decided not to take up the old man's offer. She chuckled to herself as she recalled what a friend once said about men who'd been fed love potions. Apparently, once on the drug, they'd say yes to everything—absolutely everything!

Chapter Eight

On 30th June, six months after their reunion, Ali was told that he was going on a three-month deployment to Matshelagabedi, a village on the border of Botswana and Zimbabwe. The news meant he and Duski were to be apart for three entire months—the ultimate test for their relationship.

It was on Sunday of that week, after a hurried kiss, that Ali jumped into the driver's seat of a patrol V8. He promised to SMS and ring regularly before he drove off—a promise he only kept for a month.

*   *   *

The two murder cases were still pending, and Duski was still waiting to see the forensics report on the taxi driver's murder case. Though a very dedicated police officer, she'd almost given up hope of ever bringing the killers to justice. Ali's silence and the fight to keep the relationship going were threatening to take precedence over the cases.

One evening, as Tina belted out, '*what's love got to do with it*,' she sat and pondered the subject of love. For generations, she thought, people—even great philosophers with profound wisdom—had searched in vain for the meaning of love. But nobody had touched its true essence. Her thoughts wandered off to a Marcus Garvey book she'd once read. Garvey had defined love as a '*happy but miserable state in which humans occasionally found themselves in from time to time.*' It dawned on her how true that statement was, especially in her case. She had, on numerous occasions, been in and out of that miserable state of affairs. Despite all the short-lived affairs she'd been in, she still hadn't learnt that love only temporarily sweetened life, as Garvey had once said.

In the first six months of their relationship, she would have sworn she was the happiest woman in Gaborone. Life with Ali was sweet, and she was truly happy.

Suddenly, her grandmother's voice interrupted her thoughts.

Being happy doesn't mean that everything is perfect, but that one has decided to see beyond imperfections. She smiled. That was so true, she thought.

One evening, a day before Ali's return from his deployment, she was lying on her bed smoking cigarette after cigarette, trying to figure out where her relationship with Ali was heading. Two months had gone by and still, she'd had no communication from him. He wasn't even returning her calls. That evening, she finally acknowledged the relationship was over, non-existent.

Sergeant Duski Lôcha, welcome back to spinsterhood, embrace it! With that in mind, she called a taxi and vowed to focus on nothing but work from then on. *Being single*, she mused in an effort to cheer herself up as she waited for the cab, *is the greatest opportunity to explore the most important person in the world—ME!* There were so many advantages to being single, Duski thought, desperate to get Ali out of her mind. Wearing her favourite big panties and old PJs to bed and not being kept awake by someone else snoring and farting—that was the ultimate joy of being single. She smiled—it's all about me.

*   *   *

The duty inspector looked up surprised as Duski stood to attention, stamped her right foot, and saluted him as she entered the charge office.

"Sergeant, what are you doing here at this time of the night?" he asked.

"Couldn't sleep—I thought I'd come in and sort out some of the paperwork I've had pending for some time," she said with feigned enthusiasm.

"It's midnight Sergeant," the inspector pointed out, tapping his wristwatch. "Everything okay at home?"

"Yeah, fine, sir," she replied, settling herself down at her desk to inspect the mail in the pending tray.

The duty inspector looked at her suspiciously—he could tell she wasn't telling the truth. "Had a fight with your other half or something?"

"He's away and like I said sir, I'm fine—really." She half-smiled at him before getting back to ruffling through the mail.

"By the way, Detective Sergeant Boy left this for you. It is a forensics report on Mudongo's murder case I think," he said handing her a familiar-looking brown envelope.

"Fantastic," she smiled brightly pleased to finally have something to truly sink her teeth into. She immediately buried her head in the report and shut out any unwanted thoughts.

"Did you read it, sir?" she asked the inspector as soon as she'd finished reading it.

"No. Why?"

"Apparently Mudongo's phone had a video recording of his murder," she said. "Unbelievable how sick some people are," she sucked her teeth. She was shocked and angry.

"What do you mean?' the inspector asked, a bit puzzled. "If someone videoed the murder, the murderer must be on the video too."

"Yes, the perpetrator is wearing a blue boiler suit, black boots, gloves, and a balaclava," she said handing over printouts of the video to the inspector. "Surely, someone out there must know who these killers are?"

"It'll be difficult to catch them," the inspector said, looking closely at the picture.

"When did Sergeant Boy drop the report off?" she asked, wondering whether the detective was on a nightshift.

"About half past eleven. Why?"

"I wonder if he's still in the office," she said, already dialling the CID extension number.

"CID central, Detective Sergeant Boy speaking, how can I help?"

"Hi, Sarge, this is Sergeant Duski. Thank you for letting me read the report. Have you identified the man in the video yet?"

"Nope. There were no fingerprints on the phone or on Mudongo's car. We've got nothing at all to work from," Sergeant Boy replied despondently.

"So what are you doing to try to catch these people, Sarge?" she asked, "I've a feeling Boiki and Mudongo were killed by the same people."

Sergeant Detective Boy sucked his teeth, annoyed. "What do you suggest we do *mma*? Do you know something we don't? After all, Mudongo was seeing your housemate."

"I didn't mean to sound critical," she said apologetically, "I was merely airing my views."

"We've done everything we could and we've run out of suspects. Both crime scenes were wiped clean. I'm sorry Sarge, but I've got work to do—gonna have to go," he said before slamming the phone down.

"Are they anywhere near catching the killers?" the inspector asked as soon as she'd replaced the receiver.

"Nope and I don't think they ever will," she replied, shaking her head with frustration. "An

ancient Motswana once said, *'Molato ga o bole.'* A
crime never rots. One day, whoever killed Boiki and
Mudongo will get caught," she said frustrated but
hopeful.

*   *   *

Later, back at home, Duski eventually settled
herself into bed in the early hours of morning. She
was grateful for Pecker the sparrow's loyalty. His
usually annoying tapping on the windowsill soothed
her troubled mind as she struggled to summon
sleep. Ali was now as far from her mind as the stars
were from earth—a million light years away.

Her mind was instead, preoccupied by
thoughts of the two murder cases. She was
wondering whether a new approach in the
investigations might bear more fruit. She even
toyed with the idea of approaching a psychic or a
witch doctor for help.

Who knows, she thought, *they may be able to
help.*

Duski however knew it wasn't uncommon
for such cases to go unsolved in Botswana. She
recalled a ritual murder case some years ago in
which a young girl was found mutilated. It too went
cold as soon as it was opened.

Eventually, Pecker's persistent and faithful
tapping lulled her mind into drowsiness. She closed
her eyes, shut down her mind and the throbbing
in her head subsided. The knowledge that the two

murder cases had stalled to a halt was painful. Unaware she was just about to become a suspect in the third murder, she drifted off. She was confident that one day, those responsible for the murders would be caught.

Crime never rots.

She held on to the thought until she drifted off into a restless and dreamless sleep.

Chapter Nine

"Freedom, I say freedom! Get off me!"
screamed a young, barefooted woman who was
being dragged—kicking and shouting, into the
charge office by Constable Moji with the help of
another officer. The woman's strappy purple T-shirt
was ripped and the denim shorts she was wearing
were stained with blood. She was dusty from head
to toe and her hands were covered by bloody cuts.

"*Mma* you need to calm down. You're
making quite a lot of noise," one of the constables
said in an effort to calm her.

"I'll scream louder if you don't let go of me.
I said *freedom!*" the woman shouted and kicked him
on the shin. Though handcuffed, the young woman
fought the two constables like a cornered tigress.

At the start of her shift that afternoon,
Sergeant Duski Lôcha received a call from
Maruapula Flats. A male voice at the other end of
the line reported that a woman had broken into
his flat and was attacking his girlfriend. The caller
suspected the woman was mentally ill. Being the
section leader, she'd sent the two constables to
attend to the report.

"*Dumela mma*, what is your name?" Duski
greeted, cautiously approaching the young woman.
"Please sit down and tell me what the problem is,"

she said, pointing to a bench on the other side of her desk. The young woman stopped screaming and shot a crazy and suspicious look at her.

"Where is he? He's mine! Do you hear me? Mine!" the woman growled at her.

"Take the handcuffs off," Duski ordered the two constables who'd brought the young lady in. Duski had no idea what she was on about, but she thought she'd give her a chance to explain unrestrained.

"You sure, Sarge?" Constable Moji asked, looking uncertainly at the crazy woman they were still struggling to hold still.

"Just take 'em off constable," she barked.

"Okay, Sarge," Constable Moji shrugged, reaching for his lanyard where he kept his keys. He unlocked the cuffs and cautiously took them off.

Duski walked round to the other side of the table to sit next to the young woman. Once she'd settled herself down, she took one of the young woman's bloodied and cut hands and clasped it gently.

"What is your name?" she asked, looking sympathetically at her.

The woman was tense, but she seemed ready to talk. Still, she kept throwing murderous glances over her shoulder at the two officers who'd brought her in. Duski signalled them to leave the office.

The two headed straight to the kitchen and as they opened the door, the smell of freshly fried fat cakes drifted out into the corridor and the charge office. Duski's stomach rumbled, reminding her she hadn't eaten anything since morning.

"Cynthia," the woman replied softly. "Can you ask him to come and see me?" she suddenly asked, her large brown eyes staring at Duski.

"Cynthia, who are we talking about?" Duski asked, cautious not to set her off again.

"He said he was going to marry me—he promised me, but this woman has locked him in the flat. She won't let me see him," she whispered, a bit tearful.

"Is that why you broke into the flat? Did you break the window with your bare hands?" she asked turning over the woman's left hand to inspect it. "Got to get this seen to first," Duski said without giving the woman a chance to respond.

"This can't wait. I want to tell you all about him now," the young woman insisted, almost hysterically. "Lovemore has been ignoring my calls for a week now."

Tell me about it, Duski thought, full of empathy.

"When I finished work at lunchtime today, I went round to his flat to see if he was okay," the woman rambled on, staring at the floor. "I knocked at the door a few times, and when nobody answered, I tried opening the door. It was locked, but I thought I heard someone coming towards it. I knew he was in—was just about to leave when I heard a woman's voice asking who it was. I heard Lovemore say he didn't know and told the woman not to answer the door. I went mental. I knew he was with another woman," She stood up and wrung her bloodied hands—her large brown eyes stared crazily past Duski into the unseen distance.

"Let's get you to the hospital first. Your hands need to be seen to now," Duski said, trying to calm the woman down.

"No! I haven't finished yet," she snapped, rolling her eyes and sucking her teeth. She was fuming with anger but she sat down again and broke into a sudden smile. "I told him that I knew he was in there, but he still wouldn't open the door. It was then that I started kicking the door and shouting his name. Guess what he said?"

Duski shook her head and encouraged her to carry on.

"He told me to go away or he'd call the police," she snarled.

"You're attractive and young, I'm sure one day you'll meet someone more deserving of your love than this guy," Duski said thinking more of her own plight. "Life is too short to . . ."

"You don't understand. I can't just go away," the woman interrupted. "I'm pregnant," she cried. "When he didn't come out, I piled stones by the front window and hurled them through it. I smashed the rest of the window pane with my bare hands. I then went through the window into the living room. She was there, the cow, staring at me. I went straight for her face with a piece of broken glass. Lovemore got to me before I could carve her face," she was crying, a stream of snort and tears running freely down her face. She was staring hard into the distance, her face was tormented and her eyes were wild with anguish.

Why do women always blame other women when it's clear who is at fault? Duski wondered, *I would have used the glass to cut off the bastard's balls myself.*

"He held me down until the police arrived," the woman continued, now looking intently at her. Duski sat and forced herself to concentrate on her client. "And they brought me here—but not easily," she said with a satisfied smile.

"Cynthia, we have to get you to hospital and have those hands seen to," Duski said, firmly this time. The young woman immediately stood up and obediently followed her to the staff kitchen.

"Constable, I want you to come with me to Princess Marina," Sergeant Duski Lôcha said to a motherly looking female officer a few years older than herself. "Take this young lady to the duty car, and I'll be with you in a minute. Constable Moji, can I have a word?" she asked, leading him outside into the holding cell's courtyard. "Did the man whose flat Cynthia broke into press charges?"

"No, just told us to make sure she didn't bother them again," Moji said. He stamped his right foot to attention and went back into the charge office.

"The bastard ditched her for another woman," Duski muttered to herself. Against the earlier vows—promises she'd made to herself to forget Ali, Duski started thinking about him, wondering what he was up to—whether he too, had found some other woman to replace her.

What's wrong with Batswana men, she thought. She sucked her teeth, convinced they were all the same.

Cheating bastards.

At the hospital, the duty doctor did not seem concerned about Cynthia's state of mind. Her hands were examined and treated and after a long reprimand back at the police station, Cynthia was driven to her parents' home in Tlokweng.

*   *   *

It was half past seven in the evening and the charge office was quiet after that afternoon's kerfuffle.

The smell of papa and ground beef drifted enticingly into the charge office, luring the hungry constables to the staff kitchen for the second time that day. Duski sat unmoved back at her desk. Her hands cupped her face, as she thought about the events of the afternoon. She was thinking about how infidelity—so common in many relationships in Botswana—had contributed to the spread of the HIV infection.

She sighed, wishing she could travel back in time—to the time before white people came with their so-called civilisation, back to the time when women did not have to go through the hassle of finding Mr Right. Mr Wrong, in her case. In her view, it was this endless quest for the perfect partner that had brought about the uncontrollable spread of the killer disease.

In the old days, she recalled her grandmother once saying, *the union of two individuals was a very delicate task, which could only be entrusted to the wise elders of the family. All a young woman had to do when her time came, was relax and wait for the bride price—a healthy herd of cattle to be driven into her father's kraal before being delivered to her new family.*

The repeated rattle and buzz of a cell phone dancing on the desk in front of her broke her reverie. She picked it up. "*Pshaw!*" she sucked her teeth quite loudly before hitting the red button with a determined but shaky thump to end the call. She switched the phone off and put it in her shirt pocket.

Ali was back in town. To say that she was still furious about his unexplained silence would have been an understatement. She was not mad at Ali's unexplained lack of communication, but at her own weakness. Regardless of the long silence, she was still in love with him. She knew as soon as she saw him again, she'd readily swallow any feeble excuse he cared to give. Duski took out the switched off cell phone from her pocket to put it into a lockable drawer to stop herself from calling him back.

She was about to join the others in the kitchen when the charge office phone rang. She hesitated before picking it up, wondering whether it was Ali again. She bit her lower lip, determined to tell him where to go before picking up the receiver.

"Central police station, Sergeant Duski Lôcha speaking. How can I help you?" She recited the drill, her voice full of authority and ready to suck her teeth if necessary. It wasn't Ali—it was the man who'd rang that afternoon about Cynthia.

"She's back in the flat," the caller said, anxious. "My girlfriend's alone—I'm worried she might harm her," he added hesitantly.

"Sir, how do you know she's back there?" Duski asked, wondering why the girlfriend hadn't rung them herself.

"I'm calling from work, my girlfriend just rung me to say Cynthia was at the door. She's scared officer, could you send someone round?" he pleaded, almost crying.

"We'll go right away, sir," Duski reassured him before replacing the receiver. "Constable Moji," she called out, marching down to the kitchen. "Get Constable Peba, we're going back to the Flats—same address you went to this afternoon. Looks like our young woman didn't heed my words of advice. Be gentle with her this time," she added, pushing the kitchen door open.

"Yes, Sarge. We're ready Sarge," the two burly constables said in unison. They stood at attention with their buttocks clenched as she gave orders.

Ten minutes later, when they arrived at the Flats, the headlights revealed a naked female lying on her back, one slim leg on top of the other. Her left arm was under her head and her right hand was holding what appeared to be a joint. Moji dipped the headlights before they got out of the car and cautiously approached the figure. They could smell the joint she was obliviously dragging on and was happily singing along to music blaring from inside the flat.

"Cynthia, what are you doing back here?" Duski asked, squatting down next to her.

> *"Easy skanking, skanking it slow,*
> *Excuse me while I light my spliff,*
> *Good God! I gotta take a lift . . ."*

Cynthia wailed at the top of her voice—singing along with the late Bob, oblivious to their presence and her surroundings.

"*Mma,* what have you done with your clothes?" Constable Moji, who'd followed Duski, asked. He was trying hard to remain professional at the sight of the woman's prime womanhood. Constable Peba joined them and he too, stood and gawped at the naked woman.

"Don't you think you two should be looking for her clothes instead of standing there gawping?" Duski reprimanded the two constables before turning her attention back to Cynthia.

Embarrassed, the two officers immediately snapped into action. Moji's short sharp steps shot in the direction of the smashed front window, immediately solving the mystery of the missing clothes. Both her clothes and the dressing put on her cuts earlier that day, lay smouldering in the front room.

"*Monna Peba, mmenyana yo o tshubile diaparo tsa gagwe,*" Moji announced, shaking his head while pointing at the smouldering pile.

"What? She's burnt her clothes?" Constable Peba followed Moji's pointing finger. "We need to speak to whoever is inside," he suggested after inspecting the pile. "*Koo! Koo!* Police! Open the door!" Constable Peba shouted and pounded on the door at the same time.

Cynthia continued her duet with Bob Marley throughout sergeant Duski's interrogation. Constable Peba's persistent pounding on the door, however, managed to silence her temporarily. She took a long drag and blew the smoke into Duski's face.

"Tell them she can't let them in," she suddenly blurted out before looking away. She seemed bored as she took another long drag.

"What do you mean?" Duski asked moving closer. Suddenly, she noticed Cynthia's hands were covered in fresh blood.

Ignoring her question, Cynthia resumed her singing. Duski gave up and got up to join her colleagues—they were still pounding on the door.

"You're wasting your time," Cynthia kept shouting out in between the singing. "She's dead," she finally stated, confirming what the officers were already suspecting. Her words were spoken with great coldness; they sent cold shivers down their backs.

Constable Moji, who was about to ram down the door, noticed it wasn't actually locked—they all silently walked in and were surprised to find the sparsely furnished sitting room devoid of a female corpse they were all bracing themselves for. Instead, they saw a lone, black stereo that was blaring out Bob Marley's reggae. Duski turned the music off and proceeded to search the bedrooms while constable Moji and Peba searched the bathroom.

In the main bedroom, a young woman was lying face down on a blood-soaked bed, her neck slit open. Beside the body lay a shard of blood-smeared glass.

"Oh my God, what has she done now?" Duski muttered as she stared at the scene. All sorts of thoughts, questions and mostly regrets, raced competitively through her fogged mind like a tornado.

I shouldn't have let her go, I should have detained her.

Section 203 of the penal code scrolled across her mind like end credits: *(1) Subject to the provisions of subsection (2), any person convicted of murder shall be sentenced to death.* Suddenly, she recalled something Cynthia had said to her earlier that day. *If she was telling the truth about the pregnancy, she'd probably get life.* All the while, Duski blamed herself for the tragedy.

"She's right—body is in here," she eventually called out from the bedroom. "Constable Moji, radio the scene of crime team please," she instructed as soon as the two constables had assembled themselves beside her. The thought that she could have prevented the murder had started to haunt her.

"Yes, Sarge," Constable Moji said, immediately reaching for his radio while taking in the bloody scene in front of them.

Duski went back outside where Cynthia readily confessed to the murder of her rival. She even displayed her bloodied hands in case the sergeant had any doubts.

CID would love this one. No evidence of witchcraft, no missing body parts, and a suspect waiting patiently to be arrested, she thought, recalling the still unsolved alleged ritual murders.

"Cynthia, you are being arrested on suspicion of murder," Duski stated with a heavy heart, placing her right hand firmly on Cynthia's shoulder. But Cynthia stared vacantly into the distance and dragged on her joint during the formal caution. "You have the right to remain silent, and if you wish to say something, you can do so, but whatever you say may be taken down in writing and later used as evidence." Duski recited the drill as if it were a poem in a language she didn't understand. Afterwards, she went back to the police bakkie to find Cynthia something to wear before taking her back to the station for further questioning.

The deceased's boyfriend arrived at the scene as she drove out with Cynthia securely cuffed in the back of the bakkie. Constable Moji was guarding her. Constable Peba was left with the unpleasant task of giving the boyfriend the bad news.

Chapter Ten

BP.160 C.R.No. 250
Station . . . CPS

Statement

I . . . . *Cynthia Botho* . . . .
. . . .
(Above give full name of deponent)
Age: 25 yrs Old Sex . . . Female . . . .
Present Address . . . . . . Tlokweng Village plot no.
26934 . . . .
. . . .
. . . . Employed
as . . . Shop Assistant . . . .
Home Address . . . . Tlokweng Village plot no.
26934 . . . .
. . . . Ward . . . . . . Matlapeng . . . .
Headman . . . . . . Goabaone Bogatsu . . .

States:

   A year ago, I fell pregnant. When I told my
boyfriend, Lovemore, the news, he told me he wasn't ready
to be a father. Lovemore promised me if I terminated the
pregnancy, we'd save up, get married, and have kids later.
I got very upset and disappointed that Lovemore wanted
me to kill our baby, but because I loved him very much and
did not want to lose him, I let him take me to a backstreet

abortionist. I was already four months pregnant when
Lovemore took me to see the woman. Two weeks before,
I started feeling the baby kicking and punching. I kept
wondering whether the baby knew what was going to happen
to it—that I was planning to murder it before it was even
born. I tried to talk Lovemore round, to draw his attention
to the fact that the baby was a living thing that deserved life.
But no, he had made up his mind. He told me that if I kept
the baby, I would be on my own—he would have nothing to
do with me. I was too much of a coward to stand up to him.

Early one Sunday morning, we went to see the
abortionist in Old Naledi. When we got there, the woman
took me to a back room, asked me to take my panties
off, and made me lie on a metal-framed bed. The woman
stuck two fingers inside my vagina and felt around for the
baby. She told me that she could feel the baby, and then she
replaced the fingers with a knitting needle. She poked around
for a minute or two, and then she began puncturing my
womb with the sharp end of the needle. Every time the needle
stabbed into my womb, I felt the baby kick and punch. I
wondered if it was trying to fight back. It was so painful; I
thought I was going to die. When the woman finished, she
told me that I would start bleeding in a couple of hours. She
said that I should go to the hospital and tell them I was
having a miscarriage when that happened.

Back at Lovemore's flat, at about lunchtime, I
began getting sharp abdominal pains. Without warning,
dark, bloody clots started pouring out. I was in so much pain
that I thought I was dying. Lovemore drove me to Princess
Marina hospital and told them that I was pregnant and
probably having a miscarriage. A few hours later, I went

into labour and gave birth to a grievously wounded baby girl. When they showed me the tiny corpse, I felt a massive pressure in my head. I was about to explode with shame and grief. The hospital referred me to Lobatse for psychiatric treatment. After six months, I felt much better and was released. I moved back in with Lovemore.

Two months ago, things started going badly between Lovemore and me. When I told him that I was pregnant again, he just turned round and told me to get out of his flat. He said that he did not want to see me again. He accused me of trying to snare him into marriage. He accused me of bewitching him. I was so angry and shocked by his accusation—and most of all, his coldness. I told him that I had nowhere to go (he'd made me give up my rented room in Gaborone West when I first moved in with him). He ignored me, took his car keys, and drove off without saying where he was going. I stayed and contemplated reporting him to the customary court if he forced me out. Someone had to force him to take responsibility for our child.

Later that night, when he came back, he packed all my stuff in a suitcase while I was asleep and took it to my parents' house in Tlokweng. He dumped it by the gate and told my mother to ring and tell me to leave his flat or they would soon be eating seswaa *(pounded meat) and* samp *at my funeral. As soon as he left Tlokweng, my mother rang, begging me to get out of the flat as soon as I could.*

I didn't want to leave the flat, but I was scared and confused that Lovemore didn't care for me. I left for my parents' yard, upset and shocked. I could not sleep that night. I was trying to figure out why Lovemore was behaving like he was—and suddenly it clicked: he was seeing someone else. I tried phoning him so we could talk and sort things out, but he ignored my calls.

This afternoon, after work, I went back to his flat to confront him. I wanted to remind him that I was still pregnant and that he shouldn't engage in unprotected sex if he was so against having children. He refused to let me in, and I immediately knew why. I could hear a woman's voice inside the flat.

I lost it. I piled up stones by the front window and smashed my way in. As soon as I crash-landed inside, I went straight for the woman. Lovemore managed to stop me before I could scratch her eyes out. Someone in one of the neighbouring flats must have called the police. By the time the police arrived, I think I had gone completely mad. I remember fighting with them. I was brought back here (central police station) and later taken to Princess Marina hospital where I had my hands attended to.

After being cautioned, I was released and allowed to go back home. The police dropped me back at my parents' house. I was beginning to accept the fact that I would be a single parent when someone started texting me telling me that she was Lovemore's new girlfriend. She told me that I should leave him alone because he didn't love me. I ignored the messages, but they kept coming. I knew then that I had to teach Lovemore a lesson.

I don't smoke dagga, but I suddenly had a great urge to take something that could numb the pain I felt at the moment. I knew that the Shebeen queen who lived next door sold dagga, so I went round there to buy some. After I had smoked a couple of joints, I called a taxi to take me back to Lovemore's place. I did not know what I was going to do when I got there.

The door wasn't locked, so I walked straight in. The television was on, but there was no one in the sitting room. I went to the bedroom. The woman I met earlier was lying on the bed, and there was a half-empty bottle of Amarula on the bedside table. I picked it up and hit her hard on the head repeatedly until it broke, but the woman never moved. This incensed me, so I took a big, sharp piece of it and started stabbing her on the back of the neck. I then called Lovemore to tell him that I was in the flat and had a surprise for him. He asked whether I had done anything to hurt his girlfriend, and he said that he was calling the police. I said, "Good, I was just about to do that myself." My clothes were soaked in her blood, which repulsed me, so I took them off and burnt them. I put on some music and waited for the police to arrive.
Signature of deponent—*C.Botho*

Statement read over by/to deponent in the *Setswana* language, acknowledged by him/her to be the truth* and sworn to by him/her before me at *Central* *Police* *Station,* *Gaborone* on this *Saturday* of *September* *20th,* *2009* at *2100* *hrs*

**Commissioner of Oaths* **Delete where required.*

Chapter Eleven

The smell of overcooked cabbage, disinfectant, and antiseptic spirits permeated the air as soon as she took a seat outside the hospital's psychiatric department. Duski closed her eyes and went over the events of that evening, including Cynthia's statement.

Why would the deceased text Cynthia? How did she get hold of her number? There was no cell phone in the bedroom. Did someone else send Cynthia those text messages? Why was the victim unresponsive during the attack?

The case wasn't as straightforward as she first thought. There were too many discrepancies and unanswered questions. *Let's hope we don't end up with another unsolved murder case,* she prayed.

"Excuse me *mma*," a voice rudely interrupted her thoughts. A middle-aged Asian man stood smiling at her. "I completed examination," he said in a distinct Indian accent. "Young lady is showing signs of substance-induced psychotic disorder," he added.

"Can I take her back to the station?"

"She needs further psychiatric evaluation," the man said. Duski's heart sunk. *Don't do this to me, not on a fucking Friday night,* she thought. She knew what was coming next. "She's to go to psychiatric hospital tonight," the Indian doctor explained, handing her a pink medical form with scribbled notes.

"Thank you *rra*," she said. *And thanks for the fucking seventy-odd kilometre drive to Lobatse in the fucking night, too,* she wanted to add.

*   *   *

Cynthia seemed calmer, but distant. Nevertheless, Constables Moji and Peba didn't want to leave anything to chance. They led her to the back of the bakkie and locked her in before they all piled into the front with Duski. Constable Peba squeezed in the middle, making it almost impossible for Duski to reach the controls. She kept hitting his groin every time she changed gear.

As the bakkie sped through the dark hills on the winding and undulating tarmac road to Lobatse, the three officers fell silent. Moji soon fell asleep and started snoring while Peba perched himself as far back as possible from the gear stick and placed his hands protectively over his groin every time Duski's hand went for the gear stick.

Duski stared ahead, her mind once more racing through the contents of Cynthia's statement.

Why was the flat left unlocked? This would be very imprudent given that Cynthia had broken in earlier that day.

Her mind switched over to Lovemore's statement, which she'd had a quick glance at before she left the office. He claimed not to know

Cynthia and stated he'd never seen her before that afternoon, when she broke into the flat.

Someone was lying.

*   *   *

The brightly lit rows of eucalyptus trees at the bottom of the last range of hills announced the end of their journey. She slowed down to admire the remnants of colonial Lobatse as she drove along a tree-lined avenue. It was constructed, she was once told, for the 1947 visit of King George, Queen Elizabeth, and their two daughters, Princesses Elizabeth and Margaret.

Duski followed signs for the mental hospital after the first roundabout. It was nearly ten o'clock when she finally parked the bakkie inside the hospital compound. After a seemingly endless process of form filling, Cynthia was eventually admitted and scheduled to be seen by a specialist in the morning.

*   *   *

Ali was waiting for her when she got home that night. He was lying on the bed with his legs dangling down. Duski wondered how long he'd been there in the dark when he opened his eyes to find her staring at him, expressionless. She wasn't sure what she was supposed to feel—anger, annoyance, joy?

"I rang your cell twice today—rang the office as well, and was told you'd gone to Lobatse," he said sitting up to light a cigarette he'd been fiddling with.

Duski perched herself at the edge of the bed, as far as possible from him. She pulled out a cigarette from a pack of red Peter Stuyvesant he'd thrown on the bed. He watched her with amusement as she reached for a box of Red Lion matches to light the cigarette that was now hanging between her parted lips. Ali's amusement was soon replaced by surprise as she dragged slowly on the cigarette which he k new was filled with dagga and exhaled the toxic fumes through her nostrils with apparent ease.

Duski stared back with narrowed eyes and wondered why she'd ever trusted him or believed he'd changed. Her mother's favourite saying came to mind.

Once bitten, twice shy.

Ali shook his head slowly and took a long drag on his own cigarette. She could see his disproval, but he was in no position to judge her—not until he'd explained his long silence.

Duski had smoked all sorts of things for years, but never in public. Usually, she smoked in toilets—as did most self-respecting women in Botswana.

"So how was your trip?" she suddenly asked blowing the dagga smoke into his face.

Ali immediately fanned it away, cocked his head slightly to the right and bit his lower lip. She could tell he was getting angry and she wasn't in the mood for a fight.

"By the way, I'm going out," she said inspecting her wristwatch. It was nearly midnight, but she knew the Bull and Bush would still be open. She fished out her cell from her handbag to call her friend, Thandie.

"Hi, Thandie," she said as soon as her friend picked up. "What you up to tonight? Oh good. Can you pick me up? Yeah . . . in fifteen minutes. Great, see you then, byee."

She switched the phone off and started rummaging through her wardrobe for something to change into. Although she was annoyed with Ali, events of the day took precedence over her personal problems as she got herself ready.

A young woman's life was cut short today. Her killer, another youth whose life had just begun and the man responsible for the tragedy will carry on with his life as if the two women had never existed,

She reflected sadly as she pulled out a pair of jeans and a green T-shirt. To Ali's annoyance, she sat down on the edge of the bed, lit another one of his dagga filled cigarettes and exhaled the smoke towards him through her nostrils. She looked at him reflectively, wanting to share her thoughts—but something stopped her. Life was too short, too valuable to waste fighting over meaningless things.

If he's cheated on me—so what? She thought.
*He'd used his own penis to fuck whomever he'd been seeing
and I've no right to complain about it.*

She smiled at him, but Ali was unsure how
to interpret the sudden sign of kindness. Did it
mean she was no longer mad at him? He shrugged
and kept his teeth well hidden behind his lips.

Women, he thought, *might be a trick.*

Duski finished getting ready and got
up. *Relationships are never gonna work for me*, she
concluded. *Could try the witch doctor's love potion*, part
of her thought.

But she hated the very thought that she'd
have to make Ali love her against his will. Work,
she reasoned, was what she should be having a
relationship with right now. After all, it paid her
bills and bought her clothes.

*I need to get Ali out of my life, my mind, once and
for all*, she mused while applying pumpkin oil to her
short dreads.

Suddenly, Duski felt an overwhelming urge
to make a midyear's resolution.

*I promise to be faithful only to myself, my work,—I
have been treating these aspects of my life far too lightly.*

It suddenly dawned on her that she'd been
in the force ten years. She recalled her family's
shock when she first told them that she intended to
sign up. Her father, whose love of old banger cars
had made him a regular at the traffic police offices,
had nearly choked on a piece of biltong he'd been
chewing when she made the announcement. She

smiled at the memory as her mind flitted from one topic to another.

Duski refocused her thoughts on the two unsolved suspected ritual murder cases.

I'll start my own investigation and pester CID for the taxi drivers' case file the following week, she thought. Before she could figure out exactly how she was going to carry out the investigations, her thoughts were interrupted by a car pulling up at the gate. She immediately tucked her purse firmly under her arm, stood in front of the mirror to run her fingers through her short locks before heading for the door.

As she pulled the door to, she paused for a moment and wondered whether she was overreacting or being irrational. Maybe she should stay and patiently await an explanation, she thought.

An ancient wise man once wrote, *the course of true love never did run smooth.* With the saying now fixed in her head, she shut the door and walked to the gate where Thandie was waiting in a white Toyota Tazz. She was wondering whether things would eventually work themselves out.

*   *   *

Thandie finally found a parking space at the edge of an unmarked dirt car park. Still, they'd to wait for a few seconds for the dust the car had upset to settle before they could step out. The Bull and Bush was, as usual, packed. Outside, couples leaned against parked cars snogging, drinking, and playing loud music. Night traders lined the entrance with carved elephants, giraffes, tribal figurines and African masks.

Duski and Thandie walked in and immediately headed for the outdoor bar.

That was when she first noticed him. Her heart missed a few beats as she locked eyes with him. Leaning against the counter in the far corner of the bar, stood a young white man with dark and wavy mane-like curls.

"See that white guy over there?" she said excitedly, pointing at the young man who was standing between two white women, "He's sooo gorgeous."

Thandie glanced over, pouted and said, "Not my cup of tea—God, you're into white guys?"

"We all have different tastes," Duski said and proceeded to order their drinks.

"One Hansa and one Savanna Dry please," she handed over a fifty pula note to the bar man. She was clearly hurt by her friend's curt reponse.

"Now this is what I call gorgeous," Thandie winked at the barman as he handed over the drinks.

The barman smiled and shook his head.

Duski cracked open her can of Hansa Pilsner and rummaged through the contents of her handbag for cigarettes. She pulled one out, lit it and held it high between her un-manicured fingers. She sat deep in thought while Thandie flirted with the barman. She occasionally glanced over at the white guy and dragged on her cigarette.

Duski loved Thandie to bits, but she knew that she was a malicious gossiper, a vice she enjoyed without shame. She knew that if anybody was going to spread any rumours about her fancying a white guy, it would be none other than her best friend. She reflected on why she'd always preferred Thandie's company above all her other friends. Like her, Thandie was a real 'good time girl.' She was the sort of girl who, when confronted with two indulgences, she'd always go for the one she hadn't tried before.

From the corner of her eye, Duski caught sight of the white guy walking past. She felt his eyes on her back sending tiny ripples of electricity down her spine. With caution thrown to the wind, she finished the contents of her can in one gulp and followed him inside . . . all the way to the dance floor.

He knew she was following him. The young man stopped and suddenly turned round to face her. "Would you like to dance?" A pair of deep blue eyes gazed into her brown eyes. Her heart stammered, and her breath came in long drafts as she stared dumbfounded at the pale face before her—and at the intense blue eyes.

His handsome body and the faint dimples in his baby cheeks, made him look like he'd just walked out of a Hollywood set. Duski stared, hypnotised by the intense blueness of his eyes.

"It's okay," he said teasingly. Duski felt hot all over with embarrassment, "Hope it means you're interested." He smiled, revealing the most perfect and white set of teeth she'd ever seen in a white man's mouth. "Can I buy you another Hansa?"

She nodded trying hard not to stare. But as he headed towards the crowded bar, she stared at his back dreamily.

What the hell am I doing? I should just walk away and forget all this nonsense. If anybody from work sees me with a white man, I'll be teased endlessly, she thought. She could already hear her colleagues' jeering. *Hey, Sarge, has he got a black dick? How big is it? Is it true that white men have small dicks?* Dickheads, she thought sucking her teeth angrily at her absent colleagues.

The young white guy was leaning at the bar among several black men. She watched them reflectively, suddenly realising that she'd no idea what colour a white man's penis was. *Surely all men have darker penises.* She found it hard to think of a penis being any colour other than dark chocolate. *Ali is very light skinned, and yet his penis is darker than the rest of his body*, she reasoned.

"Penny for your thoughts?" the young man said, noticing that Duski was in a pensive mood.

"Oh, you're back," she said, rather embarrassed.

"*Craig*—Craig McGhee, by the way," the young man said as soon as he'd sat down next to her. He shook her hand.

That's a promising start. At least he is not called Andres Van Niekerk, Duski thought.

"From Edinburgh, Scotland," he added, much to her relief.

"Duski Lôcha," she took a swig from the can he'd just put in front of her. "Cheers," she added lifting up the beer can in salute before putting it down again.

"Duski Lodger?" he asked, the distinct lilt in his voice floated almost inaudibly above the music.

The way he said her name was different, funny. *The lilting accent,* she thought, made her name sound foreign. "Yeah, something like that—call me Sarge if you like! That's what everybody calls me at work," she giggled mischievously.

"Don't tell me you're a copper?" he exclaimed, saluting her playfully.

"Unfortunately," she said shyly, dragging him off to the dance floor as 50 Cent's voice boomed from a nearby speaker. "You're a good dancer," she observed as soon as they started dancing.

Craig did a Michael Jackson spin. "You look surprised," he said, facing her.

"Thought white people couldn't dance," she replied. She giggled and nodded towards a group of white youths twitching painfully behind them.

"It's funny, I've always thought all black people were good dancers," Craig retorted playfully. She followed his eyes towards the middle of the dance floor where a fat black man was wriggling around the dance floor like a mophane worm being toasted alive. They both fell into a fit of giggles and watched the man's strange dance with amazement. Soon, they too joined the swaying and sweaty bodies in the middle of the dance floor.

Suddenly but gently, Craig pulled her towards his muscled chest. His arms encircled her waist, forcing her to rise on her toes. She craned her neck forward—towards his inviting lips—and closed her eyes. The music ceased—the only audible sounds were their two hearts pounding while the pleasant fragrance of his aftershave, a blend of sandalwood, lavender, and cedar, invaded her senses.

Somebody tapped her on the shoulder.

"Excuse me," a thin, blonde woman with piercing green eyes said. It was one of the women Craig was talking to earlier at the outside bar. "Could we borrow him for a second?" the woman asked. Craig planted a kiss on her forehead and reluctantly followed the woman outside. Duski decided not to wait for Craig to return. She went in search of Thandie instead.

"What happened to your *'gorgeous'* white boyfriend?" Thandie asked as soon as Duski found her in a corner of the beer garden in the company of an elderly black man. "Thought you'd gone off for a quickie."

"He's been borrowed," Duski slurred and pointed at the two women talking to Craig at the bar. Ali's dagga laced cigarette she'd pinched earlier and the two lagers she'd had, were beginning to take effect. She stared at the women who were sucking the life out of their cigarettes while Craig had his head bowed. His gaze was fixed on a pint of beer in front of him.

"So you want to shag a white guy?" Thandie asked, looking disapprovingly at her friend. "Is this because of Ali? Thandie said, her lip curling up into a sneer.

Duski dug into her purse for her last cigarette. She lit it, took a long drag on it, and said, "Me and Ali are finished and I'm trying to move on."

"But having a relationship with a *lekgoa*? Come on, Sarge, think of all the hassle—people pointing fingers, calling you names! I know you're pissed off with Ali, but that's not the way to get back at him. What you need, my friend, is a nice sugar daddy to pay for all your creature comforts," Thandie perched herself on the elderly man's lap. "If it gets out you're into white men, no one will touch you," she warned, her nose turned up in the air as if someone had just farted.

Duski studied the man who looked old enough to be her father and said, "this has nothing to do with Ali," she said, reflecting on her behaviour. She wasn't looking for a relationship, all she wanted was to feel needed, loved . . . and Ali had let her down.

"I've got a strange philosophy, nothing here appeals to me. I like my men like I like my whiskey, mmm, aged and mellow," Thandie suddenly broke into song, rudely interrupting Duski's thoughts. She gave the elderly man a peck on the cheek. "By the way, this is my benefactor," Thandie said, putting her arms around the man's suited shoulders. "He's a sweet sugar daddy, and he is LOADED. My friend, I want to shit out poverty," she said whispering and giggling drunkenly into Duski's ear.

If Thandie was a country, Duski thought as she listened to her friend with amusement, she'd be America—well developed and open for trade, especially for those with stacks of money.

Thandie was a permanent girlfriend to another married man who'd bought her a house and a car. The man was also paying her a monthly allowance in exchange for occasional small favours. Duski knew her friend had other rich clients who paid for her expensive tastes in exchange for what Thandie preferred to call, *an occasional penis massage.*

Chapter Twelve

A note was lying neatly folded on the bed when she got back home later that night.

Gone to O'Hagans. See you tomorrow. Love, Ali.

She tore it up and then threw the pieces in her mouth, and chewed them with gusto before she spat them out and collapsed fully clothed on the bed.

Five hours later, she was woken up by a thumping headache and the purring and vibrating of her cell phone on the bedside table. The screen was flashing: *Ali calling.* She angrily hit the off button, sucked her teeth, and went back to sleep. Sometime in the afternoon, she was eventually forced to get up by the intense heat that was making her nauseous. She dragged herself out of the sweat-soaked bed and headed towards the bathroom to soak herself in a cold bath.

Memories of the previous night came in dribs and drabs, clouded by a massive hangover. She recalled a kiss. How could she not? You don't kiss a man you've only just met and erase it from your memory the next day! She was shocked to realise that she wasn't as appalled as she should have been, considering her strict Christian upbringing. The cold water slowly cooled her down and quietened the thumping headache enough for her to recall the young man's name.

Craig.

She shut her eyes and revisited the events of the previous night.

A pair of intense blue eyes held her gaze. Soft, plump, beer-tasting lips teased her slightly dry ones while a pair of firm, yet gentle hands encircled her waist.

She felt a familiar, heavy and painful ache between her legs. Silently, she parted them, looking up at the invisible blue eyes. Padlocking her childhood teachings in the darkest and deepest parts of her unconsciousness—where they'd no escape route, she shamelessly gave herself to the white stranger with the intense and bewitching blue eyes.

The dusty and musky air in the overcrowded bathroom became scented with sandalwood, lavender, and cedar.

She unbuttoned his jeans and was surprised that he wore no underwear. She pulled his jeans down to reveal a magnificent bolt and upright hard on—but the colour of his penis wasn't clear.

She was still trying to work it out when her clitoris suddenly succumbed to several massive spasms in the cold bath water. She moaned softly.

"Sarge, are you all right in there?" Constable Kowa asked pounding loudly on the bathroom door.

"Yeah, I've hit my big toe on the bloody—" she began, belatedly realising her moans must have expressed pleasure rather than pain.

"You got a visitor," Kowa announced through the closed bathroom door before Duski could come up with a more convincing excuse.

"Thanks," Duski replied, not bothering to ask who the visitor was. She knew that it was Ali. She rose slowly and dried herself while trying to work out the best way to handle the Ali situation.

Should I tell him that it's over? She thought wondering how he'd take it.

"I'm sorry, babes. I know you're mad at me for not returning your calls. I mean, I couldn't ring you—there are reasons of course," Ali started hesitantly the minute she walked into the bedroom.

Duski said nothing; she just stood there and watched him with amusement. She knew he was lying—and he was good at it. A pro.

"My phone got stolen—I'm sure you saw last month's copy of *The Voice*," he said pulling out a torn off newspaper article from his jean pocket.

Jungle Man Terrorises Cops, the headline read. He placed it on the bed and she reluctantly scanned the page.

The Special Support Group (SSG), deployed along the Zimbabwean boarder near Matshelagabedi Village, are living in fear of a strange man who raids their campsite at night and loots their food and mobile phones. Strategic efforts to arrest the man have failed because the mystery man is very elusive and appears to be using supernatural powers.

"Got a new phone now," he added quickly before she could comment on the contents of the article. "Kept my old number though," Ali said. "I'm really sorry babes. I know I've let you down big time—I promise I'm not gonna let anything come between us again," he added.

Duski sat down on the other side of the bed and took out a Stuyvesant from her dressing table drawer. She lit it and took a long drag while wondering whether to believe his story or not. Everything Ali had told her so far seemed too rehearsed to be true.

"Aren't you going to say something, babes?" Ali asked, lighting a cigarette.

"What do you want me to say?" she asked, thinking of Craig and her midyear's resolution. She felt trapped and confused.

"How about we go out, have some fun—put all this behind us, shall we?" Ali said, moving closer to her side of the bed. He kissed her neck lightly.

Duski sucked her teeth. In her heart of hearts, she knew that he was lying through his teeth, but she didn't want to say anything to contradict his story—she was scared of losing him.

"I'm not entirely sure about all this—our relationship, I mean. Where is it going, Ali?" she asked instead, puffing out smoke towards the already blackened ceiling.

"Let's go to Game City, hey—discuss this over lunch . . . and do a bit of shopping after," Ali said, but he regretted his words as soon as he'd uttered them. He recalled how torturous Duski's shopping trips could be.

Gaborone has a few indoor shopping centres; unfortunately, all flung apart in the far corners of the city. Usually, Duski's shopping trips involved going around all the shopping malls two or three times, trying on heaps of jeans and stacks of shoes before making any purchase decisions.

"Not a bad idea," she said, suddenly brightening up. She threw the towel she'd had wrapped round her, on the floor to moisturise her body before getting dressed. "You could have at least borrowed one of your friend's phones to send a text," she suddenly said unable to shake off the feeling he was hiding something from her. That the rehearsed story, the lunch and the shopping trip were all a cover up—she could smell another woman in all of it.

Ali stared past her and past the bedroom walls at some invisible object, "You don't believe me, do you?" he said sounding distant.

Duski ignored him and concentrated on moisturising her body. It wasn't the lies that bothered her—it was the fear she sensed in his voice—and the troubled, distant look. She'd learnt from past experiences that when a man had something to hide, he'd always respond to a question with another question. She, however, decided to bookmark the issue, pending further investigation. Right now, she'd the shopping expedition to think about.

Her mind was already racing through a list of things she intended to buy. A pair of denim must-have jeggins, she'd seen at Truworths and a pair of red trendy wedges from Bata.

I could actually treat myself to several pairs of panties, she contemplated thoughtfully. She'd spotted a four pack of granny panties with red roses at one of the lingerie shops at River Walk Mall only a few days ago.

Later that afternoon, after a seemingly endless, exhausting and hot tour of Gaborone shopping malls, Ali finally took her back to Game City mall for lunch, and later, out to the cinema. With thoughts of the young Scot, her midyear's resolution, and doubts about Ali's fidelity, stuffed right at the bottom of her bulging shopping bags and bloated stomach, Duski headed back to Block 8 with her man by her side.

*   *   *

It was the evening of November 25th, and it was Duski's birthday. Ali was on night shift, or so he'd told her. Duski had neither the desire nor the energy to go out; instead, she spent the afternoon staring at the ceiling and thinking about the still outstanding murders. She was wondering whether the victims' private parts had been sold already and whether the killers would ever be caught when her lower lip and eyelids started quivering almost simultaneously.

A bad sign, she thought. Every Motswana knew what it meant. *What was going to upset her?* She wondered her thoughts reluctantly going back to a subject she'd been avoiding—here relationship with Ali and her suspicions that he was hiding something from her.

For weeks, she'd pretended not to notice numerous phone calls to his cell, which went unanswered whenever they were together.

Duski reached for her cell phone to ring a taxi to take her to Ali's house in Maruapula. It was just after half past ten in the evening when the taxi dropped her off outside Ali's house. *Ali will be at work,* she thought as she approached the door. Her heart was beating erratically with anticipation and dread. She'd all night to snoop around before the end of his shift. She was wondering what dark secrets she might dig out as she hesitantly knocked on the living room door. Ali's housemate Solomone answered the door and seemed rather taken aback to see her.

"You look like you've just seen a ghost, homeboy," she said, rather puzzled by Solomone's strange reception.

"Wasn't expecting to see you . . . I mean, not at this time of the night," he corrected himself. "Come in homegirl," he said, hesitatingly stepping aside to let her in.

The room was crowded and noisy. A few of Ali's workmates sat around the room, their faces glued to a game of football on television.

As she stepped in, everyone went quiet. The commentator's keen voice suddenly became audible. Her eyes followed everybody's towards Ali, who sat stiffly next to a heavily pregnant woman.

She immediately recognised her. She was his ex, the woman she'd met in Ramotswa while investigating Boiki's murder. Duski suddenly felt dizzy. An overwhelming numbness overtook her body, but miraculously, she managed to remain upright and intact.

She said a cheerful *dumelang* to everyone before marching towards Ali's bedroom where a couple of slightly damp thongs were hanging from the top of the wardrobe and an unpacked suitcase lay open on the bed. She heard footsteps following along the short corridor.

Duski sat down on the edge of the bed and waited.

"Why didn't you tell me you'd gone back to her?" she asked as calmly as she could when Ali walked into the room. "Why the lies about the phone, all the stories about thieving monkeys?" she sucked her teeth. Anger slowly spread across her face like a bush fire.

"I can explain," Ali said, looking sheepishly at the floor.

"Her bump explains it all," Duski retorted, her voice quivering with indignation.

"I was drunk, and that is the honest truth," Ali said, wishing he could remember exactly what had happened that night. His mind was blank as

129

if the memory of the night had been deliberately erased.

"Puh-lease, spare me the bloody crap," Duski screamed at him. Ali sat down at the edge of the bed and looked at her, wondering whether he should tell her the truth. The look on her face told him it was neither wise nor advisable.

"How could you do this to me? You slept with that woman without using condoms. She could have the virus," she sobbed, a stream of tears ran down her face.

"Babe, I—" Ali began, but a light knock at the door interrupted him. "Who is it?" he barked as the door was pushed ajar to reveal the pregnant woman.

"Everything okay in here?" the woman asked, looking at the two, amused.

"Ali, I've had enough of your lies. You and I are finished. By the way, congratulations *mma*," Duski said to the woman before storming towards the dressing table where Ali had just put down an unfinished bottle of St. Louis. She grabbed hold of it, aimed it at his head and watched with a satisfied smile as blood trickled from his forehead all the way to his lips.

Before she could flee, Ali grabbed her by her clothes and for a split second, Duski thought that he was going to hit her. Instead, he let go of her. But Duski glared challengingly at him before she marched back into the sitting room to ask Solomone for a lift back to Block Eight.

*　　*　　*

"Homeboy, how could you do this to me? You could have told me what Ali has been up to," Duski said accusingly as soon as they left the house. She glared at Solomone through a stream of tears.

"I'm innocent, homegirl," he said, "I only found out myself, a few days ago when she turned up pregnant at our door."

"He swore they were no longer together," she murmured.

"I'm sorry, *makhaya*, I'd no idea he was back with her."

Duski wanted so much to believe him, but she knew that SSG guys were like a pack of witches—they never talked about the secrets of the coven.

"You shouldn't be angry with him, you know. Give him a chance to explain," Solomone said cautiously. "Your anger might just be the thing that drives him into that woman's arms for good."

"What's there to explain?" Duski exploded. "What drove him back into her arms in the first place?" she said with an overwhelming temptation to slap Solomone for coming up with such lame excuses for his friend's behaviour. She knew her relationship with Ali could not be saved. She was fuming. She was angry with herself for not dumping him when she'd the chance. "Drop me off here, please," she suddenly said as they turned into Dithutwana Road. She opened the door before the car had stopped, jumped out, slammed the door without thanking Solomone, and headed off towards her local Shebeen.

Her head was in turmoil. She desperately needed a drink to numb the dull ache in her heart—after all, it was her birthday. It was already past midnight when she finally knocked on the Shebeen's tin shack door. She was surprised to find the yard deserted and the Shebeen queen in her pyjamas.

"Don't do the devil's business anymore. I closed the Shebeen five months ago," was her proud response to Duski's surprised expression as she let her in.

"Come on, let me have a few cans. I promise I'll pay you as soon as I get paid next month," Duski pleaded, not believing that the Shebeen was no more. A quick scan of the contents of the shack, however, soon confirmed it was indeed closed. The chibuku grates were gone; the big fridge where the beers were normally kept to chill was also no longer there.

"*Mmata*, I'm through with that kind of life. Anyway, what have you been up to? I haven't seen you for ages," Bontle, the Shebeen queen enquired, changing the topic.

"Look, Bontle, I've got to go. We'll speak another time, yah," Duski said, holding the tin shack door open to let herself out. She was in no mood for Bontle's late-night chitchat.

"You okay?" Bontle asked, noticing for the first time that Duski had been crying.

"Yep, I'll be fine. See ya," she replied, forcing herself to smile a little.

"Goodnight *mma*. Oh by the way—nearly forgot to mention I was getting married on Sunday," Bontle suddenly announced.

"Getting married? To whom?" Duski stood transfixed at the door with disbelief.

"Just come along to the Tsholofelo community hall on Saturday—you'll find out then," Bontle said with a mysterious smile as she handed Duski an invite. "Was going to pop round yours tomorrow to drop it off," she added.

"Thanks and congratulations," Duski said before disappearing into the dimly lit backstreets of Block Eight. She mused and puzzled over the identity of the Shebeen queen's mysterious suitor as she headed into the deepest and darkest parts of Block Eight's shanty side. She was heading to another local Shebeen.

*   *   *

Through mere physical and mental exhaustion, she finally fell asleep. In the distance, cockerels crowed to signal the breaking of another dawn—and to warn local witches of the end of the witching hour. The purring and dancing cell phone on the bedside table woke her up a couple of hours later. She peeped at the screen; it was her housemate Kowa. She ignored it, feeling a bit disappointed that it wasn't Ali—she was hoping he would call. The phone beeped to signal an incoming message from Kowa, reminding Duski she was on duty in a couple of hours.

The time on her cell display read 12:00. Duski felt nauseous, numb, and empty. She recalled her midyear's resolution. She had to pull herself together—she'd to solve the two cold cases and reinvestigate the Maruapula Flats murder.

Work is what matters, she kept reminding herself.

She got up to make herself a cup of strong black coffee. Love and relationships were no longer part of her life—she was now officially a single woman, due to be married to her work. She sat sipping the coffee and morosely contemplated the new life ahead.

Don't cry because it's over. Smile because it happened, she thought, recalling what her grandma once said to her. *Some people are born lucky: they get married, have children, and live happily ever after.* Sadly, she realised that fairy tale life wasn't for everyone.

Chapter Thirteen

"Sarge, you got a visitor in the interview room," Constable Moji announced, standing to attention in front of Sergeant Duski Lôcha that afternoon.

"Why the interview room?" she asked in surprise, looking up from a copy of Cynthia's confession statement she'd been analysing for the past hour.

Constable Moji shrugged. "Err . . . private matter, I guess," he whispered hesitantly, leaning towards her.

"Whatever it's, I'm sure it can be discussed in here," she insisted, wondering who the mystery visitor was. Was it Ali coming to tell her the pregnant woman's unborn baby isn't his? She thought, still hopeful their relationship could be salvaged.

The charge office was rather quiet and almost deserted save for a short queue of people waiting to have documents certified. She put the report in a lockable drawer and headed off towards the interview room. Constable Kowa dived under the switchboard counter as soon as she saw Duski walk past.

Strange—why was Kowa hiding from her? She thought, utterly perplexed as she headed towards the interview room where Constable Moji was waiting outside to let her in.

"Your visitor is in here, Sarge," he said, holding the door open for her.

A stale smell of *chibuku* hit her as soon as she walked in. On a bench behind the interview desk sat a very skinny and light-skinned woman. Her slightly wrinkled skin and permanent scowl made her look much older than she probably was. The woman was holding a sleeping toddler rolled up into a bundle inside a faded green baby wrapper.

Duski sat down opposite her.

"*Dumela mma,*" she greeted the visitor.

"Duski Lôcha?" the woman asked in response.

Duski nodded while studying the woman's appearance—four top front teeth were missing.

Who the hell is she? And those deep set wrinkles, even L'Oreal's Revitalift cream would have a hard time penetrating them, she thought.

"How can I be of help?" she finally asked, baffled by the woman's scowl.

"Since you've taken my son's father— thought you might want him as well," she said, depositing the sleeping bundle on the desk before storming out.

Completely befuddled, Duski stayed in the office for a few minutes to digest the woman's words.

Her son's father? Who the hell is her child's father?

It can't be . . . She took hesitant steps towards the sleeping baby. *Ali couldn't have slept with that woman. Ali couldn't have slept with a woman like that, a woman who stinks of stale chibuku.* She sucked her teeth angrily before summoning the courage to carefully pull back the torn, knitted green wrapper.

Ali, you bastard, you sonofabitch—you've blown it now, she thought as she unwrapped the bundle and stared in disbelief at the little face. The little boy had Ali's button nose, round chubby face and smooth tawny complexion. *The fucking bastard can't keep his business in his trousers.*

"Constable Kowa," Duski suddenly yelled out, opening the adjoining door to the switchboard.

"Yes, Sarge," Kowa stood to attention and faced the fuming sergeant.

"Who was she?" she looked at Kowa accusingly—she was pretty sure she was hiding something—that she knew the woman. *Why has this woman turned up today when she's been with Ali for over six months? Kowa is somehow involved.* She was convinced Kowa had been spying on her. *That early morning phone call and text were rather odd. And why did she dive under the desk when I walked past?*

"What woman, Sarge?" Constable Kowa gave her a deliberate and vague look.

"The woman with the baby—you know her, don't you?" Duski looked her straight in the eye—she could tell she was lying.

"What makes you think that Sarge?" Kowa shrugged.

"You haven't answered my question, Constable," Duski interrupted, getting annoyed.

"To be honest—haven't got a clue what you're on about . . . excuse me, got work to do" Constable Kowa said as one of the lines on the switchboard started flashing.

"Central police station, Constable Kowa speaking. How can I be of assistance? She's right here, hold on," she said before covering the mouthpiece and whispering, "Sarge, it's for you. I'll transfer it to the interview room." She waited for Duski to pick up on the other side before she replaced the receiver and stared with a satisfied smirk at the cubicle's glass panel in front of her.

"Ali's on his way to pick up his son. In the meantime, make sure that the baby is okay," Duski barked at Kowa before slamming the door shut behind her and marching back into the charge office.

How did Ali know his ex had just dumped his son with me? she wondered, still convinced Kowa had something to do with the woman's visit.

But why?

She searched every corner and crevice of her brain for an answer, but found nothing. She was still trying to figure out what was going on when she recalled a famous Shakespearian quote:

I hold the world but as the world: A stage where every man must play a part, and mine is a sad one.

Reflecting on her own life, Duski recited the lines inside her head—somehow she found them soothing.

*   *   *

When Ali arrived just before half past three that afternoon to pick up the little boy, Duski refused to talk to him. Ali did not persist, he knew her very well. He knew she wasn't the sort of woman to let lying dogs lie. He knew she'll eventually let him explain, and that all would be forgiven and forgotten, he told himself. His hopes of getting back with her hung on an ancient Setswana saying:

If you once owned a dog, it'll never forget your whistle.

With the saying swirling round and round his head like a dose of ecstasy, Ali drove back to his house with the little boy and a firm belief that everything would soon be back to normal. All he needed to do, to get the ball rolling was to get rid of the pregnant woman and the child.

*   *   *

The air was fragrant with the smell of damp earth and the scent of the much-needed rain. Black clouds had gathered and clung together in thick folds. They were accompanied by distant, loud rumbles of thunder, a few scattered showers, and an occasional flicker of lightning.

The wedding wasn't until noon that day.

Duski was up and ready when Thandie's little white Toyota Tazz pulled up at the gate, followed by a great cloud of dust. She picked up a blue clutch bag and the wedding present and did a final catwalk in front of the wardrobe's full-length mirror.

Thandie hit the horn impatiently.

Thandie as usual, hadn't left anything to chance—*you never know who you might bump into,* was her philosophy. She was wearing a black mini-dress with a matching handbag, a pair of red stiletto shoes, and a black super-afro wig.

After Duski had strapped herself in, Thandie mounted a pair of poppy red animal sunglasses on her chubby button nose.

"So who's the groom?" she asked as she reversed out into Ditjaube Road.

"Don't know," Duski replied, surveying Thandie's attire.

She looks like she's going for a jamming session with the Jackson Five, she thought, slightly amused.

"My ideal husband would have to be one who keeps his mouth shut and chequebook open," Thandie said. "I sincerely hope she's marrying someone nice . . . and rich," she added.

*   *   *

The community hall was covered by a cloud of white fine dust that had been unsettled by cars driving in and out. It hadn't rained as much as Duski had hoped, and the heat was becoming intense.

Thandie stirred the Tazz round to the back of the hall where there were fewer cars.

At noon, a white balloon-decorated Toyota Corolla pulled up, dust and all, in front of the hall's reception. Bontle, the Shebeen queen, was wearing the most dazzling yellow and blue gown. Accompanied by a priest, wolf whistles and ululations, she stepped out of the car and into the hall towards a makeshift pulpit just below the stage. The priest stood beside her and soon began the ceremony.

The guests took their seats and the ceremony began.

"Everything that happens in this world happens at the time the Lord chooses. God sets times for births, times for deaths, times for planting. And today . . ." the priest paused to scan the congregated guests. He continued, "Today, we are assembled here to witness the union of Sister Bontle Mothootsile and God."

Duski and Thandie exchanged puzzled glances while the priest wiped sweat from his brow with the back of his hand.

"And now, it's time for my sister here to give herself—body and soul—to the Lord Himself." He paused and looked at the guests before shouting, "*Hallelujah!*"

"*A-men,*" the guests chorused.

"*Mma,* repeat after me: I, Bontle, commit my life to you, God. With deepest joy, I come into my new life with you. As you've pledged to me your life and love, so I too happily give you my life. And in confidence, I submit myself to your hardship. I will live only unto you God—loving you, obeying you, and ever-seeking to please you. Therefore, throughout life, no matter what may be ahead of me, I pledge to you my life as an obedient and faithful servant." The priest stared intently into Bontle's eyes as if he were in a trance.

Bontle looked up with a fixed smile at the corrugated roof and recited the vows after the priest.

"Poor Bontle, she's clearly lost the plot," Thandie whispered, pinching Duski's thigh to get her attention. "We've got to get out of here now," she added, dragging her out of the hall and all the way back to the car.

"Your friend and her priest are barmy," Thandie said shaking her head as soon as they were back inside the car. "Is this what religion does to people?" she mumbled, perplexed, as she reached for a beer-filled-cooler box she'd brought with her and helped herself to a bottle of Savannah.

"This reminds me of a similar incident a year ago, of woman we'd to take to Lobatse mental hospital." Duski paused briefly to drag on a cigarette she'd just lit. "Her family had rung the station, concerned about her mental state." She paused again to fan out smoke through her nostrils. "Do you think a broken heart can lead one to madness?"

Thandie stared broodingly at a packet of cigarettes she was about to open before absently saying, "Do you think that's what happened to her? That's why I prefer relationships with sugar daddies . . . no emotional attachments—uncomplicated—just like the surgeon and the victims on his operating table. Strictly business."

"Thing is, Thandie," she started, "in this HIV/AIDS era, do you think it's safe to do that? Even with condoms? What if the condom splits?" Duski blurted, wondering if her friend had already caught the dreaded disease. "Life's precious, you know," she added.

"Never heard of anti-retroviral therapy?" Thandie retorted.

"But it doesn't mean people should deliberately get themselves infected, does it!" she reproached.

"Come on, let's stop talking about AIDS. It's a depressing subject, especially on your friend's wedding," Thandie said, starting up the car and reversing out of the compound.

"You're right, let's get the hell out of here," Duski said. "I wonder why poor Bontle has decided to devote her life to God," she suddenly said, staring at a passing dust devil as if the answer whirled in the middle of it.

"You never finished the story of the woman you took to Lobatse. What happened to her?" Thandie asked, changing the subject.

"She was convinced that God spoke to her, telling her that she was the chosen one."

"Chosen for what?"

"God knows—no pun intended. I don't think she knew either—the family said she'd been through a lot. The usual story—failed relationships," she said, thinking about her own relationship perils.

"Poor thing, what happened to her?" Thandie asked as she stirred the car into an unmarked parking space in front of the Liquorama bottle store.

"She was later diagnosed as suffering from some kind of psychotic disorder," Duski concluded sadly as Thandie parked in front of the liquor store for the second time that day.

*   *   *

Disappointed by the so-called wedding, Duski and Thandie decided to visit the infamous George's Pub and Grub in Tsholofelo that evening. George's was a favourite haunt for local prostitutes. It was a British style pub that was deliberately designed to make British expats feel at home.

Thandie swerved the car, with the expertise of a drink-driver, into an unmarked parking space in front of the pub. As usual, the place was heaving. Local men wearing Manchester United and Liverpool football shirts perched on every available seat in the tiny pub. In one corner, a large overheard screen televised a match between Man United and Liverpool.

"Hi, Sarge. Long time," a familiar voice with a caressing lilt said behind—her heart rate went on the double. She turned round to find herself staring into Craig's blue eyes. If she were white she'd have gone all red at the memory of her erotic scene in the bathroom the morning after meeting Craig at the Bull and Bush. She hung her head in shame.

"What happened to you? You disappeared without saying goodbye," he said. He held her hand, his blue eyes focused on hers intently.

"Too noisy in here, can we talk outside?" she asked.

"Who's she—the woman you were with at the Bull and Bush?" she asked as soon as they were out on the veranda.

"Me brother's wife—hope you didn't think we were together," he searched her eyes.

"She made it obvious she didn't like what she saw."

"What I do is none of her business," Craig said stamping out the cigarette stub he'd just thrown on the ground.

From Craig's response, Duski realised she'd been right in thinking she was the subject of the lecture Craig was given that evening by the two women at the bar. She slowly walked away from the veranda to lean against Thandie's white Tazz in the car park. She lit a cigarette and stared at the moon deep in thought.

Craig followed. He too leaned against the car and watched her as she dragged nervously on her cigarette, all the way to the butt.

She was about to light another when Craig suddenly cupped her face and turned it gently towards himself to meet her gaze. Her heart rate went on the double again and rapidly gaining momentum like a village crier's drum. His hands slid inside her top—sending tiny explosions through her entire being—before exploring the contours of her curvy butt. He withdrew his right hand to trace the skin around her slightly parted and anticipating lips.

It was a starry moonlit night and the dimly lit and dusty shopping complex was empty—save for the sea of white bakkies and saloons tightly parked together in the dry dirt car park. The air was breezy and alive with the smells of barbecued meats and loud music from neighbouring bars and Shebeens.

"Can't wait to explore the rest of you," he whispered his voice hoarse with emotion as their eyes locked under the moonlight.

"I want to get to know you first," Duski protested weakly and pulled away a little to search his deep blue eyes. She wondered what he really wanted from her . . . and what a good-looking bloke like him was doing in Botswana.

Was he running away from something?

"Have you got a girlfriend?" she suddenly asked.

"Been single for a year now," he said kissing her parted lips as if his very life depended on it.

"*Whore!*" somebody spat out. It came from a group of men zigzagging through the tightly parked cars.

Her sensual moment came to an abrupt halt.

"I don't think this is a good idea," she looked over Craig's shoulder at the men walking past. To her horror, she recognised one of the moonlit faces. It was Ali's. She wondered whether he'd recognised her and whether it was he who'd shouted 'whore' at her.

"Got to go now, sorry—think I've had a lot to drink—we've been drinking all day," she rambled on as she rummaged through her handbag for her cell phone so she could ring to ask Thandie to come out.

Duski was reluctant to go back inside, she knew if Ali didn't recognise her when he went past, he would surely know as soon as she walked in that she was the slut they'd just seen kissing a white man.

"Can I give you a lift home?" Craig asked, wondering what he'd done wrong. "or would you prefer to go back inside to find your friend?" he carried on, unaware of the cloud of anxiety that had suddenly masked the glow in her eyes.

Duski shook her head and looked at him briefly. She wondered how he would feel if she told him she was embarrassed about being with him. She surveyed her un-manicured fingernails in the semi darkness, fiddled with her phone and said, "I'll ring a cab. Thanks, anyway."

She was about to dial the taxi company she'd stored in her contacts when a commotion at the pub door caught her attention. Two women rolled out, their arms locked around each other's necks like two male kudus.

"Thandie, what the hell is going on? What happened?" She rushed to her friend's side as soon as the bouncers had pulled the two women apart. Thandie's strappy top was torn and bloody and it now barely covered her big breasts.

"This prostitute had the nerve to call my mother names," Thandie screamed.

"Who you calling a prostitute?" the other woman screamed back, ready to resume the fight.

"Thandie, we need to go before someone calls the police—you don't want to spend the night in a cell," Duski warned. She fished out the car keys from Thandie's handbag and dragged her back to the car. Craig held the door open while the bouncer picked up and threw Thandie into the passenger seat.

"Please call me," Craig said, quickly scribbling his number on an old receipt he'd managed to dig out from his wallet. He put it firmly in her hand.

"I am not sure if this is a good idea," she said looking anxiously past Craig at Ali who stood staring at them from the veranda.

"Thought you liked me," Craig said, perplexed.

Duski briefly studied his face, the earlier glow in his eye, now replaced by disappointment and hurt. She touched his hand before winding up the window and driving off—just before a police van pulled into the car park.

Chapter Fourteen

The first week of December would have been just like any other if it weren't for the way it ended.

It was Sunday evening when Duski eventually woke up to get ready for her night shift. She reported for duty at ten o'clock at night. The station was fairly quiet, which was typical for a Sunday night.

After a brief handover, she brought out copies of the Maruapula murder case statements and went over them several times and took notes. She needed a distraction, something to stop her from thinking about the mess her life had recently descended into. She thought about Craig.

A white boyfriend—is that what I really want?

Ali had to be dealt with first, of course. She'd to make it clear to him they were finished—history. She knew he was still in love with her—she saw it in his eyes when he stared at her from the veranda at George's. She reflected on her own feelings.

Don't cry because it's over. Smile because it happened, she thought and smiled as she recalled the quote. *Where did I read that?* She wondered.

"Sir, there are a few things I need to check out on the Maruapula murder case," she said, standing to attention in front of the duty sub-inspector. She handed him the notes she'd been scribbling. "I've got a feeling the victim's boyfriend hasn't told us everything about the night his girlfriend was murdered," she explained.

"The case is out of our hands now, Sergeant. CID are dealing with it," the sub-inspector reminded her as he studied her scribbled notes.

"I know sir, but what if they've missed the clues? That poor girl might hang for a murder she hasn't committed! I can't help feeling she's innocent," Duski said, looking at her boss pleadingly. "Let me do this, sir—let me go and clarify a few things with the boyfriend."

"I'm not sure this is a good idea—leave CID to deal with it—better speak to the officer in charge of the case about your suspicions."

"Promise I will—as soon as I've confirmed my suspicions."

"Okay, okay," the sub-inspector said, putting up his hands in mock surrender. "Just be careful and report to me as soon as you get back," he added handing back her notes.

"I'm taking Constable Moji and Constable Peba with me, sir. Nobody would dare mess with me with those two," she stood to attention and waited to be dismissed.

A quarter of an hour later, the three officers knocked on Lovemore's door at Maruapula flats.

"One of us will have to go in through the window," Duski advised when nobody responded.

The flat looked deserted, as she expected. The front window that Cynthia had smashed in hadn't been repaired.

"Sarge, I'm afraid you're the only one small enough to fit through the window—unless you want us to break the door down," Constable Peba said, preparing to use his body as a battering ram.

"We haven't got a search warrant and at the moment, we don't even know if he is guilty," she cautioned.

"What do we do now?" Constable Moji asked, clearly disappointed.

"I'll go in through the window. If there are any problems or I don't come out after a few minutes, break the door down," she said, putting her hand through the broken pane first to open the window.

"Yes, Sarge. We'll be on standby," the two burly constables chorused as they positioned themselves strategically at the door.

"Looks as if he's moved out," she shouted from inside the flat. "His clothes, lounge and bedroom furniture are all gone," she added.

"What are we going to do now? Shall we speak to the neighbours? Somebody might have his forwarding address," Constable Moji suggested.

"The lights are still on next door," Duski said as the two constables helped her out through the window.

"Okay, time waits for no man," Constable Peba said, trotting off ahead of Sergeant Duski

Lôcha and Constable Moji, heading towards the next flat along from Lovemore's.

*   *   *

It was nearly two o'clock in the morning when Duski and her two constables eventually left the Maruapula flats. She was now convinced Lovemore had something to do with his girlfriend's death. Her biggest challenge yet was to find out where he'd disappeared to. The neighbours they spoke to didn't seem to know who Lovemore really was or where he came from.

"The man in the first flat thought Lovemore was from Metsimotlhabe. Yet when I spoke to him on the phone, he didn't sound like a southerner. Moji, you recorded his statement. What do you think?" Duski asked. She'd been mulling over Lovemore's real identity since they got back to the station.

"He wrote the statement himself, but when we spoke, I detected a northern accent. He could be Zimbabwean," Moji concluded, recalling his conversation with Lovemore.

"Do you think Lovemore is an alias?" Peba asked.

"It's possible. We need to search Cynthia's room tomorrow night for his photographs. *The Voice* might help us find him if we run the photos on next Friday's edition—could also alert other police stations to be on the lookout," she said.

153

"Someone who knows him might come forward and if he is innocent, he will contact us himself.'

"Sarge, what do we tell CID? They're in charge of the case—don't want to step on their toes," Constable Moji cautioned.

"I'm sure they'll have to find him when the case goes to court, after all he's a witness—we're doing them a favour," she said as she went to the inspector's office.

"We are back, sir," she announced, stamping her right foot to attention in front of the sleeping sub-inspector. As usual, the sub-inspector jumped, sending the paperwork his head had been resting on, flying.

"I can see you're back, Sergeant. As I told you so many times before, there is no need for all that noise," the Sub-Inspector said, clearly unamused as he picked up his paperwork from the floor. "It's not funny, Sergeant! Do you think I can't see that smirk on your face?" he sucked his teeth as she disappeared through the door, back to the charge office.

"Sarge, you have a phone call," a constable shouted from behind the switchboard screen. "I'm transferring it over to your desk," she added.

"Central police station charge office, Sergeant Duski Lôcha speaking. How can I help?" she recited the drill. "Yep. Partial? Plot number? Yep—will send officers over as soon as possible," she said, replacing the receiver before scribbling an address down in her police notebook. "Constable

Peba, could you ask the radio operator to call officers on Beat Three to ask them to attend a case in Partial? Plot number 3221. Apparently, a naked woman is hiding behind some hedges. Looks like she's being chased by a mob."

"Yes, Sarge," he said as he threw the newspaper he'd been reading on the table to stand to attention before disappearing through the short corridor leading to the charge office.

"Sarge, their radio is breaking up—can't hear a word of what they are saying. Why don't we just drive down there and check it out ourselves. It'll be quicker," he reported back after a couple of minutes.

"Who's on Beat Three? Let me guess, Constable Peter and Constable Moeng. They're up to their old tricks again," she said sucking her teeth. She recalled her first experience with the two constables as a police recruit. That was the trick they played every time when they were out on patrol—always pretending there was interference when someone radioed them.

"Have their radio checked out as soon as they get back," she ordered. "Peba, let's go. Moji, you tell the sub-inspector we are out on a call," she said, throwing her police hat on.

Five minutes later, they arrived at the hedged yard at the back of the Middle Star Shopping Centre. As they drove past the centre and into the Partial housing estate, their headlights immediately picked out a naked figure cowering behind the hedge, arms held tightly across her bosom. Peba, who was driving, turned off the lights and rolled the car slowly towards the yard. The mob that had been milling around with stones and sticks chanting *moloi* (witch) melted into the darkness as soon as they noticed the police car.

They reformed some distance away from the woman. Fortunately, the cloudy sky hid the moon, providing much-needed cover for the woman from the bloodthirsty mob. Duski drove closer to the hedged yard and parked between the naked woman and the witch hunters.

She got out of the car and approached the woman.

"It's the police *mma*. What are you doing here at this time of the night? Where are your clothes?" she asked, offering the woman her hand to help her up. "Peba, get me a blanket from the back of the bakkie please?"

"I can lend her a dress," a woman said behind her, she'd come from a nearby house. "By the way, I'm the one who called you," the woman added before disappearing back into the house. She came out shortly carrying a cotton dress.

"*Tankie mma*," Duski said immediately helping the scrawny, shivering figure into the dress.

Though it was a hot night, the naked woman was shaking like a leaf.

"Let's get inside the vehicle so you can tell us what's going on," she said as she studied the victim's face. She could tell from the woman's distinct facial features, she was Zimbabwean.

"We can talk inside my house if you prefer," the Samaritan woman offered. "The man who got the mob on to this poor woman lives in the third house from here. His name is Monageng," she said, pointing out the house with her torch.

"We need to pick up this man first then. And if you don't mind, we'll need you to come with us to the station to make a statement," Duski said, jumping into the driver's seat with the two women while Peba went into the canopied back ready to escort the man who'd incited the mob.

*   *   *

"Please tell us what happened to your clothes *mma*," Duski asked the Zimbabwean woman in English once back at the station.

"This man tore them up and chased me out of his house. He called me a witch," the woman started in heavily accented English. She glanced accusingly at the man in question sitting not very far from her.

"Had to. I needed to get my cell phone back. She stole it and hid it in her underwear," the man protested.

"He owed me some money. He'd been messing me around for weeks about the payment. He took a bedspread on credit. I'm going back to Zimbabwe in the morning, and I need the money."

The man hung his head in shame as the woman cast another accusing look towards him. "I went to his workplace in the afternoon to collect the debt. He told me he didn't have money on him and asked me to come back in the morning instead. He promised to pay me then. I told him I didn't mind waiting until he'd finished work. I went back to his house with him at four o'clock, but when we got to the house, he told me to wait outside while he went to a money link. I waited for hours, and at midnight, he came back and went straight to bed without saying a word to me.

I sat outside, hoping he would eventually come out again. When he didn't, I threatened to call the police. He let me in and started threatening me. He told me to leave him alone or else I would be sorry. I noticed, as I walked in, that his cell phone was on the table. I grabbed it and told him that he could have it back after he paid me. He went mental, grabbed hold of me, and tore my clothes up. He called me a witch and tried to get the neighbours to attack me too," she sobbed.

"Yes, people were ready to stone her to death," the Samaritan woman added.

"She'd taken my cell phone, and all I was trying to do was get it back," the man protested. "She's lying—I didn't refuse to pay her or call her a witch. I told her I would pay her in the morning, but she wouldn't have any of it. I had to get her out of my house," he added anxiously.

"Why did you tear up her clothes?" Duski asked looking at the man disapprovingly.

"As I said, I was trying to get back my cell phone. She'd hid it in her bra. What was I supposed to do?" the man said. He was staring—seemingly embarrassed—at the shiny charge office floor.

"But you didn't have to tear the woman's panties off as well," Duski said accusingly.

"She'd it in her bra, and when I tore that off her, she put it in her . . . her . . . panties! I had to tear those off too—I had to," the man confessed, feeling a little bit foolish. "I couldn't let her take my cell phone . . . that phone is my life," he protested.

"*Rra*, I'm afraid we'll have to charge you with indecent assault," she said without sympathy for the shamefaced man in front of her. "Constable Moji, take a witness statement from the lady please. Constable Peba, you take the gentleman's please. Thanks."

*   *   *

It was nearly five o'clock in the morning by the time Duski and her men finished recording all the statements. Constable Moji and Constable Peba drove the man to the nearest money link to withdraw cash so he could pay the Zimbabwean woman.

Duski felt sorry for the woman, she knew how hard it probably was for the woman to support her family back in Zimbabwe given the present crisis. She thought of how ordinary Zimbabweans were bearing the brunt of their country's political and economic crisis. Legal and illegal immigrants were flooding neighbouring countries, particularly Botswana—a large number of them were responsible for almost half of the street crimes in the country's towns and cities. Still, the Batswana were becoming increasingly intolerant of their less fortunate neighbours.

She recalled an incident a few years ago when Mugabe was consulted about the problems his people were causing in the country. His shocking response to the problem was, "Shoot them if they are causing you a problem." Left with no choice, the Botswana government reacted by erecting a large electric fence along the border to stop Zimbabweans from entering the country illegally.

The problem faced by the government was that many illegal Zimbabwean immigrants refused to claim asylum. All they wanted was to get what they could out of the country and then go back to feed their families back in their own country.

Who could blame them? She thought sympathetically. *There's no place like home.*

Fortunately for the assaulted Zimbabwean woman, she had a visitor's visa. Duski was therefore, saved the unpleasant task of having to arrest and detain her as an illegal. She however decided to overlook the fact that the woman had come into the country to sell goods on the streets without a hawker's licence.

It was nearly six o'clock in the morning when Dusky drove back to the station after dropping off the Zimbabwean woman at the bus station. As she dragged herself back into the office—exhausted after the night's drama—she was immediately summoned to the inspector's office.

"Take a seat, Sergeant," the duty sub-inspector said. He looked at her with a sombre expression—her heart somersaulted. She could tell something was very wrong . . . a senior officer never offered a junior a seat for no reason. "*O lepodisi ke batla gore o itshware*," she heard him say, his voice sounding distant.

Her mind raced through a list of relatives who the anticipated bad news might relate to.

"Had a phone call a few minutes ago from Superintendent Kang," he began but paused as he moved to other side of the table to sit next to her. She could tell from his tone that something bad had happened. She knew that a phone call from a senior officer such as *Rre* Kang meant something was seriously wrong. The sub-inspector's voice was unusually solemn. He was using the tone of voice she'd heard not so long ago during the Maruapula Flats murder case when she'd accompanied him to Motlatsi's family to inform them of their daughter's murder.

The sub-inspector was a traditionalist, well versed in the intricate and traditional ways of announcing death. This usually involved elaborative condolences, often punctuated by Setswana proverbs and solemn expressions—before one got to the really bad part.

As he rambled on, her mind went on a hundred-metre trot to search for what Ali might or might not have done after he'd left George's on Saturday. She recalled a very disturbing dream she'd had on that Saturday night. She'd briefly wondered whether it was a premonition.

In the dream, she and another female officer were chatting when a white police Land Cruiser pulled up by the SSG armoury. Six armed officers who'd been on an armed escort jumped off the vehicle. As it pulled to a stop, Ali left the group and walked determinedly towards them, an AK-47 strapped to his right shoulder. He'd inserted a magazine, which he had in his left hand and had released the safety catch before corking the gun to fire indiscriminate single shots at them like a lunatic.

She'd woken up sweaty and shaky, but relieved it was only a dream.

Her mind wandered off to crimes of passion she'd dealt with since joining the police force. She shuddered involuntarily as a recent case came to mind—a very tragic homicide and suicide case involving an SSG Assistant Superintendent. The officer had become suspicious his wife was having an affair. He'd heard rumours she was having an affair with one of his bosses. One early morning, after a night of heavy drinking, the officer had gone to the armoury and taken out an AK-47 rifle with a full magazine. He took it to his house.

His wife, who was a nurse at a local clinic, was up and ironing her uniform when he shot her at close range and killed her in front of their two children. After shooting his wife, he went to his boss's house and shot his way in. Fortunately, his boss was away for the weekend with his family. Frustrated, he shot himself in front of his boss's neighbour who'd come over to investigate the source of the shooting.

"He was found hanging from a tree in some bushes near the airport," the sub-inspector's voice pierced through her heart like a machete. Duski stared absently at his head before refocusing her stare on his mouth to make sure she'd caught the words correctly. The sub-inspector's mouth suddenly multiplied into a dozen mouths as she started to sway.

The exhaustion from the night shift and the impact of the tragic news suddenly took their toll. The rest of the sub-inspector's devastating message filtered into her unconscious state like a dream. His solemn voice kept repeating the same thing over and over.

"The body of a pregnant woman was found in his bedroom with fatal gunshot wounds. The body of a pregnant woman was found in his bedroom with fatal gunshot wounds."

Finally, she drifted into oblivion.

Chapter Fifteen

"Sergeant, can you hear me?" a distant voice called out from somewhere above her head.

Duski's eyes were sore and swollen—her heart felt sore and swollen too. She kept her eyes shut while summoning all the energy she'd left to shut the voice out too. A strong smell of cleaning chemicals mingled with the fresh smell of overcooked cabbage, circulated nauseatingly around the room. Slowly and painfully, she opened her eyes and surveyed the bare and cheerless walls around her.

"Yes, I can hear you," she whispered at a pair of eyes peering at her from a little white-capped and corn-rowed head. "Are you a nurse?" she asked. She knew it was a silly question—it was obvious from the woman's attire that she was a nurse. The question she had intended to ask was *'why am I here?'*

"Yes, I'm a nurse," the woman said before she'd had the chance to rephrase the question. "You fainted at work, that's why you are here." The woman handed her a little blue tablet and said, "You need to rest now, and this will help you sleep."

Her head was pounding. There were some questions she wanted to ask the woman, but she couldn't bring herself to. She took the tablet instead and the nurse handed her a glass of cold water.

"Thank you," she murmured before she went back to rearranging her thoughts and recalling the events of the previous night. She remembered going over to Lovemore's house at midnight and later driving to the Partial housing estate to rescue a naked Zimbabwean woman from a bloodthirsty mob. Finally, she recalled being summoned to the inspector's office at six. After that, everything became a blur.

"Sergeant, I'm glad to see you're back with us again. You gave us quite a scare this morning," the sub-inspector beamed as he walked towards her bedside. "How're you feeling?" he asked, leaning against the bed rails.

"What's going on, sir? The nurse said I fainted." Her swollen eyes looked suspiciously at the sub-inspector.

"Don't you remember what happened this morning?" the sub-inspector asked cautiously, "The nurse said it's okay to take you home; I've given constable Kowa a week off to stay with you at home until after the funeral."

"The funeral? Whose funeral?" she looked at the sub-inspector, terrified. She tried to sit up.

"We need to get you home," he said. "We'll talk about this later," he added as he helped her off the bed.

Duski let herself be led outside the hospital building, into the blinding rays of the early morning

sun. The soreness in her heart, lack of sleep
and the warm rays on her heavy swollen eyelids
made everything seem surreal. The early morning
Gaborone wake-up calls of kombi conductors
luring passengers with flirty compliments, traffic
noises and a sea of white cars queuing up on
the shiny tarmac leading towards the hospital
roundabout seemed out of place.

She knew something was very wrong—she
felt strangely alienated. Though the morning sun was
already getting hotter, she felt an unusual chill. She
desperately wished someone would tell her what was
going on. Her head was throbbing and her mind was
in turmoil as the sub-inspector led her into a police
Hyundai waiting in the hospital's car park.

Back in Block Eight, Constable Kowa,
Constable Solomone, Ali's housemate and a few
neighbours had congregated in the living room.
They all fell to a solemn silence as soon as she was
walked in.

"I've run a bath for you, Sarge," Constable
Kowa said quickly getting to her feet. She'd
spent the morning scrubbing and tidying up the
bathroom just the way Duski liked it. She hugged
her and said, "We're all with you," and sniffed back
a couple of unruly tears.

Duski nodded and smiled. She wanted to
know what was going on, but she was too scared
to ask who'd died. She shut the door as soon as she
was left on her own. Her towel and bathrobe were
already in the bathroom on top of the washing

basket. She undressed, stepped into the warm and foamy bath and sat staring blankly at the rusty bathroom window. She was unsure what she was supposed to do.

*   *   *

It was already dark when she eventually woke up with a dull heartache. She felt numb, dazed and disoriented. There was a filter of light coming in through the corridor, which gave her bedroom a moonlit effect. She switched the bedside light on. It was then that she noticed it.

The letter was addressed to her. She recognised the handwriting immediately. Duski stared at it for a while, her hands shaking before she eventually summoned enough courage to pick it up.

Carefully, she tore open the envelope, immediately noticing the letter was written in English. Her mind went into protective mode, and she became a spectator in her own show. She watched herself read the letter.

> *My love,*
>
> *My sugar, by now you have realised why I'm writing this small letter to you. My honey, I'm missing you very much right now, My heart is perambulating with every word that I write, If words of love could ride a bicycle, I would be competing against Diego Maradona right now*

to win you back. I'm missing you like sugar misses tea. I love you spontaneously, and as I stand horizontal to the wall and perpendicular to the ground, I only think of you. Please stop haranguing with the feelings in my heart because I love you more than snake loves rat. To me, each day starts by thinking of you and ends by dreaming of you. When I saw you on Saturday night at George's with a white man, my metabolism suddenly stopped and my peristalsis went in reverse gear. My medulla oblongata also stopped functioning.

Crazy, you may say, but this is true. If only you knew what was going on in my encephalon, you would understand. That's why I can't live without being with you face to face. Sleep tight and don't let those bed bugs ever bite 'cause you are too sweet a thing for them. Remember, I love you more than snake loves rat.

Ali

She read the letter several times, trying to digest its meaning. In dribs and drabs, fragments of the morning's events started coming back. She recalled someone saying something about Ali . . . and something about hanging from a tree. The fog in her traumatised mind lifted as the fragments finally became whole. She recalled Sub-Inspector's heart-wrenching message before she'd blacked out:

*He was found hanging from a tree in some bushes
near the airport, and the body of a pregnant woman was
found in his bedroom with fatal gunshot wounds.*

Duski stared at the letter and recalled their
fight—their last ever fight.

You weren't writing me a love letter, were you?
she thought, *It is a fucking suicide note. Thanks.* She
sobbed, wishing she could have had a chance to tell
him it didn't matter that he'd got another woman
pregnant. *We could have talked about it, sorted it all out,
planned to give away the baby, etc.* Her mind rambled on
with the *'could haves'* and *'should haves.'*

In the days following Ali's tragic death,
Duski lived in the deepest and darkest parts of hell.
She was constantly consumed by an unbearable
guilt. Her mind replayed the events of the past days
and recounted the contents of the letter as if on
auto play—time after time. There never seemed
to be a quiet moment in her troubled mind and
every passing second was occupied by purgatory
thoughts. She stared vacantly day and night, at her
bedroom ceiling, leaving chores such as sleeping,
getting out of bed, bathing, brushing her teeth,
getting dressed and eating to the living.

*   *   *

One late afternoon, a week after the tragedy,
she got a long overdue visit from CID. She wasn't

surprised when Detective Inspector Marvellous and Detective Sergeant Boy knocked at her bedroom door and summoned her to Broadhurst police station. She'd known that sooner or later, rumours would reach the investigating team about her row with Ali over the pregnant woman.

"Sergeant, can I start by saying how sorry we are about your loss," Detective Inspector Marvellous started hesitantly as soon as they arrived at the station. He cleared his voice and said, "I know you are still grieving, but we do need to ask you a few questions." Duski stared at him vacantly and then at his partner, Detective Sergeant Boy.

"We need to know where you were between two and five o'clock in the morning last Sunday."

Again, she looked at them, confused. She could not recall what day it was and she wasn't even sure how long she'd been bedridden. "I never left my bed," she said a bit perplexed.

"Sergeant, we are talking about the night your boyfriend died. Can you remember where you were at those times?" Detective Sergeant Boy repeated the question, his tone, a bit unsympathetic.

"I went to George's with a friend on Saturday night—we must have left the place around midnight," she said slowly recalling the events of that fateful weekend. She wondered whether Ali would still be alive if she hadn't met Craig.

"Do you remember where you went or what you did after leaving the pub?" Detective Inspector

Marvellous asked, trying to make his interrogation as sensitive as he could.

"I drove my friend home because she was over the limit and I stayed over at hers," she explained. She wondered whether the detectives thought she shot the pregnant woman. "Where is all this leading?" She sucked her teeth, anger slowly rising from the pit of her empty stomach and spreading like a plague through her traumatised body.

"Well we've reason to believe Ali was murdered soon after shooting his girlfriend," Detective Sergeant Boy said, dropping the bombshell. "Somebody clearly wanted it to look like he'd committed suicide," he said, looking at her challengingly.

"Murdered?" She felt dizzy but she knew she'd to keep herself together—intact. "Why do you think this has anything to do with me?" Her chest constricted with fear, pain clouded her sunken and haggard face.

Duski recalled the Mariette Sonjaleen Bosch case, the first white woman to be hung in Botswana. The evidence used to convict her was circumstantial—there'd been no direct forensic evidence linking her to the alleged murder—not even fingerprints on the gun or in the victim's house. Duski suddenly realised she was going to have a tough job convincing them she was innocent. She knew if CID couldn't find evidence clearing her from the case, they could easily use whatever they could dig out about her relationship with Ali to build a case.

"Sergeant, you'd a domestic with the deceased a few days before his death when you found out he'd got his ex-girlfriend pregnant," Detective Inspector Marvellous stated.

"Whoever killed Ali wanted to teach him a lesson," Detective Sergeant Boy added, looking her straight in the eye. "Castrated him to take away his manhood" he said. "The killer must have been pretty pissed off, don't you think?"

"And you think I am that killer?" she asked, stunned by the Detective Sergeant's accusation.

"Well you tell us. Did you? You were the last person to ring him on that Sunday morning before he was murdered." Detective Sergeant Boy looked at her accusingly.

Duski thought about the phone call she'd made soon after leaving George's that Sunday. She didn't even get to speak to him. She'd rung to apologise even though she didn't know why she'd wanted to do that. She'd done nothing wrong. She tried to quieten a little nagging voice that kept reminding her that dating a white man was wrong—it killed Ali.

"Sergeant, nobody is accusing you of anything," Detective Inspector Marvellous said, looking reproachfully at Detective Sergeant Boy.

The DI moved to sit next to her before putting a protective and affectionate hand around her stiffened shoulders. He looked at her reassuringly and said, "Everything is gonna be all right, Sarge. You just tell us what you know and that will be it."

"Sir, if you are not accusing me of anything, why have you brought me here? Why are you asking me all these questions?" she shrugged off the DI's hand from her shoulders before looking at him with eyes brimming with unshed tears.

"If you were the investigating officer, you'd do the same. Remember our motto: rule no one out or in," he said. He moved even closer to place his hand on her shoulders again—firmly this time. "We all know you're not capable of murder, but when people are hurt by those they love—"

"With all due respect, Detective Inspector, if I was the investigating officer, I would have made sure I did my job properly instead of going around and randomly accusing innocent people," she interjected. She knew what he was going to say. She stood up, hyperventilating with anger. "In case you've forgotten how to do your job, Detective Inspector, every police officer has their fingerprints held by CRB. If I were the investigating officer, I would have checked the prints picked up from the crime scene against—"

"That's where our problems start, Sergeant—if the killer hadn't been smart enough to wipe off every single bit of evidence from the crime scene, including vacuum cleaning the deceased's car, then you wouldn't be here. Only someone with knowledge of crime scene investigation would have been so thorough," Detective Sergeant Boy interrupted. He had been pacing around impatiently. "And that's why, Sergeant, you're here. You can help us build a picture of what happened that morning," he added with an accusing sneer. "Sergeant, we know you rang the deceased and that his car was last seen parked at your house," he added.

Her face and body suddenly went hot with fear. Should she tell them he was there to leave her a letter? She decided not to.

"Ali didn't commit suicide, Sergeant. We all know that," he carried on pompously. "By the way, we've got the autopsy result as well," he added, shuffling through the contents of a brown envelope in front of him. "For your information, the medical examiner found no signs of asphyxia and no lividity in legs, forearms, or hands as one would expect in a case of hanging." He paused to see what effect the revelation was having on Sergeant Duski. Not sure whether her stunned silence was a sign of guilt or not, he continued, "What was found instead was stagnation of blood in the victim's back and buttocks. Do you know what that means, Sergeant? Ali was dead, lying down somewhere—not hanging from the tree where his body was discovered," he concluded, satisfied that he'd crack her in the end.

Detective Sergeant Boy was one of those officers who knew how to look after number one. He knew that if he could get Duski to confess to the murder, he would be a sub-inspector before the end of the year. He'd only been in the police service three years, and his ruthlessness and ass-licking work tactics saw him promoted soon after his probation. Duski realised she'd to pull herself together, be strong, and not allow herself to be intimidated—bullied into confessing to a crime she was innocent of.

"Detective Sergeant, you seem pretty convinced I've something to do with Ali's murder," she said calmly. "I've told you where I was on the night Ali died, what more do you want from me?"

"We've questioned your friend already. Funnily enough, she doesn't remember you driving her home. She only remembers seeing you in the morning," Sergeant Boy said with a smirk that sent chills of fear down into her empty stomach. She knew that she could end up being the scapegoat if CID could not identify a suspect soon.

"Okay, Detective Sergeant, if you've got evidence to prove my guilt, why don't you arrest me—charge me with murder?" she fumed, sucking her teeth incessantly.

"*Hoo,* hold it there, Sergeant! Nobody is accusing you of anything. As my colleague explained earlier, we're only trying to build a picture," Detective Inspector Marvellous intervened, staring sternly at Detective Sergeant Boy.

"Sergeant, we're sending a uniformed officer to search your room," DS Boy continued persistently, "so you had better tell us what you have done with the victim's private parts—you don't want us finding them, do you?"

Missing body parts, did I hear that correctly or am I beginning to hear voices? Duski's felt herself go into temporary paralysis.

"Did you just say the victim's privates were missing?" she asked, stunned by the news but trying her hardest to keep herself intact.

"Don't pretend you didn't already know that, Sergeant," he said, clearly still not convinced she was innocent.

"Enough, Detective Sergeant Boy, nobody's said the Sergeant is guilty," the DI reminded the power hungry sergeant.

"Sorry, sir, but we do need to know if she knows where the victim was killed and who else was involved. If she gives us that information, we'll let her go," the DS said before resuming his interrogation. "Lack of blood on the scene tells us the butchering of the victim was done elsewhere. As you probably didn't do it yourself—to save your neck, Sergeant, you need to tell us who did it and—"

"We've obviously got a serial killer on our hands, Inspector," Duski interrupted him. "I'm not the one you should be interrogating right now, the killer is out there, stalking the next victim while we are wasting time here." She quickly got up to leave the office.

"We'll be keeping a close eye on you, Sergeant," the DS said, following her out.

"And thank you for your cooperation—please do let us know if you recall anything that might help move the investigation forward," he added.

*   *   *

Back in Block Eight, Duski went over the interview in her head, still utterly gobsmacked that she was seen as the prime suspect. It had been confirmed that Ali himself had fired the gun that killed his pregnant girlfriend, but who mutilated his body?

It might have been mutilated after he'd killed himself? Perhaps some witch doctor stumbled upon the body and cut off the sexual organs for muti. Duski surmised though somehow, the entire hypothesis seemed like an improbable coincidence. Her thoughts suddenly wandered off to DS Boy's accusations.

The fact that the car was vacuumed rules out coincidental mutilation by a passing witch doctor. At the moment, I am the only one who knows about the suicide note and has a motive for castrating the cheating bastard, she thought despondently. She was pacing around the bedroom like a caged animal, wondering how she'd ever be able to get CID off her back.

There were overwhelming similarities
between Boiki's, Mudongo's, and Ali's murders that
suggested all were committed by the same person
or persons.

*CID are misguidedly or deliberately overlooking this
fact.* She thought, frustrated.

They seemed hell-bent on pinning the
murder on her. Duski realised as she paced around
the room that the only way of ever catching the
killer and clearing her name was to seek the old
man's help. She held on to the thought as if her
very life depended on it. Eventually, she drifted off
to an uneasy and troubled sleep.

That night, she dreamt she'd been convicted
of Ali's murder and that she'd been sentenced to
death. In her dream, she heard the judge's harsh
sentence: *'You will be returned to prison and hanged by
the neck until you are dead. Your body will be buried in such
a place as the state president may determine. May the Lord
have mercy upon your soul.'*

She was held in the maximum-security
prison, and she'd been put in a single cell
that housed an old mattress, a couple of
government-issue blankets, and a bucket. In her
dream, on the day she was returned to prison, a
female officer had entered the tiny cell she'd been
put in, to give her a brown and shapeless prison
dress and a bowl of gruel. The next day, the same
officer had returned, accompanied by two others.

They'd handcuffed her to take her down to a workshop where she was to be measured for a coffin.

Nobody was talking to her, not even to tell her when she would be executed.

"Can I ring my family," she'd asked the female officer as soon as she'd been taken back in her cell. *"Are they allowed to come and see me?"* she'd asked, looking at the woman with pleading eyes.

"It's not up to me," the guard had said before leaving her in the cell.

In her dream, early the next morning, she'd heard marching footsteps along the corridor. They'd stopped by her cell. She'd known then it was time; they'd come to take her to the gallows. Two uniformed male officers she'd never seen before had taken her away without bothering to shackle her.

She'd been so scared she couldn't even walk. They'd dragged her to a scaffold behind the prison building and had handed her over to two men whose faces were hidden behind black balaclavas. One of the men had put a black cloth round her neck and the other, a cotton hood over her head before the noose was placed around her neck. The plank under her feet gave way and had immediately felt herself fall. Sharp pain had radiated through her body as her neck snapped—and she couldn't breathe.

She was kicking and coughing when Constable Kowa eventually managed to wake her up.

Chapter Sixteen

Attending Ali's daily prayer meetings was mandatory for Duski. It was one of those chores even a grieving suspect who was in an in-between-the-dead-and-living state had to comply with. She knew that if she didn't attend the prayers, people—especially the investigating team—would start speculating about her absence.

The evening before the funeral, she summoned all her courage to sit through accusing stares and whispered damnations from fellow mourners. People from all over Gaborone had attended the prayers . . . not because Ali was famous, but because a rumour was circulating that she might be the castrating murderess.

The funeral was held a couple of weeks after Ali's death. It transpired on a Saturday in his home village, Molepolole. She was relieved that the funeral would be her last public appearance. Her biggest challenge though, still remained—facing Ali's parents and relatives at the funeral. She'd never met any of his relatives and she was terrified at the thought of meeting them.

Since the tragic incident, she'd not stopped blaming herself for what Ali did. She felt responsible for his death. She had come to the conclusion that God was punishing her for consulting a traditional doctor, using *muti,* and kissing a white man.

That Saturday, at five o'clock in the morning, Duski arrived in Molepolole. She was dressed in full police ceremonial dress and she was in the company of constable Kowa, Constable Solomone and Ali's work colleagues.

The police bus that took them to the village, pulled up outside a clean-swept compound just in time for the viewing of the body. Duski, supported by Constable Solomone and Constable Kowa, hesitantly joined a queue of mourners heading for the dark wooden coffin that stood in the middle of an empty sitting room. As she approached the half-open coffin, her knees gave—she passed out as soon as she caught a glimpse of Ali's face.

Duski had dealt with many hanging cases in the past, but she'd never seen anything like that before. She could still see in his partially closed eyes the fear and terror he must have faced in those last moments.

I see why DI Marvellous is treating his death as suspicious, but who could have done such a thing? Duski had thought before losing consciousness.

The funeral service took place soon after the viewing of the corpse. An hour later, mourners made a procession and followed the hearse to the village burial grounds. Like a zombie, Duski let herself, after gaining consciousness, be led into the police bus to accompany Ali to his final resting place on the outskirts of the village. Later that morning, she watched in a daze, as Ali's coffin was suspended on ropes over the grave. She waited with dread, for the sound of the lone trumpeter to bid him farewell.

The smell of moist soil, the sound of sorrowful hymns and the occasional crying outburst all came to her fogged mind as if from a distant dream. Before the coffin was lowered into the grave, she was again led towards it to help remove Ali's uniform and police flag, which had been placed on top of the coffin during the ceremony. She buried her face in the uniform and sobbed her heart out as the coffin was slowly lowered into the grave.

Ali's mother was the first to bid her son farewell before the solemn-looking men—waiting with shovels at the ready—filled the grave. Duski's sorrow-stricken body was helped towards a pile of soil—her shaky hand scooped a handful that was offered to her on a shovel. Her heart-wrenching sobs and the sound of the dry, dusty soil hitting the wooden coffin made the reality of Ali's death sink in. His brothers, cousins, uncles, aunties, and grandparents followed one after the other and they too, filled their sweaty grieving hands with the soil and threw it on top of the coffin. Soon—shovelful after shovelful—dust, sweat and gravel filled up the grave.

The mourners' sorrowful yet melodious voices suddenly soared towards the heavens, drowning the unbearable sounds of shovelfuls of dry earth hitting the coffin at a steady rhythm. For the first time since the tragedy, the reality of what had happened—the finality and what Ali did hit her like a smack in the face.

In many African cultures, wailing for the dead was a common custom during funerals. It seemed to have a therapeutic effect. The Zambians, for instance, encouraged all mourners to wail to their hearts' content—it gave those close to the deceased a rare opportunity to communally and truly mourn the dead. It also lessened the pain and sorrow caused by the loss. Unlike their Zambian neighbours, Batswana saw funerals as a celebration of the deceased's life—not an occasion to be spoiled by excessive wailing.

Duski, on the other hand, saw Ali's funeral not as a celebration at all. She saw his funeral as retribution. She'd defied the Christian God by consulting a witch doctor. Whatever she did, she just couldn't shake off the belief that Ali's death and mostly what he did, was some kind of punishment.

She recalled the preaching against traditional doctors that she'd been subjected to as a child. As shovelful after shovelful landed on the coffin, she could hear her father's voice reciting the Book of Proverbs. *There are certain things the Lord hates and cannot tolerate. A proud look, a lying tongue, hands that kill innocent people, a mind that thinks of wicked plans, feet that hurry off to do evil.*

Though it was a hot sub-Saharan morning, she felt a chill run down her spine as she realised that a visit to the old man was one of the things the Lord supposedly hated. By going to the witch doctor and using *muti*, she'd wilfully and callously driven Ali to murder and suicide. Like Cain, her feet had hurried her off to do evil.

As the pillar stone was placed at the head of the grave, Duski overwhelmed by a feeling of emptiness—she felt forsaken and cursed. The sound of the police rifle salute, (to bid their colleague farewell), ripped her heart apart with guilt and an overwhelming sense of loss. For the first time since the tragedy, she truly sobbed. She was devastated. She could not believe that the man she loved so much was now lying cold under the earth that buried his wooden coffin. She'd never again hear his voice, feel his touch, smell his breath, or see his smiling face. Ali's uniform and police flag she was still holding onto got drenched by streams of tears and snort.

* * *

Soon after the funeral, Kowa and Thandie became part of her bedroom furniture. They were both reluctant to leave her alone for fear of what she might do to herself. To everyone who knew her, it was clear how much the tragedy had affected her. Against the advice of her station commander and the doctors, Duski had insisted on going back to work soon after the funeral—but she rarely spoke to anyone and seemed to have developed an unhealthy obsession with the Maruapula murder case. She was spending hours going over Cynthia and Lovemore's statements and writing down notes—over and over.

At home, Duski kept to her room. This forced Kowa and Thandie to sit on her bed and bicker like old fishwives. She'd learnt to tune them out and focus on her purgatory thoughts.

One afternoon, as the three sat quietly in her tiny bedroom, Thandie suddenly and randomly said, "*Mmata,* I'm so sorry I wasn't here to tell those bastards you'd nothing to do with Ali's death." She was prancing in front of the wardrobe mirror, pausing now and again to readjust an oversized afro wig she was wearing.

"But you'd already told them you couldn't remember if she stayed at your house that night," Kowa said with a condescending sneer.

Kowa and Thandie were very much alike in character, personality and appearance, which was probably why they hated each other's guts. One would have thought that the two women were related or even twins—they were both of a very light, sandy-brown complexion and were both stocky and wobbly bellied. They both suffered from stunted hair growth—the only noticeable difference between them was the size of their bottoms.

Thandie had a European-type bottom—flat and rectangular—and Kowa, a true African butt

which stuck out and was complemented by a
pair of large and well-stuffed hips. But unlike
the ever-smiling Thandie, Kowa always wore a
permanent scowl—it was as if the whole world was
to blame for her looks.

"Why didn't you ring me when they took
you to the station?" Thandie asked Duski after
casting a condescending look at Kowa. She
readjusted her wig for the umpteenth time in
front of the mirror. "When that bastard detective
sergeant interviewed me, I didn't know about
Ali—that he'd died," Thandie added and carried
on prancing around. To the annoyance of Kowa,
she even performed a short catwalk in front of the
mirror, admiring her flat butt.

"What would you've done—stop them from
dragging her down to the station?" Kowa asked,
her flat nose snobbishly turned as far up as she
could get it.

"Would have told them where to go,"
Thandie said, swaggering proudly in front of the
mirror to adjust her miniskirt this time. "*Mmata,* Ali
was a decent guy—he really loved you," Thandie
prattled on, sitting down on the bed next to Duski.
Meanwhile, Duski stared vacantly at the ceiling,
silently smoking and oblivious to Thandie and
Kowa's bickering.

"I know is bad to speak ill of the dead,
but in all honesty he was a good for nothing
arrogant bastard—in a way," Kowa paused as a

faraway—pained kind of look clouded her eyes. "He cheated on you, had a child or children, to be precise, that he gave shit about—in short, the guy deserves that death," she suddenly said, rousing Duski from her purgatory thoughts.

Cigarette posed mid-air, Duski sat up and stared gobsmacked at Kowa's stocky and heavily loaded behind as it disappeared into the corridor. *What did she mean, "Ali deserved that death"?* She wondered hurt by her house mate's insensitive comments.

How could she have said something like that? Ali wasn't perfect and she'd been the first to acknowledge it—but he didn't deserve that type of death—to be castrated, probably while he was still alive.

"Pshaw! What's up with her?" Thandie asked, sucking her teeth at Kowa. "Anyway, what are you going to do?" She looked at Duski briefly before plastering a thick layer of blood-red lipstick on her big lips.

"What do you mean?"

"To clear your name," Thandie said dabbing the excess lipstick with a tissue.

"I don't know," Duski said flatly before resuming staring at the ceiling.

"*Mmata,* you really cannot afford the luxury of falling to pieces, not while CID still think you're their prime suspect." Thandie was looking at her with concern. "You really got to pull yourself together. I know this may seem harsh, but Ali is gone, and no amount of staring at the wall or ceiling is going to bring him back."

A tear rolled down Duski's cheek and found its way into the corner of her mouth. Thandie's words were painful, but she knew that she was right. Nothing was ever going to bring Ali back.

"You need to go back to the old man. Maybe he can help you find out what really happened," Thandie said sounding rather hopeful.

"I've done enough sinning and now I am being punished for it." A stream of tears rolled freely down her cheeks until they merged at the chin. She made no attempt to wipe them away.

"What do you mean 'you've done enough sinning'? Don't' go all Christian on me, girl," Thandie said and looked at her suspiciously. *Is she losing her mind?* she wondered, a little bit worried.

"I've killed Ali," Duski looked at Thandie, despondent.

"Don't be ridiculous. Ali killed himself—or somebody else did . . . certainly not you."

"If I hadn't gone to the witch doctor for the *muti*, Ali would probably still be alive."

"I've never heard such bollocks," Thandie said before heading towards the kitchen. "Here, drink this. It will make you feel better," she said as she returned and handed her a glass of an orange liquid.

Duski sat up, sniffed the drink, took a sip and grimaced. "Don't you think it's a bit too early for this?!" she exclaimed, putting the glass down on the bedside table.

"It's just a drop of Pushkin—it'll make you feel better—and hopefully stop you talking so much cow dung. I still think you need to see the old man, though."

"Thandie, I do appreciate your concern, but I think it's probably best if I stayed away from witch doctors from now on." She sat up and reached for a packet of cigarettes from the bedside table drawer. "I've been doing a lot of thinking and repenting this past week. I'm the daughter of a preacher and I know Ali's death is a sign of God's disapproval of what I did to get him back," she lit the cigarette. "I know it sounds crazy, but at the end of the day, I've sinned. When I was young, the term *traditional doctor* was synonymous with witchcraft. I'm a Christian—I shouldn't have gotten myself involved in such unchristian things."

"Duski, Ali's death has nothing to do with the old man's *muti*, and you know it. Traditional doctors are not witch doctors and I'm sure you know that too. They were called that by people who knew nothing about our culture. Unfortunately, these negative views about our culture have convinced our people that our culture is based on witchcraft. *Mmata*, the fear of the unknown usually leads people to draw unjustified and irrational conclusions." Thandie shook her head sadly and resumed, "Anyhow, why don't we go and see the old man and tell him your suspicions—that his *muti* has killed your boyfriend."

"Maybe I do need to go back and find out more about the *muti*." She finished the last drop of her Pushkin and orange mix thoughtfully and dragged on the cigarette.

Thandie reminded her so much of her paternal grandmother—a true African and practising traditional doctor. She recalled she too used to tell her how important traditional doctors were before a white man called Livingstone came to Botswana.

"*We looked after the whole nation. People like me had and still have unlimited knowledge of medicinal herbs for all sorts of uses,*" she would say sadly while pausing from time to time to stuff snuff into her toothless gums and nostrils. "*When that white man came, he turned our people against us, the very people who have served and protected the nation for generations. What did he know about our culture? Nothing!*" she'd rant on, "*But people like your father—like an old banger with faulty brakes going down a hill—accepted without question his condemnation of our culture.*" Finally, she'd conclude. "*Luckily, I haven't got much time left to witness any more of this nonsense.*" She'd usually suck her teeth after the rant, to express her annoyance at the long-dead missionary.

"So are you going to see him or not?" Thandie interrupted her nostalgic reverie.

"I think I should. Can we go now?" To Thandie's surprise, Duski suddenly got up and pulled on a pair of jeans and slipped off her dressing gown to replace it with a T-shirt.

"Yeah, why not? He'll probably be at lunch now, and I'm sure he won't mind having his lunch interrupted if we take a few bottles of Savannah with us," Thandie said, excitedly picking up her handbag and car keys from the dressing table.

"Do you mind driving to Tlokweng first? I need to see someone before we go to Mogoditshane." Duski had a different plan—she wanted to test the old man's powers on the Maruapula murder case. If what her grandmother had told her about traditional doctors' limitless powers was true, the old man should be able to help fill in the missing clues and tell her about the whereabouts of Lovemore.

* * *

Half an hour later, after a brief visit to Tlokweng, the white Toyota Tazz sped past the Spar Shopping Centre before taking a right turn into the heart of Mogoditshane Village. As usual, the sky was an unstained carpet of blueness. The bright and baking sun's rays leeched, unhindered, every drop of moisture from the already patchy and dry soil. The afternoon sun forced chickens and people alike under trees or corrugated tin roofs. Just before the four-way junction, Thandie turned into a compound of three tin-roofed huts, the last one in the row was a small hut used by the old man for his consultations. Thandie parked the Tazz in front of the consulting room.

"Koo, koo," they announced their arrival as they approached an elderly woman sitting under the shade of one of the huts.

"*Ee tsenang bo ngwanaka,*" the old woman called out to invite them in.

"*Dumela mma,*" they both said and curtsied to greet the old lady. "We've come to see the old man," they both said.

"He's sitting in that corner over there, but it's his lunch break, though," the old lady said pointing towards the back of an unpainted two-roomed hut. "I'm sure he wouldn't mind being disturbed," she said, nodding knowingly at the Liquorama carrier bag.

"*Tankie mma,*" they both said and curtsied again before disappearing round the side of the third hut. The old man was sitting on an animal skin armchair and listening to a small transistor radio. Next to the radio was a half-empty bottle of Savannah.

"*Dumela rra,*" they said and curtsied before sitting on a bench in front of the old man. "We've brought you something," Thandie said, putting the drinks on the small coffee table before relaying the purpose of their visit.

"Is this some kind of bribery?" he asked giving them a toothless grin before gratefully accepting the drinks. "What can I do for you?" He shielded his eyes with a withered hand and peered at them to take a closer look.

"Could we see you in the consulting hut please *rra?*" Duski asked.

"*Bo Mma,* this is my rest hour?" the old man grumbled, reminding them that he had specific consultation times.

"We are sorry *rra,* it's rather urgent—otherwise we would have waited to see you after lunch," Duski begged.

"Okay, let's go in then," he said, gulping down the remains of his lunchtime Savannah. He burped, got off the chair with some difficulty and led them in to the hut.

In the middle of the hut was a hyena skin mat with two identical traditional carved stools on either side. "Take a seat," he said looking at Duski. He pointed to a traditional stool on the far end of the rug. "I'm afraid you've got to sit on the floor," he said to Thandie who looked suspiciously at the cow dung smeared floor before sitting down.

After they'd all sat down, the old man fetched a leather pouch and a black wild horse tail from a red metal rack that was piled high with dried herbs. He opened the pouch and emptied its contents on the mat. Out of the pouch tumbled small, oddly shaped bones. The old man picked them up and gave them to Duski.

"*Di khuele* and say after me, '*Bola bolela, ke kopa thuso,*' and then throw them on the mat."

Duski blew into the bones and repeated after the old man: "Divining bones speak, I have come to seek your help," she said and threw them on the mat.

The old man's critical eye hovered over the bones and analysed the pattern they'd made as they fell. "You've been here before," he said looking at her. The old man mumbled something and moved the bones around with a sinewy middle finger. "*Mma,* the pattern formed by the bones indicates you are not a very happy person at the moment—in fact, you hardly sleep due to a recent tragic event." The old man looked at her again before he picked up the bones. "Ancient divining bones, bones of the dead, diviners of the living, tell me why there is so much pain in this young lady's heart." The old man mumbled and threw the bones onto the mat again. He studied the newly formed pattern and said, "*mma,* the bones show you've lost someone very close to you recently, but this isn't why you've come to see me." He picked up the bones and gave them to Duski again. Her face was a picture of scepticism. "I see you still doubt my powers," he said, looking her straight in the eye as he handed her the bones.

"I wouldn't be here if I had any doubts about your powers *rra,*" she lied before blowing into the bones and throwing them down for the second time. She wanted so much to believe everything the old man had just said, but her deeply

ingrained mumbo jumbo scepticism overshadowed
everything.

She recalled once reading Dr Merriweather's
(a Scottish missionary doctor) views on traditional
doctors. *They are usually jolly fellows who love to boast
about their powers to divine and to heal. They are expert
psychologists and know just how their patients will react
and they know the exact word to say to each patient,* he'd
written in his book *The Desert Doctor.* But how did
the old man know she'd lost someone? Moreover,
when she first met him, he also knew she was a
copper.

Duski wondered whether Dr Merriweather's
sceptical views were clouding her power of reason,
but with so many HIV/AIDS deaths, almost
everyone who came to the old man would have lost
a relative, spouse, boyfriend, or girlfriend.

"These divining bones can tell you are a
non-believer," the old man said and grinned as he
surveyed the pattern they'd formed on the mat.
"You're blaming me for what happened recently, is
that right?" he suddenly asked, sounding a little bit
hurt.

"No, I blame myself," Duski was
startled—she shifted uncomfortably, nearly falling
off the stool.

How did he know what I'd been thinking? She
wondered—completely baffled.

"That's exactly what the bones are saying,
you blamed yourself for coming here," he said and
grinned toothlessly at her. "But I can set your mind

at rest. You're not to blame for what happened," the old man added reassuringly, his eyes hovering over the bones. "This type of pattern indicates that we are dealing with witchcraft."

Duski's face fell with disappointment at the mention of the word *witchcraft*. The old man registered her disappointment, but he carried on regardless.

"Your loved one's death was a result of witchcraft, and it has nothing to do with the *muti* I you bathed in. But as I said earlier, you are here for a different reason."

The old man's voice seemed filtered, as if it was coming from a distance before heading into her confused mind. She was beginning to have faith—believe there was something in the mumbo jumbo he was feeding her, but she felt a bit disappointed by his prognosis.

"The bones show your quest today has to do with a young woman accused of murder. You don't believe she's guilty, is that right?" the old man suddenly asked, jolting her to an upright and attentive position.

"*Ee rra,*" she confirmed excitedly, looking up at him with renewed confidence and hope. She immediately cast Dr Merriweather's psychoanalytic views aside. "And what you want to find out is the whereabouts of a young man you suspect is guilty of the crime?" the old man asked, his face contorting as he closely scrutinised the bones.

"Unfortunately, I'll need something that belongs to this man to find out where he is."

"Will this do?" she asked, whipping out an old pair of men's socks from her pocket. "I got this from his ex-girlfriend's house," she explained and put the socks on the mat. The old man gave her the bones and instructed her to ask the bones to reveal the identity of the man.

"The man is not a Motswana, he is from across the border and this is not his first victim." The old man looked critically at the bones. He picked them up and mumbled some praises to his ancestors before throwing them on the mat again. "He's a family man with a child, or children and a wife. Something is driving him to commit the murders," the old man said, moving a few bones around as he analysed the pattern. "You need to focus your search in the north, right up to the border. I'm afraid that's all I can tell you at the moment," he concluded looking at her apologetically. "By the way, I can see a young man—he really loves you," the old man suddenly said, his wrinkled face grinning mischievously as he took one more look at the bones. Her heart skipped. She wondered whether the old man was referring to Craig. "I can give you something to make sure nobody comes between you and this young man."

Thandie looked up expectantly and encouragingly at her.

"And of course, this is entirely up to you," he added quickly, sensing the reluctance in Duski's suddenly stiffened posture.

She declined the offer with a polite but firm shake of the head. She knew that her relationship with Craig would never develop into anything and she wasn't even intending to see him again anyway.

"You know where to find me if you ever change your mind," the old man said.

"*Tankie rra,* I'll keep that in mind. And thanks for your help today," she said, putting a twenty pula note on the divining mat to pay for the old man's services.

Chapter Seventeen

"I didn't realise you were working on the Maruapula murder case," Thandie said. She looked at her friend with admiration before she turned the ignition on. She'd always loved detective work—in fact, she was an avid reader of crime novels.

"I'm not—my team was the first on the scene. I cautioned the accused on the day of the murder," she said as she sat down, shut the door and stared hard into the distance.

"And you don't think she's guilty?" Thandie asked excitedly, "And that's what the old man said."

"I don't think she is a murderer, that's all," Duski said.

"If that is the case, why do you think she confessed to it? Why would she lie about something like that? Is there any evidence to suggest she didn't do it?" Thandie took her eyes off the road briefly to glance at her.

"No, it's just my gut feeling," she said, biting her lower lip thoughtfully. "Would you mind if we drove to Tlokweng again? I need to speak to Cynthia's mother to see if she kept any photographs of Lovemore."

"Yep, why not? I love detective work. By the way, did you tell Cynthia's mother you were taking Lovemore's old socks to a witch doctor?"

"Told her we needed them for a DNA sample," she confessed guiltily.

"Don't you know lying is a sin?" Thandie teased.

"It was a harmless lie," she said, opening the glove box to bring out a packet of Stuyvesant.

"Do you mind?" Thandie shrugged and Duski took out a cigarette, lit it using the car cigarette lighter and dragged on it slowly as she pondered the old man's divination.

"*Dumela mma*, sorry to bother you again," Duski and Thandie greeted Mma Cynthia for the second time that day.

"*Ee dumelang, ditilo ke tseo*," Cynthia's mother said, pointing to a couple of faded, light green kitchen chairs. "Were the socks any good?" she asked, looking at Duski with eyes full of hope and trust.

"*Ee mma*, and thank you very much for lending them to me," she said as she fished them out of her handbag and gave them back to her. "I was wondering if we could take a look at Cynthia's hut again to see if we could find anything that might help us trace Lovemore."

"Of course you can," *Mma* Cynthia said before leading them to a breeze-block hut at the end of the clean-swept yard.

"I'm sorry I can't offer you tea—I haven't got any sugar or milk," she said apologetically after showing them into Cynthia's hut.

"It's all right. Thank you, *mma*. We've just had a drink in the car," Duski said as she surveyed the crammed little hut.

It was cheaply furnished. A double base bed dominated the centre, and there was a little homemade wooden bedside table beside it. A cheap manufactured board double wardrobe stood in one corner.

"I'll search the wardrobe first," Duski said as soon as *Mma* Cynthia had left the hut. "What have we got here?!" she exclaimed as her fingers brushed against something hard on the top shelf of the wardrobe, just a few minutes into the search. "Let's see who we've got in here," she said, bringing out a reddish-brown photo album. "Bingo!" she shouted excitedly as she turned the first page of the album. "Well he is a good-looking devil, it's no surprise the poor woman lost her marbles over him," Duski commented, looking at the picture of a mixed-race young man in his thirties.

"I know this guy. His name is Jerry. He was one of my two-week-affair victims," Thandie exclaimed, taking the photo album from Duski to scrutinise the photo more carefully. "Yep, it's him," she said and handed the photo album back to Duski.

"So our Lovemore is also Jerry. Are you absolutely sure this is the same person?" she asked, looking at her friend doubtfully.

"Absolutely positive—had a brief affair with the man—who can forget those beautiful yet

201

deceitful eyes? I could not take my eyes off him! Besides, he was so good in the . . . you know," Thandie giggled and peeped out to check whether *Mma* Cynthia was within earshot.

"What happened? I mean to your relationship with him," Duski asked, even though she already knew the answer. The poor man probably could not afford Thandie's expensive tastes.

"You know me—I've no time for *bomagogoshane*—good-for-nothing guys . . . even the good-looking ones. The guy had the nerve to ask me for a loan."

"What? He asked you for money?"

"He gave me some cheap and boring explanation about a business he was planning to set up with a friend."

"How much was he asking for?"

"Didn't stick around long enough to find out," Thandie said, shrugging her shoulders.

"What's the time?" Duski suddenly asked, staring into the distance deep in thought.

"Nearly half past four. Why?"

"I need to speak to Detective Inspector Marvellous," she said. She was thinking about her last encounter with the detective—she hadn't spoken to him since the interrogation. Duski peeled back the photo album sleeve to take out the photo and handed it to Thandie. "I wonder if he's still in the office." She said punching several numbers on her cell phone and waited impatiently for him to pick up.

"This is Sergeant Duski. Good afternoon, sir! How long are you going to be in the office for? I want to talk to you about the Maruapula case, sir. About fifteen minutes, sir. Thank you, sir." She put the phone back in her handbag. "Could you drop me off at the station? Oh . . . and could you do us another favour please? Drop that photo off at *The Voice* offices—ask them to run it in this Friday's paper." She scribbled her contact details on a piece of paper. "Ask them to get anybody who knows who this man is, or his whereabouts, to contact this number ASAP. Thanks, *mmata*," she added and handed her the note.

"The case is no longer a murder case. We are now treating the death as a suicide," Detective Inspector Marvellous said when she arrived at his office that afternoon. She was disappointed.

"Autopsy results revealed the wounds inflicted by the broken Amarula bottle were superficial, but fatal amounts of Valium and alcohol were found in the deceased's blood," he said.

Duski was disappointed in part, but she was also pleased that Cynthia was no longer a murder suspect. Her efforts to convince the DI to look into the possibility that the Amarula was deliberately spiked had fallen on deaf ears. She could not help feeling that Lovemore was somehow responsible for the victim's death.

"It is suspicious, sir, that this man also calls himself Jerry," she argued trying to get the DI to start a murder enquiry. "He might have spiked her drink with the intent to kill her."

"Motive?" he asked.

"That's what we need to find out," she said, "I've got a feeling that neither Lovemore nor Jerry are his real names. What if he's hiding something? This man is . . ."

She managed to stop herself before confessing she'd taken the man's socks to a witch doctor. She knew she'd no evidence to suggest that Lovemore aka Jerry was a murderer and not just a Casanova. She did, however, manage to get the detective inspector to part with the deceased's home address. He also agreed to provide a vehicle and a driver to take her to Gabane, the deceased's home village.

"I still don't see what you hope to find, Sergeant. We've already spoken to the family," he said, "The woman was depressed, and that is why she took her own life," he added.

Fortunately, Detective Inspector Marvellous's driver had been to the deceased's home before. This saved valuable time—with no street names, finding any dwelling in a village in Botswana could be a very exhausting and unfruitful adventure.

Duski recalled directions she was once given when trying to find a place in a village not far from Gaborone.

It's over there! Follow this road until you see some donkeys beside the road. Turn left and you will see the yard, a young man they had met as they entered the village in question had directed. They'd driven along the said road for a while, unfortunately the donkeys in question, had that day probably decided to move house—still they'd followed the road until they'd come to a dead end. *Oh you missed the turn. It is back there along the road you came on. Turn off after passing a big tree on the left*," another villager had said, but they couldn't help but notice she pointed *right* when she said left. They forgot to ask her what type of tree it was when they suddenly realised that there were several big trees lining both sides of the road. In the end, they'd resorted to an old-fashioned door-to-door enquiry, which did prove more fruitful.

The deceased's family members were very helpful. They let Duski look through all her belongings. And while rummaging through the deceased's bank statements, she came across a loan agreement for P30, 000.00 that Motlatsi, the deceased, had signed a couple of weeks before her death. As the family hadn't yet closed the account down, one of the brothers, who fortunately knew Motlatsi's pin number, agreed to go with them to a nearby ATM with the deceased's money link card to check whether the money was still in the account. The visit revealed the money had been withdrawn. Though Duski wasn't sure how relevant the missing cash was to the case, she'd a feeling however, that it was a vital piece of information.

Another visit to the bank the following day revealed that Motlatsi's reason for taking out the loan was to buy building materials. Far more interesting was the fact she withdrew the entire loan in cash the day before she died.

Why would anyone intending to commit suicide withdraw such a large amount of cash? And what did she do with the money? The old man was right. Duski was puzzled.

*　　*　　*

The Monday following the publication of Lovemore aka Jerry's photo by the newspaper, Duski sat expectantly by the phone and picked it up hopefully every time it rang. Eventually, later that afternoon, when she was about to give up hope of anybody ever ringing about the photo, the phone rang.

"Sarge, it's for you," Constable Moji said and handed her the phone.

"Is that Sergeant Duski?" an anxious and rather hesitant female voice asked at the other end of the line.

"*Ee mma* it is. What can I do for you?" she asked, excited.

"It is about the photo, the one in the paper." The woman hesitated again.

"Yes, go on please *mma*," she encouraged.

"Lovemore Masunga died two years ago," the woman sniffed at the other end of the line. Duski could tell she was crying.

"Is that Lovemore in the picture?"

"You don't understand. That man claims to be from Jackalas Number One *mma*, there was only one Lovemore Masunga in Jackalas Number One." The woman hung up before Duski could take down her details.

Thandie has been doing a bit of detective work! Duski thought with a smile, *But where did she get all those details?*

After dropping off Duski at the station, Thandie had gone off to Bank of Botswana where Lovemore had worked as a security guard, to get a copy of his *Omang* card. Duski could only imagine how Thandie managed to get hold of such a personal and confidential document. She was about to check with the switchboard constable to see whether he could trace the call when the phone rang again.

"CPS, Sergeant Duski Lôcha speaking. How can I help?"

"His name is Reazon Jonga," a heavily accented and unmistakably Kalanga voice said at the other end of the line.

"Do you mean the name of the man in the newspaper?" she asked the caller, reaching for a pen—she found a blank page on her police notebook.

"Yes, we have been looking for him for the past year. He disappeared after my daughter went missing," the man explained. Duski detected anger in his heavily accented Setswana.

"What was your daughter's relationship with . . . Reason?" she asked as she scribbled notes on the clean pad.

"They lived together. He was my daughter's fiancé."

"What's your daughter's name?"

"Melita Tafila," he said. She scribbled furiously as she fired endless questions at the man.

"Thank you very much *rre* Tafila—you've been most helpful. We'll do anything we can to help you find your daughter as well." she said and replaced the receiver before adopting a deep-thought pose.

From the information she'd gathered from the caller, she surmised that Lovemore (aka Jerry, aka Reason) was a Zimbabwean man from somewhere near the border, most probably Plumtree.

The old man was right about the mysterious Lovemore; he was indeed from across the border, she thought excitedly. The only problem she now had was how to convince Detective Inspector Marvellous that the man was a murderer and probably courting his next victim.

Her heart sank when she realised she still hadn't established a motive yet. *Maybe I need to go to Francistown to pay Mr Tafila a visit, to see if I can find anything more regarding Melita's disappearance before I approach the DI*, she pondered despondently. However, she realised she'd another problem—getting time off work to go to Francistown. She knew there was no way the station commander, Mma Kenosi, would give her time off.

In the end, Duski decided that telling another little harmless white lie was her only option. As she left the station that afternoon, she mentally composed a leave of absence application letter to the station commander. She was so preoccupied—racking her brains for a plausible reason for wanting leave of absence that she almost walked right into Constable Solomone, Ali's housemate, at the main entrance.

"*Sori rra . . . ao Solomone*, I'm so sorry, I was miles away. What are you doing here anyway? Aren't you supposed to be working?" she enquired, stepping aside to let him pass.

"It's my day off and I was just passing by. Thought I would call by to see how you are getting on," he said hesitantly.

The truth was, Solomone had had a crush on her for a long time, and way before Ali came onto the scene. After Ali's death, Solomone had been waiting for the right moment to confess his love to the sergeant—before it was too late again. He wasn't just passing by—he knew Duski's shift ended at two that afternoon, and he'd come with the sole intention of asking her out on a date that evening.

"I've just finished work, actually. You can walk me to the kombi rank if you like," Duski said, throwing her police hat on and hurrying towards a kombi that had just pulled into the rank.

"I can give you a lift home," he said, waving off the kombi.

"You sure?"

"Positive." he said, taking her hand.

"If you insist," she replied, gently disengaging her hand from his. She was aware Solomone had feelings for her and she didn't want to encourage him. She'd noticed it during her visits to Ali's house.

"My car is over at the President Hotel car park," he said gesturing at a yellow Ford Bantam parked across the road opposite the police station. "So you're no longer a suspect then?" he suddenly asked while they waited for the traffic lights to turn green at a pedestrian crossing between the main mall and the police car park.

"Not officially. The case is still open. I'll only cease to be a suspect when someone is arrested for the murder," Duski replied and smiled when she realised that it was the first time she'd mentioned Ali's death without sniffing back tears.

"My housemate was stupid to mess up a relationship with an attractive woman like you," Solomone said shaking his head, "I wish one day you and I—"

"You're a good-looking guy, Solomone
and I'm sure many women find you attractive,"
she interrupted him, guessing what Solomone was
about to say.

"But not the ones I find attractive though,"
he said, looking into her eyes longingly before
opening the passenger door to let her in the
car. Duski looked out of the passenger window
thoughtfully as soon as she'd made herself
comfortable.

Solomone was not a particularly
good-looking man, but he was not completely
unattractive either. He was of a very light brown
complexion and heavily built. His physique often
reminded Duski of Mr T and his five-foot-five
stout frame was not her idea of Mr Right. What
she particularly found unattractive about him was
his nose. It was long and rubbery at the end—*A bit
like a displaced penis,* she'd often thought.

"My housemate finds you attractive—she
likes you very much," she suddenly said, taking
out a *stompie* (a half-smoked cigarette) from her
cigarette packet. "Do you mind?" she asked before
lighting the *stompie*. A cloud of disapproval quickly
spread across Solomone's face. "My housemate
doesn't smoke," Duski added, winding down the
window. "Judging from your reaction there, I'm
sure you wouldn't want to go out with a woman like
me."

"I must admit, smoking is a very unladylike
habit," Solomone said as he kept his eyes on the

road to avoid eye contact. "What is this about your housemate, anyway?" he asked after a long silence, just before he turned into her street.

"She likes you and she is an attractive woman. She has all the necessary female contours that you guys like—a big fleshy bum and childbearing hips," Duski said, stifling a giggle as the exotic stuffed-turkey image of her housemate flicked across her mind.

"*A o ikgatha ka nna ne mma?*" Solomone asked with a hurt expression.

"I'm not making fun of you, she really likes you," Duski said defensively as she dragged on the *stompie* with a serious face. "So what do you say? Do you like her or not?"

"She is not my type," Solomone snapped and slammed his foot on the brakes in front of the gate.

"Thanks for the lift," she said opening the door, ready to leave the car.

"I'm going to the Fashion Lounge later . . . would you like to come?" Solomone asked, feigning a smile. "Bring your housemate along if you like," he added when he noticed her hesitant expression.

"I'm really busy tonight," she lied, "How about next weekend?" she added quickly as she noticed the hurt and disappointment on Solomone's face.

He just shrugged and drove off.

Chapter Eighteen

Solomone didn't give up hope of ever winning Duski's love. He occasionally went around her house to help her with groceries, and sometimes he picked her up from work.

Subconsciously, Duski started to grow fond of him, and she occasionally entertained the idea of having a relationship with him. Whatever she wanted, Solomone was always a phone call away to make sure she got whatever it was she was after. His devotion to his chauffeur duties during her extensive shopping trips slowly but surely transformed their relationship into a more intimate one. Never once did Solomone complain about her protracted shopping antics. She knew he would gladly take her to the same shops ten times in one day if she asked.

What more could a woman want? She had thought on more than one occasion. *Love, if there was ever such a thing,* she often contemplated, *will come later. I will learn to love him,* she'd reasoned before eventually letting him share her bed.

One weekend, Solomone even got his doctor to sign him off work so he could drive Duski to Francistown to see Mr Tafila. She was so appreciative of this gentlemanly and knightly gesture that she decided to reciprocate his declaration of love. On the night that she finally gave in to his advances, she'd been on a high. The meeting with the Tafila family in Francistown had proved very fruitful.

"So the loan Melita took out was fully withdrawn in cash the week she disappeared?" she asked. Duski stared in disbelief at Melita's bank statements and loan agreement for P30,000.00. "Do you think your daughter could have run away with . . . someone else?" She was going to say *another man,* but she thought better of it when Mr Tafila's deeply furrowed and weather-beaten face contorted in disapproval at her insinuations.

"Melita was not that type of girl," he said. She sensed a restrained anger in his voice. "She only moved in with that scoundrel after the engagement," he said with a hint of injured pride. Mr Tafila and Mrs Tafila were, after all, among the respectful members of the elite society in Francistown. Their only daughter could not just run off with another man only a few weeks after being engaged to another.

"Melita took out the loan to help pay for the wedding. She was a very proud and independent young woman," Mrs Tafila interjected, "There was no reason for her to run away. Besides, if she didn't wish to marry Reason, she'd have said something to us—I am sure." Mrs Tafila sniffed and wiped away a solemn tear running down her chubby brown cheek.

"Did you report her missing to the police?"
Duski asked, looking at them both.

"We did. The police came round and
searched her room. However, based on her missing
clothes and the P30,000 withdrawn from her
account, they concluded she'd probably run away."
Mr Tafila stared into the distance in apparent
agony.

"They said she would probably contact us
when she was ready to come back home," Mrs
Tafila added, holding her husband's hand.

"Do you mind if I keep this?" Duski asked
before taking out a copy of Melita's bank statement
showing the withdrawal of the P30, 000 and the
loan agreement letter from a pile of statements on
the table.

"Keep it if you think it's of any use," *Rre*
Tafila said dejectedly.

"Take this as well and please do ring us as
soon as you find her," Mrs Tafila said, handing
Duski a photograph of a very beautiful and
dark-skinned tall young woman.

"By the way, do you mind if I take one of
Melita's dresses—for DNA analysis, of course,"
she added quickly when *Mma* Tafila looked at her
suspiciously.

"Of course you can," the woman said
and disappeared into the corridor of their
four-bedroom townhouse. She returned with a light
green dress. "She left this in the washing basket
and I couldn't bring myself to wash it . . . I felt like

215

I would be washing her away . . . silly, I know," she cried.

"*Tankie mma*, I really do appreciate your help," she received the dress politely with both hands before the couple walked them to the main gate.

*   *   *

On Sunday, following the meeting with the Tafilas, Solomone and Duski set off early towards Ramokgwebana, the Botswana and Zimbabwe border. Later that morning, after they'd had their passports stamped, they headed towards Plumtree with no idea of where they were going to start their search. At two o'clock in the afternoon, the Ford Bantam pulled up at the Plumtree colonial style shopping centre where they were immediately swamped by a mob of *Bomashonisa*—black market currency exchange dealers.

"Do you want some *Zim dorrahs* my friend?" a heavily pregnant woman asked, pushing in front of the other *mashonisas*.

"No thanks, but we're looking for this man," Duski replied, holding out a photograph of the suspect. The woman looked at it and shrugged her shoulders. The other black marketers rushed off as another Botswana-registered vehicle pulled up in front of a grocery store. "He's a friend, we're on our way to Bulawayo. We just want to call by and say hello," she added, pulling out a twenty pula note and looked at the woman pleadingly.

"His wife lives in Teaspoon Street, just across the railway line," the woman eventually said, trying to grab hold of the note.

"What number?" Duski asked. She held on tightly to the note. The woman looked around hesitantly. "Can you take us to the house?" she asked, adding a ten-pula note to the twenty. The woman nodded.

Teaspoon Street wasn't that far from the shopping centre. Ten minutes into the journey, the woman announced their destination.

"It's that big, tiled house over there," she said and pointed at an unfinished bungalow with a red tiled roof. "I'll get off here," she said already opening the door.

As soon as the car had stopped, the woman jumped off, grabbed the notes off Duski and hurriedly walked back towards the shopping centre. Duski and Solomone drove on to the house where a very skinny woman was hanging some clothes on a washing line running between two posts at the back of the house. They parked the bakkie outside a chicken wire fence and walked towards her. A cute little boy—about four years old—came running towards them.

"Hallo, have you brought prezents from daddy?" the boy greeted them in English, eyes wide with expectancy.

"Before I give you any presents, young man,
I need to know your father's name—just to make
sure I'm giving the presents to the right person,"
Duski said, winking at Solomone.

"Wellingtone," the boy said in a heavy
Zimbabwean accent.

"Wellington who?" she asked the boy and
gave him a stern but playful look.

"Robart," the little boy replied.

"Are you sure this is your
father—Wellington Robert?" she asked, showing
him a photo she'd taken from Cynthia's photo
album.

"Yes! Where iz my prezent?" the boy asked
expectantly.

"Be patient, young man, we'll give the
present to your mother," Duski promised before
she approached the woman who'd just noticed their
presence. "Hello, we are friends of your husband's.
We are from Bulawayo, we thought we would call
by to say hello . . . if he's around," she said, shaking
the woman's hand.

"Wellingtone iz still in Haborone," the
woman said.

"The truth is, I owe him some money. Do
you know where I can find him in Gaborone?" she
asked. "He's moved from his last address," Duski
added quickly.

"He doezn't tell me where he livez, but I can
give you hiz cell number," the woman said, bringing

out a rather flashy mobile phone from her dress pocket.

"Do you know what he does for work at the moment?" Duski asked, suddenly realising that ringing Wellington might not be a smart move, he might become suspicious if he got a call from the police.

"He haz got a new job. He iz a barman at a place called Buyani," she said.

"Thank you. Oh by the way, if your husband rings, don't mention our visit," Duski said and gave her a twenty-pula note. "We would like to surprise him. We haven't seen him for a while," she quickly added when the woman looked at her suspiciously.

It was obvious to Duski that the man was, indeed, up to something. He was building a big-tiled house, which was obviously costing him busloads of Zimbabwean dollars. The little boy looked well fed and well dressed, unlike many malnourished Zimbabwean children they had just seen at the Plumtree shopping complex. The woman did not look too bad either—she was good looking despite stress lines that made her look probably a lot older than she was.

Before they said their goodbyes, she asked Solomone to take a photograph of her and Wellington's family posed in front of the unfinished house.

"To prove to Wellington that we've been here," she explained as they posed.

*   *   *

A week after her trip to Plumtree, Duski
compiled what she thought was the evidence
needed to convince Detective Inspector Marvellous
to launch a murder investigation. She'd also
managed to get Wellington's bank statements.
The statements showed that shortly after Melita's
disappearance, he deposited thirty thousand pula in
cash. He'd also deposited another thirty thousand
pula a few days after Motlatsi's death. A few days
after she obtained the bank statements, she went to
see the DI with the evidence.

"So what do you think, sir?" Duski asked.
She looked at the DI anxiously after he'd finished
examining the documents. "It can't just be a
coincidence that the man happened to deposit the
same amounts that both his girlfriends took out as
loans, right?"

"Pretty suspicious, I would say, but it still
doesn't prove the man is a murderer. Besides, we
don't know what happened to Melita," Detective
Inspector Marvellous said, shaking his head
thoughtfully. "Without a body, we cannot prove he
murdered her."

"Can't we bring him in for questioning
anyway, sir? We've got enough evidence, the man
is a murderer, sir," she said, recalling what the old
man told her when she took Melita's dress to him.
His divining bones revealed that Melita had been

murdered and that her killer was someone she knew. However, Duski kept that bit of information to herself. The inspector would have laughed had she dared mention it and he would probably not take her request seriously.

"Give me some time to look at the bank statements again, I will give you a call," he said, re-examining the documents while playing with his goatee thoughtfully.

Two days following her discussion with the detective inspector, Wellington was brought in for questioning. It was seven o'clock in the evening when Sergeant Duski Lôcha and Detective Inspector Marvellous ushered him into the interview room and switched the tape recorder on to signal the beginning of the interview.

"What do we call you, *Lovemore, Reason, Jerry,* or *Wellington?*" Duski asked as soon as they'd all sat down.

"Wellington," he said, looking sheepishly at the floor.

"Wellington, we know that you have killed both Motlatsi and Melita, all we want to know from you is the location of Melita's body," she stated.

Wellington wrung his hands anxiously and hung his head in silence.

"We know you made both women take out loans so you could build this house," Duski said and handed him a photograph of his family posed in front of the unfinished bungalow.

Wellington looked at the photograph, eyes brimming with tears.

"Wellington, where did you bury Melita's body? We know you've killed her. Her account hasn't been used since the day she disappeared, which could only mean one thing—that she is not alive."

"What is going to happen to them?" Wellington suddenly asked, he stared hard at the photograph. "I did it for them, to keep them alive," he added, looking at Detective Inspector Marvellous. "You're a man and know what it's like not to be able to provide for your family, to watch them die of hunger," he said to him.

"Can you tell us exactly what you did?" the DI asked. He walked around to where Wellington sat and placed a sympathetic hand on his shoulder. "I know how difficult life is in your country at the moment, but we do need to know what happened to these two women. Their families need to know, Wellington." The DI gave him a stern look and said, "You are a father. Imagine if this little boy went missing or got killed." He picked up the photograph and put it right in front of Wellington. "Wouldn't you want to know where he was . . . or who killed him?"

"For years, we've struggled to keep going, my wife even resorted to prostitution to keep the family alive. Watching her young face become lined with stress and exhaustion broke my heart. I felt helpless and useless. My wife serviced several men a night to get enough money to put half a loaf of bread on the table. The competition was fierce, she only had a few customers. With just one meal a day, you can't expect a struggling woman to have the sexiest body. Most men were looking for curvaceous and fleshy bodies," Wellington said before pausing. Suddenly, he gave a short, dry laugh and shook his head.

Inspector Marvellous stared at him, stunned while Duski sniffed noisily. She tried in vain to stop a flood of tears now running freely down her face.

"We both worked as teachers. Between us, we earned about Z400 million a month. I know it sounds like big money, but we were the poorest millionaires on Earth. We roasted rats to eat with our mealie-meal sometimes. This is all there is to eat in Zimbabwe these days—rats and more rats." He gave a short, rueful laugh again. "I couldn't sit and watch my wife fade away and get fucked by other men." He paused to look at them both. "Two years ago, I decided to do something to provide my family with more than just roasted rat meals," he continued. He held his head in his hands for a while and said, "I went to Francistown with a couple of friends, which is where I met Melita. We couldn't get jobs, so we resorted to petty theft and burglary. That's how I came by Lovemore's *Omang* card. The man in the ID photo looked so much like me that I decided to keep it."

"Did Melita know what you did for a living?" Inspector Marvellous interrupted.

Wellington swallowed hard before saying, "She thought I was a street hawker. I sold things that we stole," he said and hung his head in shame. "Melita wanted us to get married. I told her I couldn't afford to get married, but she told me not to worry about money—she would get a loan to help us out once we were married. A few days after cashing the loan, she found out I was married and my name wasn't Reason. She flipped and threatened to report me to the police. I couldn't let her. I panicked; I didn't know what to do. I strangled her and cut her up to make it easy for me to carry her body without arousing suspicion. I buried the parts in four shallow graves by the Tati River." Wellington stared vacantly at Sergeant Duski Lôcha and the DI. "Could I have a glass of water please?" he suddenly asked.

"Yes, of course," Duski said, leaving the room to get a glass of water from the kitchen.

"Thank you," he said, gulping down the water thirstily. "I knew I had to leave Francistown. That's why I came down to Gaborone and used Lovemore's ID to get a job as a security guard at Bank of Botswana."

"Why did you kill Motlatsi?" Duski asked, looking at the distraught and haggard figure on the other side of the table.

"She also found out I was married, and she—" Wellington began before staring at the photo of his wife.

"When did she find out—before or after she gave you the loan money?" Detective Inspector Marvellous interrupted, pushing Motlatsi's bank statements and loan agreement confirmation letter in front of him.

"On the day she cashed the loan, I accidentally left my cell in the bedroom when I went to the shops. She'd been suspicious I was still seeing Cynthia, so she went through my messages and found messages from my wife instead."

"And?" Duski prompted.

"Naturally, she was very upset and angry," Wellington replied, continuing to stare at the photos of his family. "I told her I was planning to leave my wife, unfortunately she didn't believe me and she threatened to leave me."

"And you decided to kill her?" Inspector Marvellous asked.

"I was desperate. I told her we needed to talk about it. I had to think of something to stop her from taking away the money. Motlatsi always kept a bottle of Amarula in the fridge. I ground up several of her Valium tablets and mixed them with the Amarula. She always loved a drink whenever she was upset," Wellington said and sniffed back tears. He looked at the ceiling and continued, "I'm not a bad man. Do you think God will ever forgive me for what I've done?" he looked beseechingly at

Sergeant Duski Lôcha and Inspector Marvellous as
if they'd the answer. "Please tell my wife and my
son that I'm sorry." Wellington finally broke down
and started sobbing uncontrollably.

The day after interrogating Wellington,
Sergeant Duski, Detective Inspector Marvellous
and the forensics team, drove him back to
Francistown so he could show them where he'd
buried Melita's body.

As soon as they arrived at the burial site,
Wellington directed them to the four shallow graves
he'd marked with flat boulders. The first grave held
a pair of decomposed arms, the second revealed
a decomposed head, with a face that had already
been eaten away beyond recognition. The third
contained the woman's torso and her lower body
was discovered in the fourth.

Duski was numb with horror at the sight
of the remains the forensics team had assembled
inside the fibreglass coffin. The body was
dismembered and it had decomposed beyond
recognition. The only part that could possibly be
used to identify the victim was strands of braided
synthetic, mousey-coloured hair which was still
miraculously attached to the skull.

Duski looked over at the haggard and
handcuffed figure of Wellington sitting dejectedly
inside the police car. She found it difficult to
believe he could have committed such a horrific
and brutal murder. Suddenly, her recent grief over

the loss of Ali seemed petty and insignificant compared to what the Tafila family were about to experience when they found out about the gruesome way their only had daughter died.

Later that day, Detective Inspector Marvellous called at the Tafila household as the bearer of bad news. Mr Tafila answered the door to let him in.

"*Dumela rra*, Detective Inspector Marvellous from central police station in Gaborone," he introduced himself, shaking Mr Tafila's hand.

"*Dumela rra*," Mr Tafila replied. "We've met before, Sergeant," he said immediately turning towards Sergeant Duski Lôcha. He looked at her uniformed person suspiciously. "You better come in," he said, "I'm on my own. My wife has gone shopping—I'm afraid I can't offer you a cup of tea. Making tea is a woman's job," he smiled at Sergeant Duski Lôcha and winked at the inspector mischievously.

"I can't agree with you more, sir, making tea isn't a man's job—people might suspect his wife had sprinkled some *muti* in his food," Detective Inspector Marvellous said, making an impression of a bewitched husband.

"Don't worry about us, sir, we've just had something to drink a minute ago,' Duski interjected, feeling a bit queasy at the thought of drinking or eating anything. The smell of the decomposed body parts that hung in the area around the shallow graves still clung to her uniform.

"I'm sure you're wondering why we're here, Mr Tafila," The DI said carefully. Mr Tafila visibly tensed. He realised he'd to break the news before the old man got too relaxed. "*Rre* Tafila, following the sergeant's visit a couple of weeks ago, we managed to trace the man who was engaged to your daughter," he said before pausing and wondering how to break the news to the old man. "This morning, the young man in question showed us where he'd buried your daughter. I'm so sorry *rra*. Unfortunately, you'll have to officially identify the body."

Duski looked sharply at the inspector, wondering whether he'd lost his mind. *What was there to identify? Dusty synthetic hair extensions?* She decided to keep her mouth shut though.

Mr Tafila aged in an instant. He held his grey head in his hands, stood up and walked around the sitting room mumbling as if he'd suddenly lost his mind. "How am I going to tell my wife that our beautiful and only daughter has been murdered?" he muttered like a traditional doctor talking to his divining bones. "God, what have we done to deserve this? Have we not served you and praised you? Why are you punishing us like this? Why didn't you take me instead?" he cried.

"Sir, you need to sit down. Sergeant, find the old man a strong drink in the kitchen or something," Marvellous instructed Duski as he sat Mr Tafila back on the sofa. "You need to get yourself together, sir. Your wife is going to need your support."

"Here *rra*, drink this," Duski said, giving him a glass of a clear liquid. She managed to find a bottle of Martell VO brandy in one of the cupboards. Mr Tafila downed the contents and marched into the kitchen to pour himself half a glass of the brandy.

"*Koo, koo,*" a neighbour called out to announce her presence and walked into the sitting room. "*Dumela rre* Tafila," a woman greeted, sitting herself down on the sofa without waiting for a prompt. "What is the matter, *rre* Tafila? You look troubled," she said, looking at Mr Tafila with concern.

"I'm not well *mma*. The police have just brought us some painful news. Melita's body has been found. She was murdered," Mr Tafila said, staring through the walls of his house with a face clouded by pain.

"*Ao batho*—how could God be so cruel?! Where is *Mma Melita*?" the woman asked, looking around to see whether Melita's mother was around.

"Mrs Tafila is out shopping *mma*, she doesn't know yet," Sergeant Duski Lôcha informed the woman.

"I'll go and inform the neighbours," the woman said, "She'll need a lot of support when she gets back."

Chapter Nineteen

"I need time to think," Duski said, taking out a dagga-filled cigarette. She lit it and resumed staring reflectively at the ceiling. She was very upset about Wellington's sentence. He'd been found guilty of two counts of murder and he was given a death sentence. Wellington had opted for a fast-track case and pleaded guilty in the hope of getting away with a more lenient sentence.

Duski could not stop thinking about Wellington's family, wondering how they were going to survive without him. She wished, for the first time in her career, that she'd turned a blind eye to his crimes.

Somebody had to stop him though, she kept reminding herself. She knew that he would have carried on killing to feed his family.

"What is there to think about? I thought you loved me," Solomone said, looking disapprovingly at the dagga-scented smoke drifting towards the ceiling.

"I'm sure it didn't just occur to you now that you wanted to marry me. You obviously have been thinking about it for some time. I need time to think too," Duski protested. She sat up and looked at him challengingly. "Marriage is a serious commitment."

"Is there someone else?" Solomone asked, wondering whether there were other reasons for her reluctance to accept his proposal.

"This is nothing to do with how I feel about you. I just need a little bit of time on my own, that's all," she said. She made no attempt to stop him from leaving. She resumed staring at the ceiling. "It is Wellington's family," she suddenly burst out. Solomone turned round and walked back into the room, wondering what Wellington's sentence had to do with his proposal.

"I didn't realise the case had affected you so much," Solomone stated, trying to sound sympathetic.

To most of her colleagues, Duski was a tough officer who would perform, if ever the opportunity arose, midwifery services for a lioness without fear. However, Solomone knew that underneath the hard core, there was a very sensitive person who really felt the pain of others.

"I don't understand how the world can stand by and let Zimbabwean people suffer so much," she cried helplessly. "Despite the gruesomeness of his actions, the truth is Wellington killed to feed his family."

"The man is a murderer, those women didn't deserve what he did to them," Solomone reminded her cautiously.

"How would you feel if I was forced into prostitution in order to put food on our table?" she asked as she sat up and glared at him angrily.

"Would you not have felt less of a man?" she challenged him. Solomone nodded and hung his head. "Exactly," she said before taking another long drag at the cigarette. She exhaled the dagga-scented smoke towards the ceiling. Solomone kept quiet. He knew that when she was in that kind mood, it was better to leave her alone.

As he drove back to his house, Solomone puzzled over the female nature. He knew, or assumed, at least, that Duski loved him, but he suspected it wasn't as much as he loved her. Solomone knew his bedroom performance wasn't up to scratch, but he didn't see it as a big deal. His view had always been that a decent woman would not turn down a marriage proposal on such trivial grounds. With that belief closely held to his heart, Solomone was positive that her indifference to his proposal had nothing to do with his below average performance.

Duski was still staring at the ceiling when Thandie arrived an hour later. Her thoughts were floating between Wellington's pending execution and Solomone's sudden proposal.

"*Wa ga mma*, what is the matter?" Thandie greeted her as soon as she sat on the bed beside her. "Was Wellington cleared of the murder charges?"

"He's on death row," Duski said, gloomily.

"You should be celebrating, you've helped put a serial killer behind bars," Thandie said, trying to cheer her friend up. "We should go out for a drink tonight."

"What is there to celebrate? That a man who was only trying to feed his family is sentenced to death? Pshaw!" Duski said, sucking her teeth impatiently.

"Duski, the man murdered two women. He could have found other ways to support his family," Thandie said in an attempt to make her see sense and stop blaming herself. "Change of subject, are you going back to see the old man?" she asked.

"Why?"

"Duski, don't tell me you still have doubts about the old man's skills. He helped you track down Wellington for God's sake."

"No, you helped me track down Wellington, remember? All that detective work you did before putting his photo in *The Voice* was what helped me track him down. Tell me, how did you manage to get all that information?" she asked, genuinely curious.

"This did the trick," Thandie said, holding out one of Duski's old police notebooks. "I told them I was from CID," she added giggling.

"*Nxa, nxa,* you are one very naughty girl, you know!" Duski scolded playfully, shaking her head and wagging her finger at her. "Where did you get that from?"

"Right here. After dropping you off, I drove back here and got it. I knew you wouldn't let me borrow it if I asked, so I didn't," Thandie said, clearly proud of her detective work. "We got to give the old man credit, though, he was able to detect you were suspicious about Motlatsi's death and he did say Wellington was guilty, didn't he?"

"I know—I've been trying to work out how he knew all that stuff. All this divining bone business is all too irrational—all crazy." Duski said, shaking her head in confusion.

Deep down, she knew that if it weren't for the old man's help, she'd not have found Wellington. The only doubt she still harboured was the old man's revelation that Ali's death was a result of witchcraft. Duski believed that she was responsible for the death—absolutely convinced that Ali's death was her punishment for going against the beliefs of the ZCC church. She had after all, consulted a traditional doctor and used *muti* to find love—and she'd been punished for it. This belief haunted every second of her existence.

"Are we going?" Thandie asked, picking up her handbag and car keys from the bed.

"Sorry, I haven't been listening," she said sitting up to look at Thandie. "Where are we supposed to be going?"

"To thank the old man? And most importantly, to find out who killed Ali," Thandie explained impatiently. She was standing in front of the mirror to adjust her wig.

"I think you are right, we do need to thank the old man. As for Ali's death, I think that one is best left to CID to work out," Duski said, standing up to put on a pair of white trainers.

Ali's death was something she still found very difficult to accept. Duski had been having a vivid recurring dream that always started the same way. She'd fall into a deep slumber and as she started to drift off, she'd feel someone enter her bedroom, followed by the creaking of the bed as if they were sitting down. This would be followed by a smell of damp earth—the kind only left by the first rains. She'd try to sit up, but her body always felt paralysed. Bizarrely, whenever she'd had the dream, she'd always feel very much awake. Although the intruder always had his back to her, she knew who it was.

Every time she'd had the dream, she would wake up to tormenting thoughts and would spend hours trying to rationalise something she knew was completely irrational. Sometimes, she'd conclude that Ali had come back to haunt her. On other nights, she'd mull over the possibility that Ali had come to tell her something.

"I wonder if the old man could give me some *muti* to make Solomone forget that he ever wanted to marry me," Duski suddenly said with a loud sigh.

"Did he ask you to marry him?" Thandie whispered excitedly. Duski nodded absently. "You don't look like a woman who's just been proposed to. What did you say? Are you going to marry him?

When is the wedding?" Thandie fired the questions at her without stopping for breath.

"Which question do you want me to answer first?"

"How about starting with the first one," Thandie said rubbing her hands together with anticipation.

"Nothing," she sighed dejectedly.

"And by the sound of it, you don't want to marry him."

"Yes and no. Does this answer all your questions?"

"What do you mean 'Yes and No'? You either want to marry the guy or you don't. I know he isn't exactly Mr Universe, but he worships you!"

"Still, he isn't Mr Right either. Remember what you once said, a woman could forgive and forget a man's faults only if his performance in the bedroom was superb."

"Are you telling me that Solomone is failing you in that department?" Thandie asked, curious.

"Exactly. The difficulty is how do you tell a guy something like that without injuring their male pride," Duski replied and looked at her friend, helpless. "I sort of love him, but I can't marry him—not with this problem."

"What exactly is the problem? Is the thing too small? Too big? Or is it because he doesn't know how to use it properly?"

"I feel bad telling you all this, but his thing is so small that I've been thinking of buying myself one of those things single women use on themselves."

"You mean a vibrator," Thandie corrected her, trying not to laugh.

"Whatever!"

"Poor man, God has really been mean to him," Thandie said, trying to sound sympathetic before she burst out laughing.

"Thandie, this isn't funny, you know. I need to know what to do," she scolded, looking desperately at her friend.

"You could marry him and take a lover on the side with a big bazooka. Or even better, you could ask the old man to give you something to make his thing big—if that's the kind of thing you are into," Thandie said and stifled another giggle.

"I shouldn't have told you this. I knew you would just make fun of me," Duski complained, now genuinely hurt.

"Seriously, you would be surprised at the number of desperate married women who take lovers on the side—they all do it to save their marriages." Thandie said, giggling hysterically. "There are quite a number of men visiting traditional doctors daily for penis enlargement treatments. I can't see why he can't have his enlarged," she concluded with feigned sympathy. "It sounds like you care for the guy anyway, so why not ask the old man for *muti*? Put it in his food or something, he wouldn't know," she shrugged noncommittally.

"And what happens when his thing starts growing? How do I explain it? Or even worse, what if there are side effects—a permanent hard on or something?"

"Why would he suspect the unexplained growth has anything to do with you? Have you ever raised any questions about his size?" Thandie looked at her friend with bemused curiosity and wiggled a little finger at her.

"What do you think I am? I'm not a whore, you know. Decent women don't discuss things like that with their partners."

"Well you will just have to suffer in silence then, won't you?" Thandie said and shrugged before adding, "If he develops side effects, personally, I wouldn't complain." She giggled and ran out the door as Duski tried to hit her playfully.

"You mad nymphomaniac," Duski shouted, sucking her teeth as she followed Thandie out to the car.

"Seriously, how small is he?" Thandie carried on, looking at her friend curiously before turning the ignition on.

"Can we talk about something else?" Duski pleaded, lighting another dagga-filled Stuyvesant before winding down the window.

"I might be able to help," Thandie said, turning the ignition off and turning to look pleadingly at her friend.

"Promise not to repeat this to anyone," Duski said after exhaling a lungful of the dagga-scented smoke.

Thandie swore not to say a word to anyone. Duski took another long drag and fanned the smoke through her nostrils thoughtfully.

"The same size as an uncooked chipolata, and that's when it's fully erect," she blurted.

"That's an exaggeration."

"Lightning strike me down if I'm lying," Duski said, swearing it was the truth. "He wouldn't even let me touch it. The thing usually flops out as soon as he . . . you know starts the business," Duski stared through the windscreen as she took another long drag. "He always pretends nothing is wrong, though—you know, when we are doing it," she said fanning smoke through her mouth and nostrils simultaneously. "The first time, I got into a panic when the thing went all sloppy and floppy inside me. I thought the condom was coming off. I shot my hand down there to check if the condom had come off, and he—"

"I know, he slapped your hand off," Thandie said.

"How did you know?" she asked, curious and suspicious. The Stuyvesant paused mid-air. "Have you two had an—"

"No, not that. I had a similar experience myself," Thandie confessed. "Mine was this small," she said and wagged her little finger as she giggled. "Only my thighs got to enjoy it—he never even

239

tried to put it in the right hole—he just shoved it between my thighs and wriggled as if he was being electrocuted," she said before they both convulsed into fits of giggles.

Thandie started the engine and joined Ditjaube Road. "When I first laid eyes on him—for the first time in my life—I was genuinely turned on. He was well muscled, tall, and drove a 4×4. Throughout the night all he did was boast about his wealth, his education and the lot. Before we went back to his house, he took me out for an expensive meal at the Grand Palm—just to prove how loaded he was."

"What is his name?" Duski asked,

"I don't know. His erection didn't last long enough for me to find out. I complained about how small he was. He called me a bitch, drove me back home and I never saw him again. He was the typical small-dick guy with an ego the size of the Kalahari Desert."

"Do you think too much weightlifting could reduce . . . you know . . . the size of a man's penis? Solomone is so obsessed with weightlifting. He practically lives in the gym," Duski said, staring reflectively at the shimmering sun-baked tarmac as the Tazz sped along the dual carriageway.

"I think it's the other way round. Men with small dicks are obsessed with their bodies. I personally think it is to make up for the shortfall in the briefs department," Thandie said, "That's why I now prefer the nice, round-bellied and mature ones.

You would be surprised what lies beneath those fat bellies—and they do know how to treat a girl."

"*I like my men like I like my whiskey, aged and mellow*," Thandie started singing playfully.

*   *   *

The Tazz pulled up inside the old man's yard, and his wife led them to the back of the consulting hut. There, they found him dozing off on a traditional folding leather chair. There was an empty bottle of Savannah on a coffee table next to the chair, a sign that he'd just finished his lunchtime drink.

"*Ntata o na le baeng*," his wife announced, trying to wake him up. The old man was snoring softly through a gap between his teeth. A brown and withered leather hat was neatly balanced on his old and wrinkly forehead. Duski felt very guilty for disturbing him during his break time, but she was reluctant to visit during the normal healing and divining times. She was worried about her reputation.

"Tell them to come back later," the old man said without opening his eyes.

"*Rra*, it's the police woman. She says she only needs a few minutes of your time," the wife explained.

"All right, all right," the old man croaked sleepily. "This is my lunch break, ladies—you'd better make it quick," he grumbled as soon as Duski and Thandie had sat down.

"*Dumela rra*," they chorused in greeting.

"I'm not well. The heat has disabled me and these old bones seem to have gone into a coma," the old man grumbled, groaning and touching his knees. "So what can a heat exhausted old man do for you?" he asked, giving them a toothless grin as soon as he was fully awake.

"We've come to thank you for helping me track down a serial murderer. I'm sure you've heard in the news that a Zimbabwean man was convicted for murdering his two girlfriends. He was given the death sentence," Duski started, still feeling bad about Wellington's sentence. "I've been thinking about what you said about my boyfriend's death. I think I'm ready to find out the truth about what really happened to him," she said, suddenly realising how much she had been mulling over the divination and the possibility of it being true.

Duski was also shaken by a recent article in *The Voice* newspaper. A newly converted Christian woman confessed to using *muti* to wipe out her best friend's entire family. Though she would not admit it to herself, it was the woman's story that made her think there might be some truth in what the old man said about Ali's death.

"We need to go into the hut and cast the bones again to refresh my memory. I see so many people. It is so difficult to remember all their problems—especially you women . . . you all have so many problems," he laughed and outstretched his thin, wiry arms to indicate the magnitude of women's problems.

The old man stood up with great difficulty, his knees creaked painfully as he led her to the consultation hut. "You girls are so cruel, denying an old man a well-deserved rest," he complained as he lowered himself onto a stool inside the hut. Duski sat on the second stool and faced the old man on the other side of the consultation mat.

He reached for his *seditse*, the horsetail whisk and his pouch of divining bones. He emptied them out onto the hyena skin mat and picked them up again, one at a time. "You know what to do," he said as he handed her the bones.

She blew hard into the bones, as instructed before and threw them onto the mat.

"A limping goat with a very sore hoof," the old man said. His practised eye hovered analytically over the fallen bones. "I am a multicoloured goat, I am limping; I have been hit by one of you goat herders," he muttered, interpreting the pattern as he surveyed the bones. "This indicates *boloi*, witchcraft. A woman who was once close to the deceased wanted him dead. This woman, it appears, is in cahoots with a local witch doctor." The old man looked at Duski before he carried on: "According to the pattern, you know this person," he suddenly said, searching her face curiously before moving the bones around. "She does not take kindly to rejection," he concluded, "which tells me that this was a revenge killing. And he wasn't her first victim."

"How do I find out this woman's identity?" Duski asked, wondering who it might be.

Did Ali have an affair with one of my friends or colleagues? She was puzzled by the revelation.

"There's the mother of his child—though I've met the woman, I can't say I know her."

The old man picked up the bones, gave them to her again and asked her to blow into them.

"*Mogolori wa mmakuikui,*" the old man mumbled, his trained eye hovering over the divining bones Duski had just thrown on the mat. "This is a positive sign. It is known as the laughing blue crane. It means you'll find whatever it is you are looking for," he said and scooped up the bones to put them back into the pouch. "Well, you've two options. You are a clever police woman—you can try and work the puzzle out yourself. Or I can give you something to help speed up the investigation a little bit."

"As for working it out, I'm already stuck—that is why I'm here. I haven't got a clue where to start. So what is option two?" she asked, looking curiously and suspiciously at the old man.

"This involves a little infusion of my special herbs known as *mhera moroga baloi*—the weed that insults witches. This will bring the suspect to you with a confession."

The old man stroked his grey stubble thoughtfully and looked at Duski's animated face. "Unfortunately, I haven't got the herb at the moment. It only grows at the very top of Mankgodi hills."

"How soon can you get it?" she asked suddenly recalling the case of the herd-boy, and hoping that the old man would be able to get it before the weekend.

"It is currently out of season, I'm afraid. It will have to be at the end of next month," he said, clearly disappointed that he could not help her immediately.

"It'll have to be option one then . . . I hate waiting," she said, knowing that facing a couple of months with more torturous thoughts and speculations would be unbearable. "If I haven't solved the case before then, I will come back," she promised putting her hand into her jean pocket to produce a newspaper cutting she'd been keeping since Ali's death. She handed it over to the old man. "Do you think you can help me figure out why he went back to her?" she asked hesitantly.

The old man studied the picture for a while, his deeply furrowed brow set in deep thought.

"What I really want to know is if the baby she was carrying before she died was his," she asked, sniffing back tears that had been hovering threateningly around the corners of her eyes.

Duski wasn't telling the truth. She'd cut out the picture from *The Voice* newspaper soon after the tragedy. Her intention was to trace the woman's family and apologise for what Ali did—and hopefully, to find out how long he'd been back with her.

"How much do you want to know?" the old man asked, putting the photo on the mat. He looked at her with eyes full of sympathy.

"Everything," she sniffed.

The old man got up and rummaged through some carrier bags of dried herbs. He pinched a mixture of herbs from different bags, threw them into a small mortar and pounded them into a fine powder. He left the hut to return a few minutes later with an enamel mug in which he stirred the powder.

"You are a nuisance, young lady," he complained playfully as he handed her the drink. "Now I've to send home all my clients this afternoon. This will take several minutes to work," the old man explained, "you need to let me know as soon as you start feeling drowsy."

Duski nodded.

She was too scared to ask why he was giving her the drink. She gulped it down and was surprised that unlike most traditional medicines, the drink was tasteless. The old man nailed the four corners of a white sheet into the mud walls of the consulting hut to make a makeshift screen before he took the mug away and left the hut again. He returned fifteen minutes later to find Duski almost falling asleep on the stool. He gently shook her and asked her to look at the screen.

Chapter Twenty

At first, the picture was hazy and blurred, but soon it became clearer and discernible. Shapes started to take recognisable forms on the makeshift screen. Ali's ex, the pregnant woman who was shot, appeared on the screen looking confused and distraught. She was walking around the house as if she'd lost something. She looked inside the mahogany wardrobe, inside the kitchen units, under a pile of exercise books on the table and under a double base bed inside one of the tiny bedrooms.

Whatever it was she was looking for, was nowhere to be found. She looked inside the huge empty fridge that dominated the tiny kitchen. She brought out a six pack of Lion Lager. Duski wondered whether that was what she was after. The woman sat down and stared at the crowned lion's head at the top of the red circular label. She pulled out one can from the pack, opened it rather aggressively and downed it in one swig. She grimaced,

"*Selfish, arrogant fuck with a selfish, arrogant dick,*" Duski heard someone say.

Duski looked behind her before she realised where the sound was coming from. It was coming from the makeshift screen.

On the coffee table—next to a copy of *The Voice* newspaper—was a packet of Craven A cigarettes. The woman pulled out one cigarette with shaky fingers and lit it up with a match. She took a long drag and coughed viciously, but not enough to stop her from dragging on the cigarette to its butt.

The screen fizzled out into another scene.

A typical African shopping complex consisting of a little bar named Auntie Bellina's, a bottle store, a butcher's shop and a supermarket. The scene was dark and hazy as if it were just after dusk. Ali appeared on the screen with three of his colleagues. He was wearing a royal blue T-shirt with a red Lion Lager circular label with the king of the jungle's crowned head at the top. The woman in the newspaper cut-out and two other women appeared on the scene. She walked up to the bar. "Lion Lager, please," Duski heard her say. She picked up the can and walked, with the determined confidence of a tigress just about to make a pounce, towards Ali and stood in front of him.

"Hi, stranger. Remember me?" she said before cracking open her can. "Mind if I join you," she asked. Ali looked at her, surprise written all over his face. He shrugged. The screen went blank for a brief moment before it came to life again.

A parade of three nude and very drunk women appeared on the screen. The girls seemed to be teasing Ali and his friends. Ben, one of Ali's colleagues, was the first to whip his thing out and approach the woman from the newspaper from behind. She grabbed his balls and guided him into her sticky and wet womanhood before he started pounding into her. It was as if he were trying to break through to the other side. The other two officers soon followed his example and mounted the two other girls.

Ali stood swaying drunkenly, watching the group of brown naked bodies writhing an arm's length away. Hairy, chocolate brown testicles slapped and pounded noisily against the woman's light brown thighs and fleshy buttocks. The frothy and creamy come dripping down between the woman from the newspaper's thighs, made Duski gag and shudder. It was common knowledge that the Ben's last girlfriend died of AIDS. The picture fizzled out and was replaced by a bedroom scene.

Ali's ex was now lying naked next to him and he had his trousers down to his knees. Duski stared at the screen stunned and watched it slowly fade away. She was still staring at the makeshift screen when the old man took it down. He slowly folded the sheet and put it at the far end of the hut.

"It wasn't his child," he suddenly said, "I know you are probably wondering if your young man had had sex with the woman."

She looked up at his withered face, confused.

"If they did have sex, the screen would have shown it," he explained sitting down next to her. "The child was another man's who'd walked out on her the day she met your young man at the bar. That's what she was looking for when she first appeared on the screen. Unfortunately,

249

your boyfriend was too drunk to remember what happened that night—apart from waking up half naked next to her the next morning.

"You took your time in there," Thandie complained as soon as Duski emerged from the hut. They bade the old man good day and drove back to Block Eight.

Over several cans of chilled Hansa, Duski told Thandie about the screen and Ali's murder. The two devised a plan of action. The mother of Ali's child in Molepolole was the first on their list of possible suspects and therefore the first on the list of people they were planning to pay a visit to. Second on the list of suspects, were witch doctors in and around the Molepolole area.

*   *   *

The following Saturday saw the white Tazz speeding along the shimmering, hot tarmac road on a fifty-kilometre journey to Molepolole village. The car was well stocked with the usual provisions—a cooler box filled with cans of Hansa Pilsner partially buried under a crushed rock of ice. Duski's plan of action was to carry out a traditional police style investigation. She realised that the only achievable option was to get the names of all the witch doctors in and around Molepolole who would not have qualms about helping an aggrieved lover to get rid of an ex-partner.

The plan to pay the mother of Ali's child a visit was scrapped after several cans of Hansa Pilsner, a few dagga-filled sticks of Peter Stuyvesant and a long-winded deliberation.

Her initial plan was to go to the woman's place in Molepolole and try to take an item of her clothing back to the old man to eliminate her from the investigation. She realised however, that the task was impossible and full of risks. She knew what would happen if she were caught sneaking out with the woman's clothes. She could almost see the headlines: "Copper Turned Witch Steals Rivals Clothes for Voodoo." She shuddered. She was already a ritual murder suspect and she couldn't afford to expose herself to any more suspicion.

It was midsummer, the dust storm season and as usual, Molepolole was under cover of fine dust. As the white Toyota Tazz entered the dust-covered village, Duski thought of how different the time of year was in her own home area. She knew Lentswe-Le-Moriti village would be perfumed by a rich scent of the *Mokoba* (Acacia) tree's yellow weeping willow-like flowers. As they ploughed through the fine dust, she suddenly remembered that she knew the village chief—she was an ex-schoolmate. Duski and the chief, Mmakwena, as she was affectionately known in the village, went to the same boarding school.

"Do you know the way to the *Kgotla?*" Duski asked, just as Thandie was about to ask her where they were going to start their search.

"From what I remember, it's along the main road somewhere. If you look out, you might be able to spot it as we drive along," Thandie said.

A *Kgotla* is a traditional meeting place where minor cases and other village matters are dealt with by the chief and heads of clans. A modern village *Kgotla* building is very distinctive. It consists of a thatched shelter with a low, traditionally decorated brick wall. As they sped along the main tarmac road into the heart of the village, Duski suddenly spotted the typical patterned walls of *Kgotla* buildings. Thandie parked the car outside the yard, in the unmarked dirt car park. They got out of the car and approached a uniformed female local police officer.

"*Mma* we would like to speak to Mmakwena," Duski addressed the officer.

"I'm afraid you can't see her dressed like that," the officer said as she surveyed their attire with open disapproval.

"What do you mean 'dressed like that'?" Duski asked. But she knew exactly what the woman meant. "Aren't you wearing trousers yourself?" she challenged.

"This is my uniform, and I work here," the officer protested.

"Look *mma*, I'm on duty. This is my uniform, too," she showed the officer her police ID card.

"I'm so sorry, Madam. I'll let the chief know you are here." The officer stood to attention immediately and saluted her before leading them towards the *Kgotla*.

The chief was inside the shelter with some village elders trying a domestic case. One of the elders, an old man dressed in a grey suit despite the heat, left the group to meet them outside the *Kgotla*.

"Have you no respect for the *Kgotla?*" The elder chastised, peering disapprovingly over a pair of thick glasses at their exposed thighs. "I'm afraid you have to go back and make yourselves decent before you can speak to the chief," he said.

"I'm sorry that you disapprove of our clothes, sir. We are police officers, and we are working undercover," Thandie lied while Duski produced her ID card again to show the old man.

"You know that in our culture, it is disrespectful to come to the *Kgotla* dressed like that. Remember, you are women, not men," the old man lectured, "I'll have to ask the chief to meet you out here." He took another disapproving look at their thighs before he walked back inside the *Kgotla* and approached a woman dressed in traditional attire.

Duski recognised her immediately. The woman excused herself, walked towards them, her eyes narrowed and fixed disapprovingly at their shorts, but her stern look softened as soon as she recognised Duski.

"Duski, I knew if anybody would dare come to my *Kgotla* dressed in shorts, it would be you. Anyway, what brings you to this part of Botswana?

My uncle said you were police officers," she said, shaking her hand.

"Sorry for coming here dressed like this," Duski said as the chief led them to one of the *Kgotla* offices. "We weren't actually planning to come here, but I suddenly remembered you were the village chief," she said apologetically, "We didn't mean to get you into trouble with the old men. Anyway, what is it like being the first female chief in the country?"

"Tough, as you can imagine. It is difficult to shake these villagers from their old ways and beliefs," Mmakwena said and sighed.

"They need some history lessons," Thandie said. "Our ancestors' traditional attire was actually more revealing than what we are wearing right now? In the old days, women walked around with breasts barely covered by beads, their thighs fully exposed under animal skin skirts that barely covered their bottoms."

The women burst out laughing as they sat down in the chief's air-conditioned office.

"That's why women were not allowed in the *Kgotla* then," Mma Mokwena said. "It would have been too much of a distraction for the men," she added, and they all laughed again. "Can I offer you anything to drink? I've got Coca-Cola, Fanta and Granadilla."

"Fanta, please. Thank you," Duski said.

"And a Coca-Cola for me, please *mma. Tankie*," Thandie said, reaching for one of the cans the chief had put on the desk.

"So what do you do all day as chief?" Duski asked, looking at the woman who was once her schoolmate with a mixture of envy and sympathy.

"All sorts of things. Last week, I presided over a case of anti-social behaviour and we held a mass caning session of the delinquents in question," Mmakwena said proudly. "And yesterday, it was a marriage wrecking case," she sighed.

"What is marriage wrecking?" Thandie asked, looking genuinely baffled.

"When a wife sues another woman for having an affair with her husband," the chief explained. "Last month, for example, a woman sued a rival for sexual deprivation. She claimed that because of the affair, her husband no longer had sex with her. The woman wanted thirty thousand pula in damages from the other woman."

"That sounds like an interesting job you have here, chief," Duski said, somewhat amused. "Do you ever find the accused guilty?"

"Yes, we do. In the case we heard today, the accused was ordered to pay the aggrieved wife ten thousand pula in compensation for wrecking her marriage," the chief said.

"What?!" Thandie exclaimed, shaking her head in disbelief. "This is the most ridiculous thing I have ever heard. Surely, the person responsible for wrecking the marriage is the husband and not the other woman. Are these *aggrieved* wives stupid or what?" Thandie looked at Mmakwena, still shaking her head in disbelief.

"The woman could not prove she didn't know the man was married," Mmakwena said, defending her court's decision.

"What about the husband?" Thandie challenged the chief.

"So what brings you here then?" Mmakwena suddenly asked, ignoring Thandie's question. She cracked open a can of Sprite and looked at Duski.

"I'm investigating a very unusual case and I thought you might be able to help," Duski said before pausing and looking at Mmakwena. She wasn't sure how to phrase the request. "I'm looking for information on local traditional doctors."

"Why? Is a traditional doctor from this area a suspect in this case?" Mmakwena asked as she looked at Duski a little bit confused.

"I am not sure yet," she said, "The case is still under investigation."

"What kind of information are you looking for?"

"Just names of traditional doctors who you think would not have qualms about helping aggrieved clients kill their rivals, enemies, or ex-partners," she said, watching the chief as she fizzled down her request with a mouthful of the Sprite.

"I neither consult nor approve of traditional medicine, as you know," Mmakwena said, wondering why Duski had come to her with such a strange request.

"I was hoping that as the village chief, you could help us find out from the villagers if they knew of any doctors with such a reputation," Duski explained, recalling Mmakwena's devotion to Christianity. At school, she was a well-respected member of the Student Christian Movement and was always preaching in an effort to convert and save other students' souls.

"It is a very difficult task you are asking me to do," Mmakwena said, sipping her Sprite thoughtfully. "My uncle, the old man you just met, is a member of *Dingaka* Traditional Doctors' Association. He's a practising traditional doctor himself—he might be able to help you." She said before she called out to the female local police officer Duski and Thandie met when they arrived at the *Kgotla*: "Could you ask my uncle to come here, please?"

"Niece and Your Highness, how can a loyal servant be of service to you?" the old man said taking off his worn hat and bowed his head respectfully to announce his presence.

"These ladies would like your advice Uncle," Mmakwena said before turning to Duski. "Ladies, I'll leave you in the capable hands of my trusted uncle. Come and see me sometime when you are off duty," she said, taking one last look at her old schoolmate's attire before leaving the office.

"So what can I do for you, *bomma*?" the old man asked. The earlier disapproval was still lingering in his deeply furrowed forehead.

"We are investigating an unusual case that involves the use of witchcraft," Duski explained. She paused to gauge the old man's reaction. "We are looking for anybody in or around Molepolole who might consider prescribing dangerous *muti* to kill others," she looked at the old man hopefully.

Thandie reached for an unopened Coke can on the desk, cracked it open and put it in front of him.

"There are many people in this country who call themselves traditional healers, but all they do is harm innocent people through witchcraft," the chief's uncle said guzzling down the Coke.

"Do you have anyone like that in the village?" Thandie interrupted, realising that he was just about to give a long-winded lecture on the subject.

"Fortunately, we only have one such person in this village and I am sure you have heard of him. He is well known for prescribing penis shrinking *muti* for his female clients who suspect their husbands of cheating," he said and put the Coke can back on the table.

"Can you give us his name?" Duski asked, excited.

"His compound is always full of bitter and twisted women," the old man continued, determined not to be denied an opportunity to slag off a man he considered a disgrace to his profession. "He's a Mokgalagadi man known as Khonou of Borakalalo ward," the chief's uncle added. "*Ee* a man like Khonou is an embarrassment to our country," he muttered angrily to no one in particular.

"Could you take us to his place, please?" Duski asked, interrupting his muttering.

"I'm not going anywhere near that witch doctor's yard," he said, a hint of fear in his voice.

"How about pointing it out to us from a safe distance, after that, we'll drive you straight back," Thandie reasoned.

The chief's uncle reluctantly followed Duski and Thandie to the car parked outside the *Kgotla* yard.

*   *   *

"There's the devil himself," he announced as soon as they drove into the centre of Borakalalo Ward. He was pointing at a tall thin man with a slightly sandy-coloured complexion. The man was dressed in a dark blue boiler suit.

"Is that him?" Duski asked, looking at the old man with undisguised surprise and confusion.

"Yes, it is. You look surprised. Do you know him?" the old man looked curiously at Duski who was still staring at the disappearing figure of the witch doctor.

"No," she replied firmly.

After dropping off the old man back at the *Kgotla*, they drove to Mafenyatla Restaurant and Bar to discuss a plan of action over a plate of *paleche* (stiff, maize meal porridge) and *seswaa* (ground meat).

"It's obvious she killed him when she found out he was seeing you," Thandie said as she rolled a lump of porridge into a ball before dabbing it onto a lump of *seswaa*, pinching a sizeable amount of meat in the process.

"We can't conclude she is guilty just because her father is a witch doctor," Duski said in between mouthfuls of stiff porridge and ground meat. What shocked her the most was that she actually recognised Khonou as the man married to her parents' neighbour's eldest daughter in Lentswe-Le-Moriti, her home village. The moment she saw the man, it all flooded back to her. She realised that she even knew the daughter, Ali's ex. She was called Fanny and they'd played together as children.

The realisation left Duski shaken. As she dabbed another ball of stiff porridge on a lump of the fibrous and juicy pounded meat, she recalled the old man's words. *The bones also show that you know this person.* "We don't even know for sure that her father is a witch doctor—it could just be allegations made out of hatred," Duski said, recalling the chief's uncle's undisguised hatred of Khonou. She knew that traditional doctors in competition had a tendency to make defamatory comments about each other's characters.

"What are we going to do?" Thandie asked, washing down the last morsels of her stiff maize

porridge and ground meat with a mouthful of
Hansa Pilsner.

"We'll go back. I'll wait outside while you
go in and ask to see Khonou for a consultation,"
Duski explained thoughtfully. "Ask him if he
could help you get rid of your boyfriend's wife or
something," she went on. Thandie was shaking
her head uncertainly. "I would do it myself, but
I'm worried that the mother of Ali's child might
recognise me. She might get suspicious that I'm
up to something," she explained, trying to reassure
Thandie.

But Thandie's eyes were widening with fear.
"What if he throws his divining bones to check if
I'm telling the truth?" she protested weakly.

"Well you will be telling the truth. You are
seeing a married man at the moment, aren't you?"
Duski looked at her friend, pleading.

"I know, but I don't want his wife dead.
What if he kills her?"

"He won't. He'll probably give you some
muti to take home or something. Please, you've got
to do this for me." Duski pushed her unfinished
meal away impatiently.

"Okay, I will do it," Thandie said
immediately stuffing Duski's leftover pounded meat
into her mouth. "What are we waiting for?" she
suddenly said and gulped down her Hansa Pilsner
before leading the way back to the car.

Chapter Twenty-One

"What did he say?" she asked half an hour later, when Thandie got back into the car. "Did he say he could do it?" she asked, trying to read Thandie's face.

"I need a drink first—then I can talk," Thandie said, opening the cooler box to help herself to a chilled Hansa Pilsner. She took a swig, burped, and said, "Yep, he said *ke dinyana*, easy-peasy. He called himself the great, fearless and pitiless crocodile of the Kgalagadi Desert. But he warned that it would cost me," she said, nursing the chilled drink thoughtfully. As she drank, she toyed with the idea of killing the married man *she* was having an affair with.

He is beginning to act as if he owns me, Thandie mused, but she swallowed the thought with another mouthful of the chilled pilsner.

"How much is he asking for?" Duski asked, wondering whether DI Marvellous would allow for such an expense. She was aware the man fancied her and would do anything for her if he thought it would eventually get him into her bed.

"He wants a deposit of two thousand pula for the ritual shrine and three thousand pula cash when the deed has been done," Thandie said before sipping her beer thoughtfully and staring into the distance.

"We only need two thousand pula. Hopefully after that I'll have collected enough evidence to bring him in for questioning," Duski said. "Did he explain how he does the killings?" she asked.

"He said he'll explain everything once I've paid the deposit. He even boasted about . . ." Thandie paused and looked at Duski uncertainly.

"Boasted about what?" Duski asked, looking at Thandie curiously.

"About some stuff he has done. I think he was just trying to impress me," Thandie lied. She put her unfinished Hansa between her thighs and turned the ignition on.

"Thandie, please, I need to know everything he said. You could be holding back information that might prove vital to the investigation," she explained.

"Some taxi guy who was in the newspapers—he claims the man was one of his victims," Thandie said as she carefully manoeuvred the car through the bumpy dirt road.

"What? Are you sure that he said a *taxi* driver?" she asked, looking doubtfully at her friend.

"That's what he said. Claimed some woman wanted him dead," Thandie added. "He's obviously lying."

"Did he say anything about any other victims? Surely, if he wants to convince you that he's good at his job, he'd have told you more." She watched as a momentary flicker of hesitation crossed Thandie's face. "He has told you more, hasn't he? Was it about Ali's death?"

Thandie nodded as she guided her drink expertly back between her thighs after taking a sip. She focused her attention on the road before responding. "But it doesn't mean he is telling the truth. The man knows about the deaths because both incidents were all over the papers," Thandie said lamely.

"At the moment, we haven't got proof he is lying about these claims," Duski said and sipped her beer thoughtfully. She lit a cigarette and dragged desperately on it in a vain attempt to clear her head. She took out her cell phone and found Detective Inspector Marvellous's number. She stared at the number thoughtfully before pressing the green button and waited a few seconds. "Hey, Inspector, sorry to disturb you, but I was wondering if you were free tonight," she said into the mouthpiece. "There is something I need to talk to you about," she added.

"I'm at Satchmo's later tonight, we could meet there if you like," the inspector said in his distinctive and heavily accented Setswana.

"Are you up for Satchmo's tonight?" she asked Thandie as she clicked her cell phone shut.

"Yep, you know me—I'm always game for anything," she said and gulped down her pilsner.

* * *

It didn't take her long to convince the detective inspector to loan her the two thousand pula. *I hope this helps clear your name and bring the real murderer to justice—I want to see that beautiful smile again,* the DI thought as he wrote out a cheque for the two thousand pula that Duski wanted.

The following Sunday evening, the two girlfriends sat in Duski's room listening to a tape-recorded conversation between Khonou and Thandie.

"How do you want to do this? Do you want to take part in the ritual, or do you want to leave it all to me?" the man's voice crackled chillingly through the tape recorder's speakers.

It was DI Marvellous's idea that Thandie should secretly tape record the second consultation.

"How are you going to kill her?" Thandie's nervous voice cackled over the little portable recorder.

"It is important to start the ritual with the victim alive," Khonou said, "There are things we need to cut off while the victim is still alive. Otherwise, the ritual won't work."

"What parts are we talking about?" Thandie's shaky voice asked nervously.

"We'll need to cut off her vagina, breasts and cut out her heart." Khonou said before adding, "Otherwise, the woman will come back and haunt you."

"Do you think that he sells all these body parts that he cuts off from his victims?" Thandie asked after stopping the recording. "Apparently, there are many business people that use this kind of stuff to attract customers and boost their profits," she added.

"I don't think the daughter is guilty," Duski suddenly said as if she'd not been listening to Thandie. She recalled her grandmother telling her that traditional doctors could not use their own *muti* to help a family member. "If the daughter wanted Ali dead, she would not have asked her father for help—she'd have gone to someone else," she said before switching the tape recorder back on again.

"Why go to someone else when your father is an expert in ritual murders?" Thandie asked just as Khonou's croaky voice went over the instructions again.

"Thandie, haven't you heard the Setswana saying: *ngaka ga e ke e ikalafa?*" she asked and looked at Thandie impatiently.

"He did it for his daughter," Thandie protested.

"The law applies not only to the traditional doctor himself, but to all his blood relations as well. Are you really a Motswana? Every Motswana knows that."

"There is a possibility that he could have bent the rules to help his daughter."

"If he had, Ali would still be alive—the *muti* would not have worked," Duski replied casting an annoyed look at her friend. "I'm afraid we have no choice but to wait for the old man in Mogoditshane to get the herb he said would bring the suspect to us," she concluded despondently before switching off the tape recorder.

"If Ali's ex didn't do it, who did?" Thandie asked.

"Who knows? Maybe some other ex-girlfriend I knew nothing about," Duski shrugged.

"But the old man said he was killed by someone you knew. So far, Ali's ex is the only person you sort of know," Thandie said, still convinced the woman was guilty. *All we need to do is get her to confess.* This was her train of thought before her mind strayed to other farfetched possibilities. "What about your housemate? She seemed a bit funny about your relationship with Ali. Do you think she had an affair with him behind your back or a crush on him?" Thandie asked, weighing her words carefully.

"She isn't the sort Ali would have gone for," Duski snapped. *Ali would never have cheated on me with a woman like Kowa*, she thought dismissively.

"It was just a thought. Anyway, I have to call it a night, *mmata*. I might call round to see you tomorrow after work," Thandie said as she picked up her keys and handbag from Duski's bed.

"I'm on lates this coming week," Duski said and yawned.

"Shall I pick you up on Friday from work? We could go out or something."

"Solomone usually picks me up. What about next weekend? It will be my weekend off," she said, lighting her last cigarette of the day.

"By the way, have you responded to his proposal yet?" Thandie suddenly asked.

"I haven't seen him for a week," she replied, fanning smoke through her nostrils towards the ceiling. "He's been ringing me but he doesn't mention the proposal."

"So what are you going to do? I mean about your relationship?" Thandie asked curiously. "Will you marry him eventually?"

"You're a very nosy woman, Thandie. If you really want to know, I would like us to be friends," she sighed, not sure how she would broach the subject with Solomone.

"*Boroko*," Thandie bid her farewell and left her to mull over her problems.

"Goodnight," Duski responded absently.

It was some time after midnight when the smell of damp earth suddenly invaded her tiny bedroom. She tried to sit up, but an overpowering sense of drowsiness held her down firmly. Against her will, she fell asleep again. As in all the previous dreams, she heard the night intruder sit on the bed beside her, but this time, the dream seemed real—she could see everything clearly. She saw him turn his head slowly towards her. As she'd sensed all along, the man was Ali. She was surprised that this time, she wasn't as scared as she had previously been. He stared at her, his eyes filled with sadness and brimming with unshed tears.

"Come with me," he whispered, "I want to show you something." Ali left the side of the bed he'd been sitting on and led her out of the room. Obediently, she climbed out of bed and followed him out into the narrow hallway towards Kowa's bedroom.

"What the hell are you doing in my room?" someone shouted. Suddenly Duski's eyes flew open to find herself staring at her housemate's furious face. "You smoke too much dagga, mate," Kowa fumed and slammed the door in her face.

"*Sori*," Duski apologised to the door and went back to her room. She was shocked and shaking as she went back into her bedroom. She checked the time—it was nearly two o'clock in the morning.

I have been sleeping for nearly four hours, Duski thought. *Thandie left at around half past eleven. I must have fallen asleep half an hour after she left.* She went around to the side of the bed where she thought her night visitor had sat. There was an indentation on the bed. She reached for a packet of Peter Stuyvesant she kept in the bedside drawer and pulled out a cigarette. She lit it with shaking hands and dragged on it as if her life depended on it. She was certain Ali was there and trying to tell her something. Suddenly, she remembered something her grandmother had said to her a long time ago:

You are a sensitive person, Duski, and sensitive people can see things ordinary folk can't see. What was Ali trying to show her? She pondered, her mind flitting from one fanciful conclusion to another.

Duski was still awake at five o'clock when Pecker landed on the windowsill. She felt comfort and reassurance from the little bird's usual rhythmic tapping on the windowpane. The usual traffic noises filtered into her room with the first rays of yet another scorching day. Car tyres screeched to a halt outside the yard gate and somebody beeped the horn. She heard Kowa's bedroom door slam shut, followed immediately by light but firm footsteps towards the front door.

Duski stayed in bed until the roar of the engine had died away. She'd the house to herself for at least several hours before the end of Kowa's shift and she was determined to find out why Ali had led her to Kowa's bedroom while she was asleep.

After she'd had a bath, a cup of black coffee and buttered bread, Duski went into Kowa's bedroom. She was convinced that whatever Ali wanted to show her was inside, but the room was locked. Fortunately, she knew the key number and was certain somebody in the neighbourhood had the same key.

After an exhausting door-to-door search, she eventually managed to find a similar key from a neighbour. As she entered the room, she was immediately hit by the same smell of damp earth she'd smelled in her recurring dream. Moreover, the room smelled the same as the stuff Khonou had given Thandie for her voodoo ritual. Duski followed the smell, which led her to the wall wardrobe. As she opened the door, she could see three clay dolls set on the top shelf with nooses round their necks and knife-scratched inscriptions. The first was initialled *B.M.*, the second was *M.M.*, and the third was *A.R.*

Duski stared at the dolls, wondering what their significance was before resuming the search to see what other strange objects she could dig out. It was clear her housemate had been to Khonou, the nasty witch doctor. She stood on a wooden stool and reached to the back of the top shelf so she could poke around in the corners. The tip of her fingers touched a carrier bag in one of the corners. She pulled it down to examine the contents. The bag was tied into a tight knot, which took a while to untie.

The bag contained men's briefs, some of which she recognised as Ali's. The underwear was smeared with strange brown stuff, the same stuff Thandie brought back from Khonou. "What the hell is this all about?" she muttered to herself and shook her head. She was stunned by the discovery. She sat on the bed and stared at the noosed voodoo dolls, horrified by what her housemate had been up to. She suddenly had an uncanny feeling that someone was watching her. She looked up.

Standing right at the door, silently watching was
Constable Kowa.

"What in the devil's name are you doing
in my bedroom?" Kowa asked in a very calm and
controlled voice.

Duski stared at her, speechless. After a few
seconds, she composed herself and held out the
clay voodoo dolls and the underwear in the carrier
bag.

"What are you doing with those?" Kowa
asked in a low and menacing voice. She took a few
steps towards her and tried to grab the carrier bag
and the voodoo dolls.

"Exactly what I've been waiting to ask you?"
Duski challenged. She held onto the items firmly.

"You've no right to go through my stuff,"
Kowa snarled at her like an enraged dog.

"You haven't answered my question," Duski
insisted.

"I've nothing to say to you, not before you
tell me what the hell you're doing in my room!"
Kowa retorted.

"Okay," Duski started slowly to give
herself time to think about how to phrase what
she was about to say. "I came in to look for some
underwear . . . I mean Ali's missing underwear."
She paused, pointed to the carrier bag and said, "I
found them in your wardrobe buried among these
voodoo dolls." She looked at Kowa and then back
at the carrier bag. Kowa sat heavily on the bed,

crossed her arms defiantly and refused to talk. She stared back instead.

"I know what you've been up to, Kowa. I'm hoping that you will be able to explain all this and prove that my conclusions are wrong," Duski said, almost in tears. Kowa stared at the dolls and the carrier bag with a defiant determination.

"Okay, then," Duski said, picking up the carrier bag and voodoo dolls. "I'll have to force you to talk," she threatened, walking out of the room.

Kowa started as if she was going to stop her, but she decided not to pursue her. "What do you think you are going to do?" she challenged, "If you dare tell anybody about this, I will sue you for defamation of character." She was staring at Duski defiantly. "Witchcraft is not a crime, but accusing someone of it is," she added. Duski stared in disbelief. She pinched herself to make sure she wasn't dreaming again. "Ali deserved what he got, and I hope he is rotting in hell right now," Kowa rambled on.

"Why? What did he do to you?" Duski finally managed to ask, staring with disbelief at the woman she once thought she knew. She recalled the Setswana saying, *"Motho ga itsiwe ise naga."*

"He left me pregnant and had the guts to say it wasn't his child I was carrying," Kowa blurted out.

The words hit Duski like bullets. She suddenly felt sick and claustrophobic, and she didn't want to hear anymore.

"Thought he was a saint, didn't you? He's a daughter," Kowa smirked, "He got what he deserved, the bastard," she kept saying.

Duski managed to compose herself. "Who are the other two?" she asked and held out the two dolls, pointing at the unfamiliar initials.

"It's none of your business," Kowa said, trying to storm out of the room.

Duski blocked her way. She had an unsettling feeling that the *M.M.* stood for Mudongo Mbulawa.

"Let me guess, Mudongo also deserved what he got? You will hang for this, you know," Duski said.

"For what?" Kowa laughed.

"You mutilated their bodies and took their sex organs. Khonou has confessed to helping you, and I have his confession on tape. And now I have this," Duski said, waving the carrier bag at her. "What about him? Who is he? Another man who dumped you and deserved to die too?" she quizzed her, holding out the third doll with initials B.M.

It suddenly occurred to her that the lion park victim's initials were *B.M.* She looked at her housemate. A typical Mokwena woman, light skinned and short with a huge bottom. She recalled the lion keeper's description. "It was you—you killed Boiki as well,' she said, trying to reach for the door.

Without warning, Kowa jumped onto
Duski, throwing her forcefully onto the bed and
pinning her down by the neck.

"Help!" Duski screamed as loud as she
could while trying to loosen Kowa's hands around
her neck. Someone knocked on the bedroom door
and Kowa loosened her grip briefly—just as a
uniformed police constable burst into the room
and restrained her.

"Are you okay, Sarge?" the constable asked,
fighting to hold Kowa still.

"I'm fine, thanks," she replied, unclasping
handcuffs from the constable's belt to put on
Kowa, who had gone completely berserk.

Though Duski was pleased with the new
development in the case—including the two cold
cases—she knew that the only thing Kowa could
possibly be prosecuted for was common assault.
She had to find the victim's missing private parts in
her possession or in Khonou's to prove their guilt.

*   *   *

Down at the station, later that morning,
Kowa was charged with common assault. Duski,
however, did not let this dampen her spirits, she
was now even more determined to get to the
bottom of the mystery. When she got back home,
she went over Khonou's tape to see whether there
was anything she might have missed, anything she

could use as evidence that the three men were victims of ritual murder.

After lunch, she half-heartedly got ready for her afternoon shift. Her head was hurting due to thinking too much and her neck was still sore. The tape recording had revealed nothing new. She realised that she couldn't use the voodoo dolls or the ritual nest to prove that Boiki, the taxi driver and Ali were victims of ritual murder.

As soon as she got to the station that afternoon, she withdrew the assault case against her housemate. She apologised and offered to drive her back to the house. Kowa reluctantly accepted the apology. The drive back to Block Eight was very uncomfortable. Duski's efforts to make small talk and apologise were met by a stony silence. After dropping Kowa off, she drove to Mogoditshane to see the old man. As usual, the yard was teeming with customers. She went straight to the front of the queue.

"I need to ask the old man a few questions," she said, showing her ID to those in the queue and apologising as she marched towards the consulting hut. "*Dumela rra* I'm sorry to barge in like this, but it is rather urgent," she said. She handed the old man the *muti*-filled carrier bag she had confiscated from Kowa's room. "What can you tell me about this?" she asked and looked at the old man, desperate for some clues.

"We'll have to consult *bola*," he said, emptying the divining bones into her cupped hands. "You know the drill," the old man said and gestured for her to take her usual seat. Duski blew into the bones and threw them on the mat. "These items belong to the victims of a ritual murder," the old man said, looking at the bones. 'The victims were killed in a manner consistent with ritual murder. Their sexual organs were removed while they were still alive so . . ." The old man paused and reviewed the pattern again. "These three men died horrific deaths. The bones show that all three had their sexual organs cut off before they were murdered," the old man said, explaining the symbolism of each bone.

"What about the body parts taken from the victims? Can they be traced?" she asked.

"Could still be in the witch doctor's possession or in some aspiring businessman's deep freezer," the old man said.

"'Could you give me a minute, please?" she asked as Sub-Inspector Bale's voice cackled over her police mobile radio. "Roger. Go ahead. Over."

"Sergeant, where are you?"

"I'm just about to leave the house, sir. Trying to make sure Constable Kowa is okay, sir," she said, winking at the old man.

"I want you back here as soon as possible, Sergeant."

"Received, sir. Over and out," she said before turning the radio off and clipping it to her belt. "But we do know that my housemate is involved in the murders. Is there anything you can do to make her tell us where these private parts are?" she asked, resuming the consultation with the old man.

"I can give you something, but I can't guarantee it will work," he said as he rummaged through packages of herbs.

"And why is that?"

"Your housemate, it seems is well protected. The witch doctor she works with is very powerful," the old man said as he burnt some kind of herb. "With luck and God's will, she'll reveal all," he said. "This is *mhera moroga baloi*, the medicinal weed that offends sorcerers and witches," the old man explained, spraying a red liquid at her face with his flywhisk before casting his bones again.

He surveyed the fallen bones, affectionately calling each one by name and studied the pattern intensely. "The blue crane fall, the rare bird of happiness," the old man smiled as he praised his divining bones. His keen eyes studied the pattern the bones formed on the skin mat. "This is a positive pattern. You will get what you are after," the old man concluded. She thanked him and drove back to the office.

Chapter Twenty-Two

Two weeks after her visit to the old man, something strange happened. It was after midnight and she had just drifted off into a dreamless sleep when she was suddenly woken up by a hysterical and demonic laugh in the hallway. She could hear Constable Kowa saying weird and bizarre things, as if addressing a meeting. She tiptoed to the door and opened it a crack. Constable Kowa was pacing up and down the corridor like an evangelical preacher.

"Can you believe that a bone from the thigh of a human being could open a grave? Ha . . . ha . . . ha," she said laughing demonically. "That's exactly what we did. We pointed the bone at graves of newly buried corpses to bring them out. We chopped up the bodies into pieces and roasted the flesh," she said, making chopping actions and licking her fingers before howling at her invisible audience. "Do you know Ali, Mudongo, and Boiki, the cheating bastards?" Kowa shouted before peering at her invisible audience angrily. "They deserved to die and I'm now the proud owner of their testicles and penises. They are mine!" she howled.

Duski decided that she'd heard enough. "Kowa, you need to go to bed," she said, interrupting her ravings cautiously. Kowa looked at her as if she didn't know who she was. "Are you a ghost?" she asked, her eyes strangely dilated with fear.

"I'm not a ghost. It's me, Duski, your housemate?" she said, holding her hand gently to lead her back into her bedroom.

"Leave me alone, I didn't kill you!" Kowa screamed and pushed her against the wall before bolting out of the house and into the darkness. Her terrified screams woke nearly all the neighbours who later formed a search party. Duski decided not to join the search. Instead, she asked a neighbour to drive her to the station. While waiting for the neighbour to bring the car around, Duski quickly changed into a pair of jeans and a T-shirt and went into Constable Kowa's bedroom. She was not quite sure what she was looking for. As she entered the bedroom, her attention was suddenly attracted by a white envelope lying on the bed. It was a letter addressed to her. She sat down on the bed, tore the letter open and began reading.

Dear Duski:

You were right about my involvement in Ali's, Boiki's, and Mudongo's deaths. The three, as I've already told you, were right bastards, and they deserved to die. Before you judge me, let me tell you something I've kept a secret from many people, including you. I've got three children by those bastards. I know I've only told you about my first, Ali's child.

The second, now ten, is Mudongo's, and the youngest, Boiki's, I had just before I joined the police force.

No woman deserves to be treated the way these three morons have treated me. For them, I was—and have always been—a slut with big tits. They never took me seriously and didn't believe I deserved to be loved. I wasn't pretty enough for them . . . or any man I've ever met. I've watched them move on. Ali has had more children with other women, Mudongo has had children with his wife, and Boiki took on someone else's child.

I guess, you're probably wondering how I carried out the killings, and most importantly, what I've done with their bits. I suppose you'd also like to know whether I had an accomplice. What I can tell you is this: I didn't physically do anything to hurt them—though sometimes I wish that I had. I don't want to get into a discussion about what exactly happened, I've no time for that right now . . . use your imagination. What I can say, though, is that I watched them die. They begged for their lives and begged for forgiveness. I must admit, I did find it deeply satisfying. In case you are wondering about the video of Mudongo's mutilation . . . yes, I took it. It was meant to be a present for his wife.

"Who killed them, then?" I can hear you ask. Let's say someone who hated seeing me in

pain. What did he get out of it? That's your
second question, right? Their private parts
of course and I really shouldn't get my friend
involved in this. I'm sorry, I can't tell you
about his involvement. He is a decent man who
happens to have a

Did you know that ground male parts
provide a potent ingredient for voodoo charms,
which can be used to bring success in business
and love? If you ever find yourself short of
suitors, go and see my friend, he'll make a very
special potion—hopefully with some of the bits
you've been looking for.

By the way, those three weren't our my
only victims. We've I've been involved in
several killings; nothing personal, just to keep
the business going. Mind you, I took the
part voluntarily. Being a single parent and
only breadwinner in a large family is quite
a responsibility. I had to find other ways of
supplementing the pittance I get as a constable.
I'm sure that you can understand that.
Unfortunately, the only way available for me
was through what society deems deviant.

Anyway, I'm sure that you want to know
what happened to the bodies of those other
victims. If you really want to know, search the
desert on the other side of Letlhakeng Village.
Good luck.

I know that, before long, you'll work out
who my friend is. Please trust me—he is innocent

in the death of those three. I brought them to him. All he did was shoot the arrows; he is funny with his arrows. He calls them his babies, and he doesn't let anybody use them. But he never touched those three. The only thing he is guilty of is taking their private bits, which I promised to let him have anyway. The irony is, he's preparing to make lucky potions with the missing bits for a couple of CID guys. Can you believe it?!

She paused, wondering what state of mind Kowa was in when she wrote the letter. From what she'd witnessed that evening—the demonic and hysterical laughter and the gibberish about opening graves with bones from the dead—she was in no doubt that Kowa was insane.

Still, how did she get mixed up with this guy? Was she in a kind of voodoo controlled sexual relationship with him? Duski wondered as she resumed reading the letter. She recalled the story of a woman who once fell in love with a witch doctor who regularly used voodoo on her whenever he wanted to rape her children. It was the woman's relatives who, in the end came to her rescue.

Sorry, I can't mention any names, but some of the guys on the investigation team are among his clients. Of course, they don't know the potions are made out of human testicles and penises. I'm sure you're probably dying to know who actually did the mutilating. I'm sorry to disappoint you, but I'm not at liberty to say.

283

Duski wondered whether Detective Sergeant Boy was one of the clients.

> *Why am I telling you all this anyway, you're probably wondering, if I'm not prepared to make a full confession? I guess what I am trying to do is cleanse my soul. I feel that this is the end of the road for me. In short, the aim wasn't to grass on someone who'd been so good to me or get into a discussion about what, where, how, or why we did what we did. That's another story, which has nothing to do with why I've decided to write to you. This isn't meant to help the investigation team reopen the cases, as I said. It's purely my attempt to cleanse my soul.*
>
> *Do I feel any remorse? Have any regrets? No—sorry to disappoint again. What I can say, however, is that I know I've done some pretty evil things over the years, and I sincerely apologise for that. Still, there's little I can do about it now . . . it's no good digging up the past. It's pointless.*
>
> *Kowa*

> *P.S. I know that you think you know who the friend I'm referring to is, but you're wrong. You mentioned Khonou's involvement in these matters the other day. All I can do is give you a word of warning: be careful going around and accusing people of witchcraft, you don't want to get yourself or your family hurt.*

She stuffed the letter in her back jean pocket, wondering whether Kowa had already contacted her accomplice. She knew they'd try to find her before she did something stupid to herself, Duski thought as she looked round the room and rummaged through the bedside drawers for Kowa's mobile phone. She eventually found it hidden at the bottom of a pile of clothes in the wardrobe. A quick flick through dialled calls revealed that she made no calls that day.

Duski quickly put the phone back where she'd found it as a car pulled up at the gate and beeped. She took one last look around before shutting the door behind her. Heavy hearted, saddened and stunned by Kowa's letter, she left the house and walked with determination towards the waiting car. She was in no doubt that Kowa was somehow tricked into taking part in the ritual murders, into leading Ali, Boiki, and Mudongo to their deaths. She vowed, as she joined her neighbour in the waiting car, to find and bring to justice Kowa's so-called friend. Khonou, Molepolole Village's notorious witch doctor, was the only person she was certain perpetrated the crimes, but Kowa was denying his involvement. After all, the man admitted to the murders to Thandie on tape. Kowa's ritual nest was also exactly the same as the one the witch doctor gave to Thandie.

She knew, however that her housemate didn't write the letter to confess to the murders.

This is a suicide note, she thought with dread. Some tiny part of her felt sorry for the constable. She wondered what would become of her children if she did commit suicide. *It must be hard*, she thought, *being a single parent to three children with three different dads who never loved you.*

*   *   *

It was nearly half past one in the morning when Duski's neighbour dropped her off outside central police station. Being a Tuesday night in the middle of the month, the station was very quiet. She was hopeful that the officer in charge would not begrudge her a vehicle and a couple of officers to accompany her to Khonou's compound in Molepolole.

"Good morning, sir," she said as she stood to attention to greet the officer in charge.

"Morning, Sergeant," the inspector responded with a yawn, surprised to see her at the station at that time in the morning. "What brings you to the office at this time?" he asked, sitting up to double-check the time on his wristwatch.

"Sir, we have a bit of a problem. Constable Kowa has just confessed to three previously unsolved murders and she seems to have lost her mind as well. I need a vehicle and some officers to go to Molepolole right now, sir. She might be on her way to warn the witch doctor she has been working with," Duski said rapidly and breathlessly.

"I am not following you, Sergeant," the inspector said, baffled by her request.

"I'm referring to the murders of Mudongo Mbulawa, the taxi driver; Boiki Maswabi, the Ramotswa man who was fed to the lions; and Constable Ali Ranoka," she recited.

"Are you sure about this, Sergeant?"

"I'm positive, sir," she said, looking impatiently at the inspector and then at her wristwatch. "Constable Kowa confessed to the murders, sir," she said, reluctantly giving the inspector the confession letter. "That's why we need to find Khonou before she gets to him. I'm sure he must be the accomplice," she concluded as the inspector read the letter.

"Do you need a driver?" he finally asked after he put the letter on his desk. "Take the duty Hilux and a couple of constables. I will contact CID. They need to know about this new development, after all they were in charge of these cases," he said reaching for the phone to dial CID.

"Thank you, sir," she said stamping her right foot to attention before ordering the two constables dozing off at the corner of the charge office to put their police caps on and follow her.

"Sergeant, I will ask Broadhurst police to help search for Constable Kowa and I will also ask Molepolole police to be on standby near the suspect's house," the inspector said as Duski hurried towards the back car park with the sleepy constables in tow.

The fifty-kilometre journey to Molepolole took her only twenty minutes.

At exactly 2:15 in the morning, Duski and her team marched into the witch doctor's compound. As they entered the compound, the team could see a police car parked some distance away. She radioed the officers to join the raid.

As the team approached the far end of the compound, they noticed a light coming from a fire burning inside a hut. The hut was partially hidden behind a couple of big-tiled bungalows at the very edge of the compound. She knew that it wasn't the consulting hut because Thandie told her Khonou used a room in one of the big bungalows for that purpose. She wondered whether the hut was the voodoo shop where he stored and sold body parts.

It was evident, given all the bungalows in the compound, that Khonou was indeed a rich man.

He could only have built this through selling human organs to desperate businessmen, Duski thought as she led her team past the posh bungalows towards the partially hidden hut.

"Koo, koo, *rre* Khonou *ke mapodise*! It's the police, open up!" she said and pounded on the wooden door. The knock was met by an artificial, yet eerie silence. She could tell that there were people inside, she could almost hear them breathing from within. "*Rre* Khonou I know you are in there," she shouted, pounding repeatedly on the door which seemed bolted from the inside.

A strong smell of something nasty seeped through a slight gap at the bottom of the door. Duski could smell something else too—human blood. *Our predator has been on the kill again tonight,* she thought as she signalled the men to kick the door in.

As the door crashed open inside the hut, it revealed Khonou and a man with a protruding belly sitting around a burning log fire. An uncovered three-legged pot was sizzling away on the log fire. She peeped to see what they'd been cooking as soon as she entered the hut. The contents of the pot included two fleshy balls bubbling in boiling water.

The sight triggered a wave of nausea that emanated from the bottom of her stomach. She steadied herself before she surveyed the contents of the hut. On the floor, in front of the two men, was a blood-soaked hessian sack with a mutilated body on it. A ball of pubic hair lay on the floor next to the chopped off penis and the mutilated body. She immediately realised what the hairy ball was—it was the man's scrotum. It looked like the man had slit it open to squeeze out the testicles before boiling them.

The sick bastard, she thought as she scanned the small hut. An okapi knife was lying on the sack beside the body.

"*Rre* Khonou, you are being arrested on suspicion of murder," she said as she handcuffed the witch doctor. She tried not to look at the gruesome scene. "You have the right to remain silent. If you wish to say something, you can do so, but whatever you say may be taken down in writing and used as evidence," she cautioned as she led the witch doctor and his client to a police vehicle.

"Take them down to the station," she instructed the two local constables. "CID will come to interview them later," she said, reaching for her radio.

"Which station, Sarge?" the constable asked.

"They are under your jurisdiction; I think they should be detained locally," she said as she walked towards a battery-operated deep freezer at the back of the hut and lifted the heavy door.

She was immediately hit by the sickening and distinctive smell of frozen human flesh. She picked up one of the little parcels in the coloured carrier bags and examined its contents. The bag contained various human organs that ranged from hearts to penises.

I hope he still remembers the names of all these people he has butchered, she shuddered, wondering how Constable Kowa had gotten mixed up with such a ruthless ritual murderer. *Did he have some kind of hold over her, or was she just as evil?* She threw the parcel back into the freezer.

"Stay here until CID arrives," she instructed a couple of her own constables before slamming the deep freezer door shut and continuing to search the rest of the hut.

Her attention was immediately drawn to an arrow pouch hanging from the rafters. *The poisoned arrows he used for slowing down the victims, just like Bushmen hunters do with big prey.*

*   *   *

At eight o'clock that morning, Sergeant Duski Lôcha and her team reported back to their station in Gaborone. They were all exhausted.

"Stand at ease Sergeant and take a seat," the inspector in charge of the night shift ordered. He'd stayed on after the shift to personally give her the tragic news.

"Thank you, sir," she said before taking a seat facing the inspector in the inspector's office. Memories of the day when Sub-Inspector Bale gave her the heart-numbing news of Ali's death suddenly overwhelmed her like a swarm of killer bees. She felt her heart choking in her throat.

Please, God, don't let it be anything to do with my family! She prayed.

"Sergeant, are you okay?" the inspector asked, concerned.

A lonely tear rolled down her cheek. "Yes, sir," she said, clumsily hitting the table and knocking over a half-empty can of Fanta as she tried to stand to attention.

"I'm sorry to inform you Sergeant, Constable Kowa was found dead this morning. She was found hanging from a tree near the airport," he said, looking at her oddly. Duski was smiling. "She hung herself with her night dress." The inspector's voice sounded distant and alien. Duski's smile widened until she broke into hysterical laughter.

"Sergeant, did you hear what I just said?" the inspector asked looking at her curiously.

"Yes sir. I have sir," she said, suddenly aware of her weird reaction to the news of her housemate's death.

Betty Keletso Knight was born in Lentswe-le-Moriti, a picturesque, privately owned religious village in the Tuli Block and a popular tourist destination in eastern Botswana. Her father was one of the village pastors who spent week days in Selibe-Phikwe, a mining town where he ran a taxi business, while her mother taught at the local primary school. Betty spent time in both the village and the mining town and later went to a boarding school in Tonota village where she completed her secondary education.

Betty undertook a year's national service before joining the Botswana Police Service, and after successfully completing training, she was posted to Central Police Station, in Gaborone. After two years of beat patrols and shift work, she was transferred to the Special Support Group and was attached to the Botswana Police band where she played the saxophone and flute in the marching band and performed backing vocals in the dance band.

After five years of service, Betty resigned from the police service at the rank of sergeant to retrain as an English teacher. She studied both English and music at Molepolole College of Education, where she met her husband-to-be, who was a lecturer at the college. After graduating with a diploma in secondary education, they both moved to Gabane where she got her first English teaching post at Nare Sereto Junior Community School.

In 1998 Betty moved to England with her husband and settled in Alton, Hampshire. Four years later, she went on to study English at Winchester University and subsequently went on to study for a master's in contemporary English literature, which she successfully completed in 2007.

Teaching English and writing crime fiction now take up most her time, but she periodically revisits Botswana to see family and friends.